AN ALIEN FOR HER HEART

A NEW HOME
BOOK TWO

AG WILDE

PETRONIE
PUBLISHING

This book is dedicated to all those humans who've loved before and have experienced loss.
This is for your heart.

AN ALIEN FOR HER HEART

Catherine

On the alien plains of Hudo III, I seek refuge from a past haunted by loss. My solitude is my sanctuary, or so I believe—until Varek appears. The alien warrior stirs something within me I thought was long dead: *desire*. He promises a bond forged in fire and intensity, one that leaves me lost—torn between the fear of opening myself again and the yearning to embrace a love that could heal my broken heart.

Varek

She's captivating. From the moment my eyes land on the human female, she becomes not just a puzzle to be solved, but the mate I desperately want by my side. I must convince her that together we can forge a future, if only she'll give me a chance. But I'm a broken male. I do not deserve her. My persistence should be tamed.

Only, I cannot stop. *I want her.* Broken or not, deep down, I know, this female is *mine*.

BEFORE YOU READ!

Hi there!

While this book is intended to be a heartwarming journey, it does contain themes and situations that some readers may find sensitive:

Passionate encounters: This book does not shy away from depicting the fiery and sometimes primal nature of the characters' connection, including an intense mating ritual that involves power dynamics.
Past trauma: The main characters have both experienced significant trauma in their pasts, including abduction, war, the loss of loved ones, and past relationship trauma. These experiences are discussed and explored throughout the story as part of their healing journey.
Possessiveness and dominance: The male protagonist, Varek, exhibits strong possessive and dominant tendencies, particularly during his mating rut. While these behaviors are ultimately consensual within the context of their bond, they might be triggering for some readers.

Injury: There is a scene involving an injury.
Animal distress: There are brief scenes of animal distress.

My goal is to create a safe and enjoyable reading experience for everyone. If you encounter any content that triggers you or that you believe should be added to this list, please don't hesitate to reach out to me on social media. I'm always open to learning and improving.

Till then,
Happy reading!
🖤 AG

CATHERINE

Life isn't meant to be a smooth ride.

No matter who you are, it's meant to build you up or knock you down. I've had a lot of that knocking down. Thought I was used to it. Stronger than it.

Years of patience. Years of growth. Years of learning lesson after lesson.

Thought I was better.

I didn't think it would ever end up like this.

Sitting here outside my homestead, those words stick as my gaze travels over the view before me. My chair leans till it touches the cottage's stone walls, my weight sinking into the worn wood. The wind is soft, the air warm. Both caress me as I pull my shawl tighter across my shoulders and release a long breath of my own. Just…breathing with the wind.

Far out in the field before me, the tall grasses sway as strange cow-hippo animals called oogas mill about, grazing without a care in the world. It's all so peaceful, so very different from the last few years of my life, that I'm caught in a sort of trance, consciously taking it all in.

This is all mine. The cottage. The field. The farm. The

animals. This piece of land out here on these alien plains belongs to me now. I blink at it, taking in the view and still blinking as if expecting my vision to clear. As if expecting it all to disappear when I lift my head from my pillow and realize that all I was doing was dreaming all along.

As far as my eyes can see, fields upon fields spread out to touch the horizon. It's quiet out here. Secluded. Perfect solitude for a weary traveler.

And I *am* weary. So very tired. The sort of tiredness that isn't etched in my muscles or my bones, but someplace far deeper.

I grip the shawl tighter, even though the air isn't remotely cold. The bright star above is warm, but the shawl tightens around me like a comforting caress. Another breath eases its way through my chest, floating to meet the wind. I gaze across the plains, not really seeing them now. Not seeing anything before me except the old memories that begin creeping in. Old dreams. Old pain.

I'm caught in my thoughts, becoming swallowed by them, when there's a sharp thud that tugs me from the depths of my own mind. I jerk, lurching back into the present and almost falling off the chair in the process. Reality snaps back as I jump to my feet, my gaze turning to the roof above me. There's a workman—or rather, a working male—up there doing repairs. So caught up in my thoughts, I'd forgotten about him. Forgotten I'd stepped outside the cottage for some fresh air, and perhaps even a chance to talk to him. Learn more about this new world I've now settled on.

Lifting a hand to shield my eyes from the sun's glare, I step back so I can see him better. "Everything alright up there?"

The workman startles—perhaps he'd forgotten about me, too—and a curved roofing tool slips from his grasp. It slides down on the thatched roof straight in my direction. I don't react fast enough. Luckily, it snags on something, hanging halfway off the roof's edge. My eyes widen as the roofer steps back, reaching for it. Retreating a further step, I watch his precarious footing. His balance seems wonky, but he keeps his foothold on a floating black tile that hovers suspended in the air just beneath him.

"All is well. Greetings," he finally replies as he grabs hold of the tool and gives me a nod in the process.

I nod back, not sure what to say now.

He's a Raki. The species I was advised to hire for all the repairs my new homestead needs. He's gray-skinned. Has a long trunk, small eyes, and bushy eyebrows. He looks like an elephant, even having the large ears to match, but he's much smaller than a full-grown one. Probably the size of what would be a baby elephant back on Earth. He barely tops my waist when we're standing side by side. But I guess that doesn't count. I'm a tall woman.

He ignores me now as he returns to his work, and I nod again. Maybe to myself this time. But maybe I'm desperate—or something. Desperate to not fall back into the void of my thoughts. It's the reason I stand here, looking up at the roof, at the alien working there, shoulders turned away from me as he deliberately ignores me, and I still open my mouth and speak.

"How's it coming on?" I ask, even though I can see his progress with my own eyes. The Raki works slowly. It's been a month since I signed up for the New Horizons Initiative. A month since their representative brought me out to live on these plains. A month since my new life began. And the roof is only halfway done. He's slow, but he's cheap and he's reliable. Turns up every day. Does his work without a fuss and then leaves again.

"All is progress." His gaze shifts to me only briefly before he looks away once more. "Greetings."

"Greetings." I press a tight smile on my face and pull the shawl so tight across my shoulders that the fibers protest. It's been like this each time I've tried to have a conversation with him. Either the Raki are not used to small talk or this one just doesn't want to speak to *me*. Which is okay...I suppose. I've hired him to work, not keep me company.

I'm no stranger to being alone. I was alone long before aliens decided to disrupt my existence. I'm used to it.

I press a brighter smile on my face and turn my attention back to the field, choosing not to focus on the fact that the Raki is ignoring me once more. If his little distraction has done anything, it's reminded me that I can't just sit here in the sun, stuck in a loop of memories and dreams. I have work to do. I stare at the field, watching the animals for a moment before I nod to myself. I should get out there. Continue clearing that field. It beats sitting in the house all day, staring at the plains and wondering how life changed so much that I ended up here.

Clearing my throat, I shoot one last glance at the Raki before I head to the barn. It's warm inside the building, probably because of the large holes in the roof that give me a view of the bright pink sky. Bits of thin clouds float by above like wisps in the atmosphere, their view unimpeded. I eye the holes, knowing the Raki will take another few months before he'll get to repairing those, too. Until then, there's not much I can do with the barn, and that slows things down. I can't move the animals in, can't start storing hay or any feed, and I certainly can't fix those holes myself. I'll just have to wait and make do till the situation improves. Heading to one corner, I stop at the tools I'd found lying about the place and stashed in a big pile there.

Leaning down, I grab something that looks like a large pair of scissors. It's the only tool out of the lot that can do the job I want and, though somewhat rusty, it's worked well so far. In the month that I've been out here, I've managed to clear a tenth of the field of tall grass. The only problem is that it's already growing back. By the time I finish cutting one side and start on the other, the field will be a full-blown grassy savannah again.

I try not to think about it. Try not to let the sheer enormity of this challenge get me down. I signed up with New Horizons because I wanted a fresh start. This is it. Nobody said it was going to be easy and I didn't come here expecting it to be. I'll push through it, and in the meantime, I'll push those forlorn thoughts away, too. I might be in my sixties but my strength is still there. God knows it is. Otherwise, I'd have given up a long time ago. And I don't quit.

So I grip the oversized scissors, the weight of it somewhat grounding as I step out of the barn. The Raki on the roof lifts his head, his gaze finding me almost reluctantly. I smile, gesturing to the scissors in my grasp.

"Just going to cut the hay." I can tell the moment the words leave my mouth that my attempt at conversation has been once again deflected by his shield of disinterest.

"A fine sol to get the job done. Greetings," he says, before focusing on his work again.

I'm dismissed. My chin lifts and I keep the smile pasted on my face as I walk around the house and head toward the field. There, with my back turned to him, the smile slowly dies, a cloud of despondency threatening to follow in its wake. I roll my shoulders, closing my eyes for a moment as I breathe in the fresh air. When I open my eyes again, the field is right before me. Grass so tall I could get lost in it. And that's the problem. I need to cut it down so I can start even a small vegetable garden or something. I'm not sure how I'll do it. I expect the first set of crops will fail. And then the next. And probably the next, too. I've never grown anything to eat in my life. I'll need time to figure this out and get things right.

If all else fails, I'll figure out how to make money with the animals. I'm good with horses. Good in the stables. Though, my lips press into a thin line as I watch the oogas lazily graze, these animals are nothing like horses. More like cows. But it can't be that hard, right? I'll just pinch the funds New Horizons sponsored me until I get a footing in all this.

Stepping into the grass, I use the massive scissors to part the tall strands. I soon end up at the small clearing I'm already making some progress in. An ooga is standing there, its ears perked at the sides of its large head.

"Hey, big guy," I whisper. "Or girl." I don't quite know which. They don't have visible udders even though the representative mentioned they can produce milk.

The animal ignores me and I shrug. "You too, huh." Removing my shawl from my shoulders, I tie it over my head instead. "Is there some kind of 'don't talk to the human pact' going on that I don't know about?"

I ask this out loud even though I'd probably pee my pants if the ooga talked back to me. I grunt a laugh just thinking about it as I use the scissors like a crutch to lower myself to my knees. "My mother used to say, 'Actions speak louder than words.'" I grunt again, glancing at the ooga who continues to ignore me. "Guess you're a firm believer in that one, aren't you?"

I chuckle as I settle fully on the ground. The position isn't comfortable but it's the only one I've found that gets me any real progress.

The first few snips of the grass are smooth. The scissors are so big they take a large chunk without a problem and I shuffle on my knees, snipping as I go. It's therapeutic, but soon my knees begin to ache, the short blades of grass like little swords poking into my flesh, and the heat of the sun like it's being amplified by a magnifying glass. I push on anyway, wiping sweat from my brow even as I worry that now that I'm on my knees, I mightn't be able to get back up. I can already feel that ache that tells me my joints are locked and I'm not moving from this position anytime soon.

I might as well stay down here and continue working then. So I keep going. I cut the grass until my whole body protests. Until lifting the scissors becomes too strenuous. Until I'm too tired to even think about the past or anything else except the fact that I'm tired and should stop soon. And until I hear a snort and a bay up ahead.

The sound wouldn't have bothered me if the grass didn't rustle and the ooga's baying didn't get louder. I stop snipping to lift my head, a slight frown on my brow as I squint against the sun. But I can't see far ahead through the tall grass. When there's another snort, more baying sounds, and the ooga closest to me begins stomping its feet in place, I know something's not right.

The oogas are usually silent. Hardly making a sound apart from their chewing and occasional release of flatulence. Otherwise, it's almost like they don't exist.

Grunting, it's an effort to rise. I hiss, pulling a breath through my teeth as I force my muscles to work. It feels like my thighs have gone dead from being in the crouched position too long and it takes a few moments of standing and stomping in place before sensation returns. Still squinting underneath the pressure of the sun, I stretch one arm to part the grass before me. Not far ahead, a group of three oogas are gathered. Just seeing them like that makes my frown deepen.

They're herd animals but still like their own space. It's a contradiction that reminds me of humans. Usually, they walk slowly, just chewing and minding their own business, often ignoring each other. Now, their heads are lifted and they're baying in unison with noses pointed skyward.

For a moment, I wonder if I'm the reason for their sudden behavior change. Did I disturb them with my unconventional methods of hay harvesting? It probably scared them to have a pale creature crawling low and cutting down their food. But no. Their attention isn't on me. Looking over my shoulder back to the cottage, I see the Raki on my roof is looking at the animals too. But then, like they're not behaving strangely, he returns his attention to his work. That's just the thing; he minds his own business. Even now, when even *I* can tell that something's not right.

I want to holler at him, ask for his input, but he's ignoring me once more. My lips press into a narrow line. I might not have much—lost everything when I was abducted from Earth—but I still have my pride.

I've been figuring things out on my own for a long time. I can figure this out, too.

Resting the scissors on the ground, I decide to venture closer to the animals to take a look. I can hear them stomping and the baying gets louder as I near the area of grass they've cleared with their grazing. Perhaps one of them is injured and they're calling for help. Horses will sometimes do that, their whinnies turning frantic when one of their own is in distress. Even as I think it, I pray that's not the case. I don't think I could bear to see one of these magnificent creatures suffering. That's when I see the reason for the oogas' upset. The scene before me is not what I expected to find.

A group of small fluffy creatures are running circles around my oogas.

I stop short, not sure what they are or if I should venture any closer. They could be dangerous, but that's a hard sell. They look like little pom poms bouncing around and it takes me a moment to notice they have feet underneath their little round bodies. They're...cute.

"Um..." Cute, yes. But the oogas don't like them. Or rather they don't like the fact that the little creatures seem to be dancing around them. I turn my gaze back to the house and the Raki working there. He's looking my way again but turns his head back to his work the moment he senses me looking, as if he doesn't want to engage.

Guess I'm all alone in this. Maybe if I leave the little fluffy creatures they'll go away to wherever they came from. In the month I've been here, this is the first time I'm seeing these things. That must mean they're just passing through.

But, again, that's not the case. I wait for a few moments before realizing the oogas are only becoming more agitated. Taking off my shawl, I wave it like a flag to get the little fur monsters' attention. Probably a bad idea if they're dangerous, but they ignore me. As a matter of fact, they move faster, becoming little black blurs. I gasp when I feel movement around my legs. A host of them appear from the long grass to rush past me and join the fray. Where there were only five of them before, now there are at least twenty. They just keep coming out of the long grass like termites from rotten wood. My eyes widen as the oogas go ballistic, baying and dashing through the grass—one nearly mowing me down in the process. I'm momentarily stunned. I didn't know the oogas could move that quickly. For Pete's sake, I'd had to ride an ooga out to these plains and it never moved like that.

Fear spikes low in my chest and I have the sense to run. As fast as I can, I shriek as I head toward the house. I make it through the little gate separating the field from the main yard with an ooga on my tail. I shut it behind me hard, the entire fence vibrating with the force as my chest heaves, my lungs burning with the sudden exertion.

The ooga misses me by mere inches. The brush of air as it suddenly turns to stop itself from colliding into the gate makes tendrils of my hair blow backward from my face.

Those little furry animals… What in the blazes are those things?

The oogas are still going crazy and one runs straight into the perimeter fence. My heart goes into my throat as the entire thing seems to bend with the force of the animal. They are, after all, built like tanks. When another does the same thing, I know I have to stop them. I can't have my perimeter fence going down. With no barn to hold them, that will only set all my animals free and invite God knows what in. Plus, who knows if I'd be able to herd them all back. My confidence in that respect is but a drop in a large empty bucket.

I stare at the growing chaos in shock. The peacefulness of the morning is gone, almost as if I'd imagined it.

Okay, Catherine. Figure this out. I square my shoulders, huffing a breath through my nose as I march around to the front of the cottage. The Raki sees me immediately.

"The animals are spooked." I point to the field even though I know he saw everything and is very aware of my sudden plight. "Some little creatures have scared them. Do you know what they are or what I should do?"

His gaze shifts to the field before moving back to me. "Wild umus," he says. "Best to tame them. Greetings."

Tame them? What in tarnation…

He goes back to his work and my brows dive. That's all the help I'll be getting from him, that's clear. But did he say I should *tame* the animals? How in the blazes am I supposed to do that? Brushing back the tendrils that have escaped my bun, I jerk slightly when another ooga collides with the perimeter fence, the sound reaching me as if I was standing right beside the fence itself. The whole structure bends outward, the wood creaking with a sound that echoes against the stone walls of my cottage.

I really have to do something.

I'm moving into the house as fast as my legs can take me, heart in my throat as I head straight to the table. I grab the communication device I have there—a rectangular thing that reminds me of a smartphone. Breath held, I tap the screen and it lights up.

I know I should, but I don't want to call. The whole reason for coming all the way out into these plains was to be self-sufficient. To live the rest of my days in serenity without the pressure of friends or relationships that ultimately fail. Yet, here I am, hand hovering over the device, considering asking for help.

I chew my lip, glancing out the window. The chaos outside is unsettling, the animals still baying and stomping, the little creatures flitting about like manic fluff balls. I sigh and tap the screen, bringing up the contact list. There are only two names there. The first is Xarion, the New Horizons representative who transported me to this farm.

Xarion had been kind, offering to check in periodically, but I had politely declined. Now, though, I wonder if I was too hasty in my hunger for peace.

I hesitate, finger hovering over his name. Can I really call him for something like this? The thought of his stern, yet understanding bunny-like features makes me hesitate further. No. I can't contact him. But as another ooga crashes into the fence, I make my decision.

My focus drops to the second name on the list and a tingle of nervous energy rises in my gut. There's only one other person I could call. A human. One who has been kind. One who has tried to be my friend even though the walls I've erected keep her at arm's length. But I have no choice.

"Computer, ping Eleanor." My voice trembles as the words come out, probably because my throat is so tight I can hardly breathe. If the perimeter fence falls and the animals get out, I don't think I'll ever get them back again. I can't let that happen.

"Pinging Eleanor Taylor."

I grimace but allow the ping to go through. The last thing I want is to burden someone else with my problems. But Eleanor's farm is up and running. She has a field. She's even planted crops. Maybe she's encountered the little fur monsters and can point me in the right direction before I lose my fence and my oogas.

I bite my lip, pacing as I look out the window just to see the complete carnival happening in the field. It seems to have escalated in the few minutes that it took me to come inside for the device.

Releasing a slow breath, I look down at my screen at the exact moment that Eleanor answers the ping.

"Catherine! So nice to hear from you! How are things going?"

I force a smile. There's light in her eyes. Eleanor's cheeks look rosy. She looks so happy. So genuinely happy, that I stare at her for a moment too long. Such pure happiness isn't something often seen on other human faces. Not out here. Not in this new reality where we've all left Earth behind.

I want to lie to her, tell her everything's going great, but that's not the reason I called. I need her help.

"Hi." I clear my throat. "Hello, Eleanor. I'm just—" My gaze shifts back to the terrified oogas. "I hope I'm not calling at a bad time. Are you busy?"

"No, no, go ahead!" I can tell she's walking through her cottage to go stand on her porch. "I was just finishing preparing some seeds we'll be planting today. Just a little tip, we have to soak them before we put them into the soil or they won't take."

In the background, I can see she's painted her cottage pink and there are flowers hanging on the walls. It looks like summer in the South of France. It looks like a home. So warm and inviting that my stressed smile becomes genuine. Peace. She's found her peace.

"I'm just calling for some advice," I start. Now that she's on the line, I feel like a fool for calling. Surely, I could have figured this out on my own. I have a supercomputer in my hands. But since she's on the line, I press ahead anyway. "There are some animals. Something called umus—"

Eleanor gasps. She goes completely still, her eyes widening as she stares at me. "Oh no. Has one attacked you?!"

Her reaction makes me focus on her fully, the knot of thoughts that have been tangling my mind going to the background for a few moments. "Well, no. Are they dangerous? I seem to have..." My gaze slides back to the field. "I seem to have an infestation of sorts. They spooked the oogas and I have no idea how to calm them down. I tried shooing the little furries away and almost got trampled by the oogas themselves. I was just wondering if you have any ideas in case you encountered them before."

"Goodness gracious," Eleanor says, and her gaze shifts off to something I can't see. "Don't go near them. I nearly died because of one."

My eyes widen. "Nearly *died*? What?"

"Zynar!"

I stiffen as she calls her mate. I don't want to take him away from his work too.

"Zynar!" But Eleanor's eyes are still wide with panic as she hustles across what looks to be her yard and to her freshly cleared field. I start to pace, her panic bleeding through the call. What sort of trouble have I found myself in? My animals are going crazy and, as I catch glimpses of the overturned red dirt of her field, I'm reminded of just how far behind I am in my own crop preparations.

"Zynar, it's Catherine! She's in trouble." Eleanor huffs, the look on her face still panicked.

"Just what am I dealing with here, Eleanor?" I look back from the chaos outside my window just as the video screen suddenly shifts.

Zynar appears. He's so tall I can't see his face, only the purple iridescent scales on his shirtless chest, which means Eleanor is holding the comm up for him.

"Umus are terrorizing Catherine's farm. I'm worried the same thing that happened to me might happen to her." I can hear the stress in her voice, and for me, a woman she only knows because our lives were both torn apart. It makes something deep inside me wring and twist. Something a part of me pushes back against. "You have to go help her."

"Oh! No!" I startle, surprised, shocked back from my thoughts to the words she just said. "I couldn't possibly take Zynar away from his duties. I know you're both busy. If he could just tell me what I should do. I—" I talk quickly but I don't think Eleanor's listening. She's rattling something about me getting hurt and how they have to prevent that.

Zynar bends and his face suddenly appears on screen. "It would be no trouble, human." He gets an elbow in his side and I see the faint shadow of a smile, giving me a glimpse of sharp fangs. "It would be no trouble…Catherine."

It's clear his mate has been teaching him to call us humans by name, but pushing that from my mind, I shake my head. "It's quite a distance between our farms and it's rather urgent. My field. The oogas. I—"

But he's already shifting the device back to Eleanor. "I cannot make it out to your homestead, Catherine," he says, loud enough that I can hear. "Not with the seeds soaked and ready for sowing. They will go bad if not sowed in the next hor and Eleanor cannot do such a job."

"I can do it." Eleanor frowns. Zynar growls.

"Much too strenuous work for you, my *kahl*," he rumbles. His kahl? God, it feels like I'm snooping in on a private moment with the way his voice deepened on that word. "Varek will go to her aid."

I blink. Varek? That's his brother. I met him once. On the same day I met them all. That first day when I had no idea what I was doing or where I was going. Only knew that there was a gaping hole inside me that nothing can fill.

Grimacing slightly, I wish I never called. The last thing I want is to make a big deal out of something I could have probably fixed myself.

"I'll Google a solution." Well, the alien version of Google. "I can't possibly—"

"It's no trouble." Eleanor faces me now. "He drives fast. He'll be there in less than an hor. You know," she nods at me "an hour."

I want to tell her this feels like something that's being blown out of proportion, but an ooga takes that moment to charge straight at the perimeter fence. It makes such a heartbreaking sound as half its body gets stuck in the wires—front half outside my property's bounds and his backside in. Oh, crapsuckles. I really need help. "Okay." My voice lowers, reality sinking in. "I'll see you then."

"Not me." Eleanor grins. "*Varek*." I open my mouth and she smiles some more. "He'll sort it out. Don't worry."

"I—"

"Talk to you soon. I'll ping him now." Eleanor gives me a reassuring smile and the ping closes.

I release a breath, pulling on the bravery I've been using for years to keep me going as I set the device down and hurry out of the house to stop my animals from killing themselves.

2

VAREK

I don't sleep. For the entire dark cycle, I remain awake, tossing and turning in my bunk. Now as dawn rises, the star's rays seem to light up the fact the room is painfully quiet, just the rustling of sleep coverings breaking the silence as I move. Every little sound is like a loud noise that threatens to shatter the stillness.

My gaze shifts to my comm where it's resting nearby. The screen is dead. No notifications. No messages. No pings. No one to speak to. My brother's absence is a tangible thing, a hollow space that seems to swallow up all the air and light.

Some of his belongings are still here. I can just make them out among the shadows settled in the room. A pair of trouse. Boots. Little things he left after moving away to his new home.

Because Zynar has a mate. The thought sends a pang of something sharp and bittersweet lancing through my chest. After so many cycles spent resigned to a fate of solitude, my brother's core-rhythm sang for a female neither of us had expected to find. The fates brought her to him.

A displaced Kari has found a mate. Zynar has found a *home*. And I...

I am alone.

I've seen the way Zynar looks at his mate, the way his entire being seems to light up in her presence. It's both beautiful and painful to witness. I try to picture it, try to imagine what it must feel like to be so certain of one's place in the universe, to know beyond any doubt that you belong to someone and they to you. But the image slips away, as elusive as the shadows that haunt me now.

I've never been lonely before; not quite like this. Not with this aching, yawning emptiness that seems to carve out my insides and leave me raw and exposed. I'm a warrior, battle-scarred and hardened. I have long ago made peace with the idea that solitude will be my only companion.

But now, in the wake of Zynar's happiness, that hard-won acceptance is crumbling, leaving behind a yearning so fierce it steals away my breath. And this yearning is like a virus. I've heard the whispers, reports of other displaced Kari becoming reckless and approaching unmated females with a boldness born of desperation.

A bitter smile twists my lips at the irony of it all. My siblingkin's mating has unleashed a flood of repressed hope among our people. A wild, reckless want for connection that borders on madness.

But who am I to judge? That madness I scoff at is the same madness writhing within me now. The same hope. The fact there might be a chance. I try to push it away, but the thought lingers still. It lingers…and I think of her. The other female who has arrived on the plains. Human, like Zynar's mate. Her name is Catherine…and she is enchanting.

Gaze shifting to the dawn sky outside, I swallow hard, forcing myself to think of something else. I only met the human once. Briefly, right after Zynar was mated. She's a stranger, a newcomer to this world who deserves the chance to find her own way without the burden of any Kari's foolish hopes and dreams. She has come here seeking peace and a fresh start, not the attention of a broken male hoping to find the one who will soothe his soul.

If she was my mate…

I stop the thought right there. It's a dangerous one. One that could all too easily consume me if I let it take root. I cannot be like the others who must have lost their minds, approaching females on the off chance that my rhythm will sing.

Shaking my head, as if I can physically dislodge the notion from my mind, I rise. I have to focus. There are jobs to do. Tasks to complete. Life goes on even if my siblingkin no longer walks by my side. Work is all I can do. Anything else is a distraction I cannot afford.

Reaching for my boots and tools, my movements are brisk and purposeful as I head into the town. There are many task requests on my list. The sooner I get started, the better.

The work is quick. Focusing on nothing else, I complete the jobs with a sort of robotic efficiency. Each time my comm pings and I accept another task, it helps push another hor behind me. At one moment of calm, I settle in my truck, claws grasping the yoke tight. The lull makes my mind wander. Makes me remember the fact that when I return to my lodge this dark cycle, it will be me and my thoughts again. That this madness rising inside of me is a form of insanity I must push back against.

I'm successful. My thoughts shift away from self-pity and self-loathing to something else. Her. My thoughts shift to the human instead.

When my comm pings, I retrieve it from my pocket with almost too much anticipation. Another job to keep me focused is exactly what I need. Except, it's not another job. It's my *kahlesta*; my siblingkin Zynar's mate.

"Good dawn, kahlesta." The comm lights up and her face fills the screen.

"Varek! So happy I reached you—"

I'm like stone as she explains that she needs my help. That it's urgent. A life-or-death situation. But what has me not even breathing is the fact it's not really *her* that needs the help, but someone else.

With a throat that's suddenly tight, I tell her I'll handle it. I can't say no, even though my core-beat fills with dread tangled up with more anticipation. Engaging the hover truck, I'm shooting across the plains a second later, my entire being thrumming with hope despite efforts to calm myself.

This has nothing to do with fate. This is simply a favor. But as the hover truck comes to a sweet stop, idling as I hop out, my core-beat stutters and beats just a bit harder. There's a soft wind in the air, carrying with it the distant sounds of baying and stomping. My ears twitch at the commotion as I turn my gaze to the homestead.

So…this is where the other human lives. Catherine.

It's a homestead much like the one my siblingkin lives in with his mate. A field. Outbuildings. And a main lodge his mate calls a ko'tehj.

There's a Raki on the roof of this one and as I shut the door of the truck, my gaze slides to him. For an unknown reason, a bristle goes through my scales at seeing him there. And, as if he can sense my focus, he turns, gaze finding me over his shoulder. I dip my head in greeting, even though his presence makes me want to snarl—again, for some unknown reason. I have no problem with the Raki. I see them all the time in the town. They do the same jobs as me and my siblingkin, except they cater to prey species like themselves. And…like the female who owns this farm.

That only reminds me that I shouldn't be here. Males like me don't usually get called to help on these plains. That anticipation that swelled in me for the entire journey becomes riddled with uncertainty. Does the human even know I was called? The last thing I want to do is scare her.

As I approach, the Raki's eyes heighten on me, and even though he dips his head and returns to his work, I can tell he's still aware of my every move. We Kari are no savages, but his caution is ingrained—and rightly so.

The unnatural behavior of those far-too-hopeful Kari must have spread farther than I thought.

Stepping into the yard, I push the Raki from my mind as my focus shifts. He isn't the reason I'm here. The human is. Catherine. Except, as I near her lodge, concern tingles along my spine. The door is thrown open wide, a soft breeze blowing the linen she's hung by the windows. Apart from that, there is no movement within.

She must be hiding, scared out of her wits. I'm about to enter her lodge, find her, and tell her I'll get her animals settled without trouble when my ears twitch. A sound reaches me through the long grass-feed. Under the commotion from the animals, there's a soft grunt, an even softer feminine voice muttering words I cannot parse, and then an exasperated huff. I stiffen. The female. She isn't hiding. She's in the field, even though she shouldn't be there. Not when the oogas are scared and mindless. They are big, powerful animals and the human is a small thing compared.

I'm moving without another thought, cutting through the grass-feed in the direction of those soft grunts. The blades are so tall I don't see her at first. But I can hear her. Hear her grunting and struggling with something, all underneath the cries of a distressed ooga. When I reach the perimeter of her land, I see her.

The human called Catherine. And she's...she truly is captivating.

She's sweating and her tunic is ripped. Her black and silver mane is pulled back away from her face. A face that's currently scrunched in equal frustration and effort combined. For a moment, I can only stare at her. For a moment, I forget my reason for coming out here.

She's trying to free an ooga trapped in the fence, her hands straining against the massive creature's weight. The ooga is panicked, its powerful legs kicking up dirt and grass-feed as it struggles, causing itself to bleed against the wires. The human is dangerously close to those thrashing hooves, her brows furrowed, her blunt teeth bared and clenched.

"Hold still, you big lump!" Her voice makes my ears twitch, perking in interest toward her. But her shout doesn't help her cause. The ooga doubles its efforts to free itself, but it only gets more stuck instead. The wires are now digging into its skin so much that the thing is slowly cutting off its air supply.

I move forward, reaching the human just as the ooga gives another violent kick. She stumbles back, losing her grip, and a flash of fear crosses her face as she realizes she's falling. Her arms instinctively spread, reaching out to stop her fall or, perhaps, to brace for the impact.

She gasps, her eyes widening the moment it's not the ground that meets her but the hard ropes of my arms. I expect to simply brace her up, but my breath stills at the moment of contact. The sensation of another being pressed against me completely derails my thoughts. I don't move. *Can't.* I can feel the human's core-beat racing, pounding like a drum against my chest. Time seems to still as brilliant green eyes find mine, wide and filled with surprise.

"Oh!" She's startled, and the word is almost like a squeak that passes her lips. She's so delicate, I can feel every breath she's taking. "You're...Varek."

I dip my chin slightly in affirmation.

She struggles to right herself as I set her on her feet. "I didn't expect you to arrive so soon."

Her voice... It's like a song. If I wasn't still reeling from the impact of her body against mine, I might be more focused on listening to her speak.

"You shouldn't be out here," I say. It comes out all wrong. Gruff and unfriendly, though that's far from what I intend.

"Oh, I—" The human takes a shaky breath, trying to compose herself, but I can still sense the tension in her frame, the way her muscles remain coiled and ready to spring. Inwardly, I groan at my horrifying social skills.

"I'm Catherine." She stretches an arm toward me and I look down at it. My siblingkin didn't tell me much about human customs. I have no clue what she wants me to do. Something of meaning, no doubt, because her arm hangs still outstretched between us.

I do the only thing I can think of. I lean down and press my nose against her skin, inhaling deeply as I take her scent in. A low rumble of appreciation hums in my throat. One that sends a spark through all the thoughts I've been having of her. I never imagined what she might smell like, but even if I had, I couldn't have ever imagined this. Her scent is subtle. A blend of earth and something distinctly her own. Something warm and comforting. It stirs memories of long, lazy afternoons on Karicek, lying in the grass with my siblingkin and watching the sky. When I stand straight again, her eyes are wide pools.

"Thanks for coming." She blinks away the surprised look and meets my gaze in earnest. "I should have probably stayed in the house until you arrived, but I couldn't just leave them." Her voice is a mixture of relief and defiance. "They're my responsibility."

I admire her spirit. That frown on her brow doesn't ease, however, even as she adjusts the tunic on her frame. The trapped animal behind her takes that moment to kick out again and the human jerks to the side, a flash of distress showing in her gaze. I would have missed it, because it disappears just a click later.

My eyes narrow slightly. She is just as I remember her. An enthralling otherworldly beauty despite the anxieties of moving to this planet on her own. Dark and silvery mane with those startling green eyes. A lithe frame, her limbs thin and long as if she's meant to sway or dance in the wind. With the chaos around us, I hope I'm not obvious in the fact I can't pull my gaze from her now.

"Your strength and effort are noted, human." Gruff again. Frakk me. I give her a nod as I turn to the trapped ooga, using it as a distraction. I wouldn't be surprised if the human runs away and hides from *me* now. Dodging another kick from the animal, I stretch an arm toward it. My grip is firm but gentle, and the creature calms down enough for me to begin guiding it from the fence. All the while, I'm aware of the human's presence. *Catherine.* She's still not hiding. She's gripping the neck of her tunic with one fist while the other arm is wrapped tight around herself.

Her throat moves as she swallows hard. Anxiety and fear waft off her in waves. And yet, outwardly, there's no trembling. None of the waters I've learned flow from human eyes when they are distressed. Her gaze shifts from my gentle coaxing of the animal to the other oogas that are still running around the field, some colliding with the fence and sending vibrations through it that work against me.

It's an effort to keep the animal calm as I work its neck from within the trapped wires. An effort to focus on the task and not on the female behind me. Every single ooga in the field is running around in confusion, and beneath all that, spots of black fur appear and then disappear in the grass at various intervals.

I manage to guide the animal out of the fence and it dashes off to join the chaos of the herd. Catherine watches, her gaze shifting across the field and I wonder what she's thinking.

"How…how did you do that?" she whispers. "How did you get it to calm down so easily?"

"Luck," I reply. I don't tell her it's simply experience. Somehow, I feel that will make things worse. Experience is not something she will have. Not yet. She's only just arrived on this world while I have lived on it for a very long time. "Now, let me deal with those umus."

I don't expect her to follow me, but she does. She has all the right to. This is her farm. Her livelihood. She has every right to be out here protecting her animals. But she is small and the oogas are panicked. Safety would be to head back to the lodge, away from this chaos. My shoulders are tight as I listen to the soft crunching of her boots. But I can't turn her away, so I let her come, slowing my pace and parting the tall grass as we move together through the field, me in front and Catherine only a stride behind. In front of us, small furry creatures scatter through the grass at our approach. The umus. They're quick and elusive, darting around in a blur of motion. I crouch down, waiting for the right moment before I catch one. Catherine's inhale is sharp at my back.

"Careful," she whispers. "It might bite."

I almost smile at her concern over my safety. When I bring the little creature closer to my face, I can tell she stops breathing.

"They don't bite." I try to reassure her though I'm not sure I do a good job. My voice is still far too gruff to soothe any female and attempting to change it is only making it worse. "They're harmless. Just playful."

Her lack of faith in my words is evident. It's so distinct, it's the only truly unmistakable emotion I've seen in her eyes thus far.

"Playful?" She echoes, her voice lilting. "They're little demons!"

This time, slight humor tugs at the corners of my lips.

"They're prone to mischief." I pause, allowing my gaze to venture to hers. "Would you like to hold it?"

She blinks at me, lids fluttering over the vivid green of those eyes. She shakes her head, hands tightening where she's still gripping the tunic by her throat and I wonder why she's holding it so tightly. To prevent the tunic from exposing her skin? Another dangerous thought as my gaze slides down her frame. She's probably pale all over. No scales.

"I don't think holding that thing is wise." She shakes her head, eyes still on the umu in my grasp, and I'm reminded of what I'm doing here. It's enough to make me swallow to wet my suddenly dry throat. It's been a long time since I've stared at any female long enough to wonder what she looks like bare. I swallow again, claws retracted as I stroke the umu's furred head, aware of every single breath the female takes behind me. Rising, I lift the umu just to show her how docile the little things are.

"Wild umus stay away from other beings. These ones are friendly. Chances are, they belonged to this very farm a long time ago." Cradling the thing to my chest, I turn to face the human. Her eyes are even larger pools in her head as she stares at me.

"Wh—" She makes a sound in her throat. As if something's stuck and she's clearing it away. "Do you think so?"

I would give her the Kari salute for assurance, but my arms are full. "I'm positive they're yours. They are little terrors when upset but they're mostly very playful. Their coats can be spun into soft threads."

That seems to have caught her attention. Her digits loosen their grip on the fabric at her neck just slightly. "Like wool?"

I don't know what or who this 'wool' is, but I'm silenced as she takes a step forward. "Now that you say that, their fur *is* a lot like wool." As she peers closer, she releases the neck of her tunic, revealing her throat and the upper part of her chest. My focus locks onto her bare skin as she continues speaking. "This is the closest I've gotten to one since this all began."

Despite the chaos still occurring in the field around us, time stills again as Catherine steps even closer. It seems she's forgotten the chaos. It seems she's forgotten *me*, and it's glorious because she stands close to me, peering at the umu in my arms.

I can't look away. Her skin is a tapestry of stories I can't begin to understand. There are tiny dots of dark pigment scattered across her chest and neck, almost like the dapples of starlight through forest leaves. Camouflage? I don't know what they are, but they captivate me enough that my digits twitch. If I was not holding the umu, I might have been tempted to reach out and touch them.

Her scent reaches me next and I find myself leaning in for a second sampling. Mm. Her scent reminds me of peace. Before the war. Before everything changed.

It's her voice that pulls me back to the present. Not the baying oogas. Not the rush of umus chasing each other in the tall grass-feed.

"You don't know wool, do you?" she asks. Her tone is different, as if curiosity has softened her earlier wariness of me.

I tilt my head slightly, still cradling the umu who has settled down in my grasp and trying not to reveal that I've been staring. "Who is he?"

She chuckles, the sound so unexpected it makes my ears flatten and I go still again. "It's not a person. It's from sheep," she explains. "Animals back on Earth, where I…where I come from." Her humor disappears like a Zilox when the sky weeps. Her expression shutters and she grasps the neck of her tunic again before taking a step backward. Curses. "They kind of look like these umus. Just much larger and not so round. We use their wool to make clothes, blankets, things like that." She gestures to the umu. And then, as if speaking to herself, she murmurs, "Almost makes me want to knit again."

I nod, trying to focus on her words rather than the gentle rise and fall of her chest as she breathes. "Knitting. A fine…task."

My tone must reveal I have no idea what she's talking about, because a small smile tugs at her lips. A brief flash of warmth brightens her eyes. But just as soon as it appears, she freezes. Her body. Her smile. Everything. She blinks and the smile is gone. Just as her humor had disappeared before, it does so again as she steps away from me.

I have offended her. I race through the interaction, repeating it in my head, but I'm lost as she wraps her arm around herself once more and doesn't meet my gaze.

"I'll…lead them to your outbuilding," I say, trying to fill the sudden silence between us that, with the chaos of our surroundings, feels as oppressive as the quietness that stifles me each dark cycle.

"Yes—that sounds…good." She doesn't sound sure about it, but I don't expect her to. The umus might remind her of animals from her home world, but they're not the same thing. She must be worried they will cause more trouble.

Dipping a claw into my pocket, I take out the sweet cubes I brought just for this. The umu sniffs and I lower my claw and allow the fluffy creature to take a lick of the treat resting in my palm. It does so hesitantly, but the moment its tongue swipes across the cube, its entire body vibrates with glee. I set it down with a bit of the cube in its mouth and watch as it races off, disappearing into the tall grass-feed.

Catherine blinks, her gaze shooting to me. The oogas are still running in circles and trampling the ground and I don't miss the moment she takes a step closer to me now that she's focusing on the chaos again. Just that slight thing and I almost puff out my chest like a fool.

"What now?" she whispers, eyes wide again, and I wish I could assure her it will all be fine. That her field will remain intact…though, now that I'm in it, I realize the Raki has done nothing to clear away the grass feed in preparation for crops. If it isn't done soon, Catherine will miss the season for sowing.

"We wait," I say, a furrow on my brow as my gaze shifts to the Raki on the roof. Crouching once more, my brows dive lower and lower as the clicks pass by.

"No crops?" I finally ask. Again, it comes out too gruff. Perhaps it's not my yearning after all but the presence of that Raki that's making me act out of sorts. The reason for which, I am not sure.

Catherine shifts, the slight movement like a trigger on my senses even with the chaos around us.

"Yes. Eventually. I just have to clear this field and then I'll be sowing some of the seeds New Horizons left me." She pauses. "That's the company that...the one Eleanor and I signed up with. I guess you know all about that since she's your..."

"My kahlesta," I murmur. If she thinks I care that New Horizons works with females who have been through trauma, I don't. I will not judge her past. It's not even on my mind as I stare at the ground at our feet.

"Right. I guess that's how you say 'sister-in-law'? Anyway, once I clear this field, I'll try my hand at the crops."

I don't tell her what I think. What I *know*. That if her field isn't cleared in the next three sols, maximum four, she'll be too late for a successful harvest this orbit. Pulling up some of the grass-feed, I look at their roots. My brow dives deeper. I stick a digit into the ground and take up a bit of the soil, turning it over, my eyes narrowing before I pull out a few more roots and bring them up to eye level.

The roots are dying. There are pests in the soil. If Catherine plants anything, her crops won't grow to harvest.

Her almost inaudible gasp is what draws my attention back as a black blur shoots through the grass-feed directly toward us. Three umus appear, all racing toward my outstretched claw. I give them each a sweet cube before standing. More appear by the time I'm on my feet once more.

"Alright, you little troublemakers. Let's go." I turn, gaze finding the wide-eyed human before I force myself to look away. My brow is still furrowed and I don't want her to think she's the reason for my rising annoyance. Instead, I shoot my glare at the Raki on the roof and direct my scorn at him instead. Dropping sweet cubes on the ground as I go, Catherine keeps my pace, gaze darting back at the line of umus trailing us from the field. Her cheeks are a strange rosy color now that wasn't there before. I've only seen such a thing happen to my *kahlesta* whenever my siblingkin does something to please her.

I almost stumble.

Am I...*pleasing* this female? The thought is absurd and yet I can't help but keep my eyes on her as we walk from the field. The furrow on my brow is erased with this new puzzle. Thank the gods she's so much shorter than I, she can't tell I'm watching her intently unless she chooses to look up at this very moment. She doesn't. Her focus is on the umus, brows still furrowed and that suspicious look in her eyes as she watches them follow us.

I could laugh. She doesn't trust the little things, though they really are harmless. But then I remember that my siblinkin's mate doesn't like them either. She's terrified of them after one caused her to fall and hit her head. She almost died and that only reminds me of how delicate these females are. That kills the humor that was rising within me immediately and I look now at the female beside me with concern.

"They will not harm you." Still gruff. I should just keep my mouth shut. And yet there's the undeniable urge to say something more. The urge to speak is unusual for me, unsettling even. I'm not accustomed to wanting to comfort anyone, let alone a strange human female. "If they tried to harm you, I would not allow it."

She looks up at me then, green gaze framed by delicate dark

lashes. "I believe you." There's a smile that follows her words but it doesn't reach her eyes. Not like before. Not like when it came naturally as if she'd forgotten who I was.

We're at the gate that leads into the main yard and I let her walk in first. Looking behind us, the line of umus bopping happily along and eating sweet cubes stretches to disappear into the grass-feed. But farther off, in the actual field, the oogas are already calming down.

I can sense Catherine's relief when she looks back and notices the same.

I nod to her before jerking my chin in the direction of the outbuilding. "I'll lead them in."

Her eyes are still slightly wide, and she's still gripping that neck portion of her tunic, but she nods in affirmation.

My eyes narrow slightly, my gaze shifting up to the Raki on the roof as I close the yard gate. He's looking down at us from where he works ever so slowly. For some reason, that annoys me, too.

"No sweet cubes, Raki?" I can't help but ask.

"None at the moment. Greetings," he replies.

Useless frakker.

He could have at least told her what to do. No doubt she has sweet cubes in her supplies. Instead, he let her risk harm by trying to solve a problem she'd have no idea how to solve on her own.

Maybe I'm snarling. Maybe I'm doing it out loud, because the moment I feel a soft touch on my arm, I snap back again like a tether pulled taut. A ripple goes through my scales and I realize Catherine *touched* me. She snatches her hand back immediately, almost as if she'd just been burned, and her gaze shifts away from me.

"I really do appreciate your help." She presses a smile on her face.

I force myself to turn away from the Raki. I'm meant to calm the human and fix her problem. Not scare her to death.

"It's the least anyone could do," I growl those words for the Raki as I lead the little creatures toward the outbuilding.

The fact his presence is adding to my irritation makes little sense. The last thing that made me emotional to the point I lost control happened eons ago. A day I never want to relive again, but one that haunts my every waking moment.

More discontent rises the moment I head around the lodge on the way to the outbuilding. The roof is only halfway done, even though I know for a fact that Catherine arrived here more than a moon phase ago. Is the Raki making her sleep in a lodge with a roof that's only half-complete? Not only that, but the high grasses choking the walkways have not been trimmed. I can see where she's been working to clear them, just so she can have a path to walk. Then there is the heavy machinery that clutters the yard, most unusable now. The only thing that seems to be in working order is the shining, new water shaft that must have been recently installed.

By the time I get to the outbuilding, I'm seething. I tell myself it's because I hate seeing subpar work and that it has nothing to do with the delicate female that owns this place. But when I pull open the outbuilding's door and see the state of the roof and the animal enclosures, I stop short.

"Is everything alright, mister um, Mister Varek?"

I stiffen. I've been seething so much I didn't realize she'd trailed behind me and the umus all the way to the outbuilding itself. I force myself to hide my fangs. To slide on the mask I usually wear. The one prey species prefer to see.

I turn, glancing over my shoulder at her.

"Everything is fine. Not to worry."

She gives me a slight smile before nodding. Her focus moves to the umus as I lead them in and when the doors close behind them all, I know she followed us inside, too.

"I'll put them here." I gesture to an enclosure that needs the least work.

"Yes, sure. Anywhere you think is best."

She's putting her faith in me and that makes me want to do an even better job. Make this work for her even long after I'm gone.

I turn and survey the space. It's functional, but far from ideal. I spot some discarded crates and decide those could be repurposed to reinforce the enclosure walls while keeping the creatures contained.

Lifting and maneuvering the crates into place is nothing. But they're large heavy things and I sense Catherine watching, her eyes widening slightly at the casual display of strength. For a fleeting moment, I allow myself to feel a flicker of pride at impressing her before I push the thought aside.

With the makeshift barrier in place, I gently coax the umus into their new temporary home, dropping a few more sweet cubes to entice them. The little creatures hop and bounce into the pen, their fluffy bodies wiggling with happiness at having the sweet treats.

Turning back to Catherine, I notice her biting her lower lip, a small frown creasing her brow as she surveys the outbuilding's dilapidated state. I fight the urge to reach out and smooth that worry from her face. Frakking Raki. He's done nothing to help her out here and she's not a fool. She knows this is no place to keep the animals. Not long-term. Not like this.

"I'll get this fixed up properly for you," I say before I even consider the gravity of my words. And frakk me with the gruffness in my tone. "The umus will be fine in there for now."

Catherine's green eyes meet mine, a tentative smile softening her features. "Thank you again, Varek." She looks away, focusing on the animals moving in their new enclosure. "This was probably all a big waste of time for you. The solution was so…simple. I'll know what to do next time."

I want to open my mouth to correct her, to tell her this was no trouble, but the words are stuck in my throat. My fangs have lengthened behind my closed lips and if I speak now I will snarl. Something is making me more than irritated. I'm qeffing angry.

Turning away, I pretend I'm looking around the outbuilding's interior and that I haven't already spotted all the things that need fixing. "It was no trouble."

Silence descends between us. It's time for me to leave. There's no reason to linger now. But there's still that thing riding on my blood. That unsettled feeling. That rising anger.

Frakk it. I face her.

"I'll be back on the new dawn with supplies and tools. We'll get this outbuilding in proper shape." I'm already mentally cataloging what I'll need to bring from my own stores.

"Oh, you don't have to—" She looks stunned, shaking her head as she speaks.

"I *want* to." The words come out softer than I intended and it stops her in her tracks. It seems I've lost all control over the tone of my voice. For a long moment, we simply gaze at each other. Did I speak too softly? What am I doing anyway? I have jobs to do tomorrow. Paid tasks for clients that booked many sols before. I shake my head, breaking the spell. I should go.

"I'll see you on the new dawn, Catherine."

"Oh..." She seems stupefied.

Good. I don't know what I'd do if she declined my help. So I give her a nod, chin to chest, before striding out of the building before she can come up with a very good reason to reject my offer. Like the fact the state of her farm is none of my business.

I don't know why I'm doing this. It's probably the start of that long-dreaded insanity that has haunted me for too many sols now.

But beneath the practicalities, a new feeling takes root—the warm glow of something precious and delicate, unfurling tentatively within my battle-scarred soul. I tell myself it's just the pleasure gained from helping another being.

It isn't.

I would be a fool to lie to myself so blatantly.

It's hope. Even though I know only the naive cling to such things so dearly.

3

CATHERINE

The sun's high in the sky today again. I stand just outside the porch staring at it. It doesn't nearly blind me as much as the sun on Earth did, but it's not comfortable to stare at either.

My focus shifts to the sky itself. To the wisps of clouds and then to the pink hue behind it all. It's still so strange to see, even now. As if someone diluted Kool-Aid and it spilled across the canvas above us.

When I first arrived here, transported by a carrier on behalf of the allied rebel camp I was staying in, I'd held my breath, eyes widening as I stared at the sky. I'd been worried I wouldn't be able to breathe. With a sky like that, the air was probably toxic despite what I'd been told. It wasn't (obviously). Unless it's slowly killing me and I have no clue. But, isn't everything else, too?

If finding myself in this new world has told me anything, it's that I have less control over my life than I thought. We think we have control, but we don't. People go. Time moves on. *You* move on—as best as you can anyway.

I shake my head, clearing my thoughts because I know

where they'll lead. Down that road of old memories and pain. Instead, my gaze drifts to the fields stretching out before me. To the grass swaying gently in the breeze and the oogas grazing calmly now. If I'm lucky, this will be my last home. This farm, this land—an opportunity to create something that heals my broken soul. Something that is wholly mine.

Even if I'm doing it alone.

There's an ache there at that thought. One that's so old, so deep, that it feels like a deep fissure embedded inside me. I sigh, turning away from the porch as I head to the barn. Pushing the large doors open, I pop my head in before I enter, bracing myself for any chaos that might ensue. But the little umus are still in their enclosure. As I step in, I can see they're all lying down on their little bellies, not a care in the world. Now and then, a slight shiver goes through one of them that makes their fluffy bodies vibrate, but apart from that, no one could convince me these were the same animals creating havoc just the day before. A breath of a laugh brushes past my lips. Just yesterday they were little terrors and today they look like soft plushies you just want to cuddle.

"You're not fooling me," I murmur as one lifts its head and watches me as I reach for my large grass-cutting scissors. I lift them and snip the air. The little umu continues watching me, before resting its head on what I'm going to assume is another's butt.

"Nice pillow." I chuckle, stepping closer to the enclosure. My shoulders are tight as I wait for the animals to react, but they don't. They ignore me and continue resting. I release a breath of relief as the first genuine smile of the morning graces my lips. "Maybe he was right," I whisper. "Maybe you really aren't that bad."

A swell of gratitude rises in my chest as I think of the alien with the pretty pink and purple scales. If he hadn't come to my aid, I'd have probably woken up to all my hopes and dreams falling apart. Because of him, I still have my farm. All the oogas are fine, and I even have a set of little alien sheep that promises a second stream of income if I can figure out how to process their fur. I owe Varek…everything. And that's why I got up early to ensure that his efforts don't go to waste. "I'll bring you some hay later," I whisper, even though the umus still completely ignore me.

With that I'm heading out of the barn, my gaze shifting to the hole-filled roof only briefly. That's something I'll have to sort out soon. Fix the roof so I can move all the animals in. Get my field ready for crops and then I'll be able to finally feel like I've got a strong hold on things.

I stretch my back, a yawn escaping my throat as I open the little gate separating the house from the field. The shawl is tied over my head to protect against the rays as I find the spot I was working on the day before. Kneeling, I waste no time as I begin snipping. At once, I'm reminded of how slow and hard work this is. I keep at it, getting maybe about a square foot done before I hear the engine of a vehicle nearby. My head pops up as I listen. With the silence of the plains, the sound of the engine is so obvious when it normally wouldn't be anywhere else. Perking my ears, I listen. Short of getting up and staring, I have to just assume it's someone passing by because these high grasses block my view of the road. That's just another reason to cut them down.

I wait a few moments but the engine sound remains. My hearing might not be one hundred percent, but I'm pretty sure the vehicle is idling at what would be my gate. A second later, the engine sound dies.

Must be the Raki. I don't have a watch but I know he's early. The sun—or whatever they call this star, hasn't fully risen yet. The only reason why I'm awake and on the field is because, like most other nights, I couldn't sleep.

I turn my attention back to my grass cutting. The Raki

doesn't give two quacks if I rise to greet him or not. It will be just like those other days when I've tried to make conversation or just be polite. I'll say hello and he'll reply with something like, "Nice dawn. Greetings." The conversation will end there.

Turning my attention back to the work in front of me, I use both arms to work the tool in my hand. It's hard going. My arms protest. It's like using one of those chest fly machines at the gym, except I'm on my knees and my goal really isn't perky breasts—although those would also be appreciated.

I get a few more snips in when I tug on the scissors as they snag on a bunch of grass. I pull and nothing happens. Grunting, I tug again.

"Gosh darn it." The blades have locked and won't reopen. Putting all my weight into it, I tug, but the grass roots are deep and the scissors aren't opening. I ease up off my knees and squat now, putting my every strength into it as I tug. Nothing. It might be anger. It might be frustration. It surely is annoyance, because I brace my shoes into the earth, giving it all my might. My stubbornness wins as the root suddenly gives. The moment of release is abrupt and I'm thrown back because of my overuse of strength.

"Whoops!" I go down, landing on my back between two dark boots. Blinking, I don't immediately understand what I'm looking at until clarity chases away the confusion.

I'm not alone.

My heartbeat quickens as I stare dumbly up into the crotch of the alien's trousers. My throat goes dry as my gaze shifts up along the hard planes of his chest, perfectly smooth iridescent scales coming into view, showing me glimpses of pink, purple, and blue under the sunlight. Corded muscle jumps as if aware of my attention as my gaze slides higher to his face.

He's back. He's *here*.

Varek tilts his head, looking down at me. "Good dawn, Catherine."

His voice is a deep rumble that sends a shiver down my spine. The fact makes me stiffen because that shiver has no place. It has nothing to do with the cool morning air.

"Are you alright?" His concern makes me stiffen, too. He's here. Why? Perhaps for payment for his help yesterday? He left in such a hurry, I didn't even offer him anything for his time.

My breath hitches as he extends a clawed hand, offering to help me up. I stare at it for a moment, my mind still trying to catch up with the fact that he's here, standing over me, looking at me with those intense yellow eyes. They're slit like a reptile's and completely focused on me. So much that his attention is making the hairs on my arms stand on end. Despite that he's so calm, I feel completely bare underneath his attention.

Swallowing hard, I nod and reach up to take his hand. His skin is warm, the scales smooth against my palm as he effortlessly pulls me to my feet. I stumble slightly, my body colliding with his solid chest before I can catch myself.

"Whoops," I mumble, my cheeks heating as I quickly step back, putting some distance between us. "I didn't expect...I thought you were the Raki."

Varek's lips twitch, and I'm not sure if it's amusement I see in his gaze or something else. His eyes are almost impossible to read. "Disappointed?"

"No!" I say too quickly, then clear my throat. "No, of course not. Just surprised. What are you doing here? Is it about yesterday?" I'm still not used to alien customs and there are so many. So many different species exist, while we humans wondered if we were alone in the universe. Oh how very wrong we were. "I can pay you for your help. Actually, I should have paid you yesterday. An oversight on my part." I smile at him. "I just have to get my comm. I left it in the cottage."

I'm about to walk around him when his next words stop me.

"I'm here to work."

I stop in my tracks, my neck snapping in his direction so quickly that I almost sprain a tendon. "What?"

"I'm not here for payment. I'm here to work," he repeats, a little bit louder this time as if he's unsure what pitch he should speak so I can hear him. But I heard him fine the first time, I just can't believe what he said.

"Work?" When did I hire him? Was his help yesterday some sort of initiation into working here? Some sort of interview? I blink at him, trying to piece together the information I have. I mean, God knows I need the help, but I haven't discussed a contract with him or anything. I'm thinking about all this, thoughts racing across my mind as my brows crease a little. And then I remember his last words before he left the day before.

"I'll be back tomorrow with supplies and tools. We'll get this outbuilding in proper shape."

Oh God. He was serious?

He crosses his arms, the movement making the muscles in his shoulders and arms flex. I force myself to keep my eyes on his face, ignoring the traitorous flutter in my stomach that's so sudden and misplaced, it arrests me.

I'm shaking my head as I speak, already thinking of reasons why this is a bad idea. "I appreciate the offer, but I'm sure you have better things to do than help an old woman with her chores."

Varek tilts his head, his brow furrowing as if he doesn't understand what I'm saying. "Old?"

My mouth opens and slams shut. I resist the urge to say *"Um, yes, me obviously."* Can't he see it? The gray hairs. The fact my skin has freckles that weren't there when I was twenty. The fact I feel so...diminished. But I guess he can't see *that*. A sudden rush of self-consciousness goes through me as I wonder if the differences between our species mean he doesn't perceive age the same way humans do.

"Yeah, old," I repeat, a bit more firmly this time. "I'm not exactly a spring chicken anymore." I add a soft laugh to the end, just to soften my words a little. But…what *does* he see when he sees me? Just a woman? Just a 'female' as these aliens say?

It's not something I considered before with any alien species I've encountered this far. You start seeing yourself a certain way and that's all you perceive others see you as, too.

Varek tilts his head the other way, his eyes narrowing in contemplation. "Age is marked by the spirit within." He leans forward and I stiffen again. He's suddenly too big. Too present. "You are radiant. Your spirit shines brightly, and that is what I see."

His words catch me off guard, and I find myself staring at him, unsure how to respond.

"Radiant," I murmur, more to myself than to him. The word feels foreign on my tongue, yet it sparks a warmth in my chest. I want to laugh it off, like I would do any polite compliment. But there's sincerity in his voice, a depth of understanding I hadn't expected. It's been so long since anyone has spoken to me like this. With true appreciation. And it's coming from *him*. Someone I wouldn't have expected to say such a thing to me.

"Yes." His voice is so soft, it sounds more like a low hiss than an actual word.

My gaze meets his, and those slitted eyes bore into mine. Dangerous. He's a predator with the eyes of a snake. I shouldn't trust him. At least, that's what my brain says. Everything else says something else. He hasn't once done anything to suggest he's dangerous to me. Heck, Eleanor is mated to his brother, and I'm pretty sure that means they're getting busy beneath the sheets every night. I'm putting a lot of trust in her taste in alien equipment here.

My cheeks flush at where my thoughts have gone and when Varek's gaze shifts over my face, I can tell he notices the change.

I clear my throat. "Thank you." Brushing non-existent dirt from my tunic, I take a step back. "That was very nice of you to say." I clear my throat again. What were we talking about before? I seem to have forgotten. Oh, right. The fact he said he's here to work. "Now, about you working here…"

Varek eases back, standing tall again. "You need my help." His gaze shifts around the farm. "You are my kahlesta's comrade and that Raki has done nothing to get you settled into your new home. I will fix that."

Right. So he's offering because I'm Eleanor's friend. That makes sense. At least she's making contacts. The only person I've managed to form any sort of relationship with since coming here is the Raki who doesn't even want to speak to me. Not really a budding friendship happening there. I have to count myself lucky that Eleanor's awesome extroversion has allowed her to settle in so quickly and that I'm bearing the fruits of that labor.

My gaze shifts over Varek now, watching as he turns in a slow circle as he scans the farm. His muscles are like guns, powerful and ready. I've never truly understood the meaning of that term until now.

I straighten as he turns to face me again, only realizing I'm staring when his lips shift into what looks like a self-conscious smile. I blink, clearing my thoughts. His words are sincere, his expression earnest, and it makes something in my chest ache. When was the last time someone offered to help me without ulterior motives, without expecting something in return? But I'm powerless in this world. I don't have much money or influence. I have nothing to offer but a few credits and maybe a cold drink from my supplies. He's not doing this because he wants to get close to someone with the Richmond name. Out here, my name means nothing.

And he's right. I need his help.

I tilt my chin, forcing myself to speak through the anxiety rising at the base of my spine, as if swelling to the beat of a drum. This won't be for long. He's probably offering to do a day's work. "Well, there's a few jobs I could ask you to help with, if you're up to it."

Varek's shoulders lower as if he'd been holding his breath. He was afraid I'd say no? Okay. What's the catch?

"Perfect," he purrs, and I try not to dwell on how the sound rumbles from his lips. "Now, let me take a look at that roof."

He gestures for me to lead the way, and I do, but not before noting that he lifts the heavy scissors so I don't have to carry them. A ball rises in my throat as we walk towards the barn. Am I doing the right thing? If he's anything like Eleanor's mate, maybe this is the best thing I can do for my farm. I can't help but sneak a glance at him from the corner of my eye as we walk, taking in the strong lines of his profile, the way the morning light plays across his iridescent scales.

He's...beautiful. The realization comes suddenly. A wayward thought that makes me frown as I stare at him. He *is* beautiful. Not just physically, but in the way he carries himself, the quiet strength and gentleness that seems to radiate from him. His long green hair flows over his shoulders, not a tangle or knot to be seen. His jaw looks sculpted by female hands that truly appreciate the male form—strong and chiseled, yet not harsh or overbearing. His prominent brow and cheekbones make his face an angular masterpiece. And his eyes...those yellow depths seem to see straight into my soul.

And they're looking at me now.

I shift my gaze away, clearing my throat again. It's so silent between us, only the sounds of our shoes hitting the ground as we walk, that I can even hear the insects I'm going to pretend are crickets chirping in the long grass.

We reach the barn and I open the door. Stepping inside, I look up at the hole-filled roof. It's a mess, and I feel a pang of embarrassment even though he's seen it all before. I've been giving the Raki the benefit of the doubt, but with Varek here now, it's very clear that maybe the Raki wasn't the best hire.

"I don't know how much you'll charge to do the roof, but I'm willing to pay your full rate." I hope he understands what I'm saying. That although he's Eleanor's brother-in-law, that doesn't mean I expect the job to be done for cheap or free. If I cultivate a business relationship from the start, it will work in both our favors. "How much would you charge to get the barn roof recovered?"

Varek sets down the scissors he's been carrying and looks up at the roof, assessing the damage. His expression is unreadable as his gaze flicks across the rotten beams and over the holes above us. He turns in a slow circle, hands on his hips, and I try not to look at the muscles bunched in his back with the pose.

I frown at myself, partially ashamed and partially horrified.

"New support needed there." Varek points at a spot before his finger shifts to another section. "And there. There too. I'll need to strip the whole thing. The fibers are rotten. Need replacing."

I nod, as if I understand it all. It sounds like a lot of work, but there's something reassuring about his confidence, about the way he seems to know exactly what needs to be done.

"That's fine. As long as the pom-poms have somewhere dry to sleep before it rains." I don't miss that his lips twist in slight humor at my nickname for the umus. "Do you need anything? From me?"

When he turns, his gaze shifting to me, expression still unreadable, his stare is so intense that I run the question through my mind again.

Oh crud. I need to be specific.

"In terms of supplies." But even as the words leave my mouth, I realize that my attempt at clarifying may have only made the unintended insinuation worse. Heat crawls up the back of my neck. "Is there anything you need me to get? Supplies? Or anything I need to help with?"

For a moment, he doesn't reply. So much so that I wonder if

he heard what I asked. I clasp my hands in front of me, wondering if I should ask again, but I'm sure he heard me, right? He was hearing me fine before.

"Yes," he suddenly says.

I nod, glancing around the barn even as I wonder what specifically he was answering to. Probably all the above. "I'll try to find everything you need. This was once a functional farm, I'm told, and most of the things around here still work in one way or another." Or I hope, at least.

"What I need is…" He pauses again and when my gaze shifts to him, a slight furrow on my brow, I realize there's a slight furrow on his brow, too.

"Yes?" I prompt gently.

"Catherine…" He says my name in such a disarming way, it doesn't sound like my name at all. As if he's calling someone else entirely. I have the urge to look behind me just to check if there's anyone else in the room with a name pronounced so tenderly.

"Yes?" This time it's softer. I suddenly feel like I'm walking on eggshells here. He hasn't moved since I asked him what he needed from me. His attention has only heightened, the intensity of his gaze growing more potent with each passing second.

"I must go to the town for supplies. The beams for support. Bolts." He pauses. "Would you like to accompany me?"

His question has my eyelids fluttering. "Accompany you?"

My heart does a little thud that feels like it lifts its head for the first time in a while. Going to the town feels like a trip away from this farm that would do me good. The last time I saw the town was when I first arrived. There was no time to look around because Xarion, the New Horizons representative that accompanied me here, was already there waiting for me. He'd escorted me directly to the farm. But I can't go to the town just to walk around. Not until things are settled here. There's a lot to do and random trips will just eat away at the little time I have to get this farm in order.

"You'll need to choose the right beams for the repairs," Varek continues, his voice steady. "The type of material you want for the roof fiber and the trim. I'd prefer if you were there to make the final decisions."

His reasoning is practical, but there's something in his tone that makes me feel like there's more to it. I turn his reasons over in my mind. They're valid. The barn is my responsibility, and I should be involved in the choices that affect it.

"Well," I breathe, blinking up at him. "I suppose that makes sense."

Varek nods, and it seems like his eyes get brighter. "We'll take my hover truck."

It's that same moment that I realize something else. Going to town with him will mean being stuck with him for a few long hours.

An uneasy feeling rises within me at the thought. Being alone with him for that long, confined within the small space of the truck… It's not that I don't trust him—I do. But the idea of being in such close proximity is unsettling. It would mean conversation. Relationship building. I might have to open up parts of myself that I've been keeping locked in a trunk without a key for years before I was even taken from Earth.

"The journey to town will also give us a chance to discuss the repairs in more detail." Varek's gaze shifts back to the roof as he speaks. "I'd like to make sure we're both in agreement about what needs to be done."

It's almost like he's convincing himself too, and that helps. I'm not the only one wary about this impromptu trip. *There isn't more to this, Catherine. He simply wants to do the job well, which is admirable.* We still haven't discussed how much his rate will be for all this so I suppose we can discuss all that on the way, too.

"You're right." I give him what I hope is a convincing smile. "It's important that we get this right. For the sake of the farm."

He blinks at me before I'm sure I see the faint ghost of a smile.

"For the sake of the farm," he agrees.

My throat is dry again, so I clear it and swallow. It doesn't help. With my thumb, I gesture at the barn doors and toward the cottage. "I'll go get my comm and meet you out front."

Varek dips his head slightly in affirmation and I spin on my heels and hurry out of the barn.

For the sake of the farm. Yes. I'll go with that because anything else is absolutely ludicrous.

4

CATHERINE

Turns out I don't just go to the house for my comm. Once inside, I notice my tunic has dirt stains from when I'd been kneeling and clearing the grass. Thanks to a mirror Xarion supplied, I catch a glimpse of my reflection and realize just how disheveled I look.

I run a hand through the wisps of my hair that have fallen out of the French braid I'd done today. Grabbing the piece of linen I use as a hair tie, I let my hair down, staring at myself in the mirror. I can't remember the last time I took a moment for self-care. Truth be told, it didn't feel like there was much of a reason to anymore. And that's saying something for a woman that's always taken care of herself.

But there are no more charity dinners to attend. No more hosting events. Out here there are no manicures. My eyebrows have grown out. I haven't even had the chance to figure out what sort of makeup exists in this world, though I'm sure there must be some that work on my human skin. I'm completely just...me. But now, with the prospect of spending the day with Varek in town, I find myself running my fingers through my hair. I tug at my clothes, wishing I had something nicer to wear. My hands flutter to my face, feeling the lines and imperfections that seem more pronounced now than before. I can't go to town looking like *this*. I may have lost a lot, but I haven't lost my self-respect.

I head to my room and quickly change into a different tunic. They all look the same, just boxy brown linen, but at least I'm clean now. Running a brush through my hair, I let the strands rest over my shoulder, not bothering to put the hair tie in. A glance in the mirror shows a face that's still flushed from the morning's exertion, so I splash some cool water on my cheeks, hoping to calm the redness.

It hardly makes a difference.

With a sigh, I gather my comm and tuck it into my pocket. Dresses with pockets. Just one joy of intergalactic travel. As I'm about to leave, I notice my boots are caked with mud. Sitting on the edge of my bathtub, I quickly scrub them clean with an old piece of cloth. It's a small thing, but it makes me feel a bit more put together.

Grabbing a satchel that looks like a large tote bag, I throw it over my shoulder as I step out of the house. My gaze finds him immediately. How could it not? The pink sky is like a backdrop to his iridescent scales. Like a painting you'd see on computer wallpapers.

He's leaning against his truck, eyes scanning the horizon. He straightens the moment he sees me, his entire being coming alert.

"Sorry to keep you waiting." I offer him a smile as I head toward him.

His gaze sweeps down my frame and I pretend I don't notice as I come to stop a few feet before him.

"I have no problem waiting."

Why does everything he says sound like it has some deeper meaning?

I give him another smile. This one more genuine than the last as my gaze shifts to the vehicle behind him.

It's a vehicle that hovers off the ground, suspended in the air itself. The front of the truck where the driver and passenger sit is a transparent cab that gives a wide unobstructed view. The back is open and has an array of tools and materials I couldn't name if I tried, but it's clear he's capable. Clear he does this type of job all the time. Turning, he opens the door of the truck for me.

I ignore the heat that rises in my cheeks as I dip my head and duck into the vehicle. Seats that feel like leather greet me. Firm and in perfect condition. The cab itself is spotless, and my eyebrows shoot up as he closes the door and hurries to the other side.

He's clean. Somehow that makes me a little bit impressed. I relax a tad more.

I'm adjusting the empty tote in my lap when he hops into the driver's seat and his door slams shut behind him.

"All set?" he asks, glancing over at me.

I don't understand it. He's a big male. I'm tall. Five foot ten. He towers over me; and yet, his tone is so gentle when he speaks.

I nod, trying to match his easy confidence. "Ready."

Varek gives me a slight jerk of his chin, and as we drive away from the farm, I can't help but feel a mix of anticipation and trepidation.

My confidence in all this wanes as I watch the farm disappearing behind us.

Popping out my communicator, I press through the options on the little device. It takes me a while but I finally figure out how to send Eleanor a message instead of a ping. Apparently, some alien godsend uploaded our language to the universal server. All us humans who were captured are slowly finding our place outside of Earth. Typing is awkward, but I punch in what I want to say. Partially for safety, because, well, no one knows I'm randomly heading off with an alien hunk. And partially because I need to focus on something else than the alien riding in the vehicle beside me.

"Good morning Eleanor, I'm heading into town with Varek. Let me know if you need anything while we're there."

I hit send and tuck the comm back into my pocket, stealing a glance at Varek. He's focused on the road ahead, his hands steady on the steering wheel that's shaped like a T. The landscape around us changes from the familiar fields of my farm to more fields, only unfamiliar. Random buildings dot the expanse and I soon realize they're abandoned homesteads just like mine.

I gaze out of the truck, fully appreciating the fact that nothing is in the way of the view when I turn in Varek's direction to find him watching me. If he didn't have such good control of the vehicle I might have panicked. Instead, I pretend I don't notice that either.

He's staring. Not blatantly. Side glances, as if he doesn't want to make it obvious he's looking at me, and now that I've noticed I'm completely aware of it. I try not to focus on it. He's probably trying to figure out why I decided to come to his world. Or probably just curious. I am an alien after all, one of few humans this world has ever seen. The first day the Raki came to start working on my roof, I was out of sorts. It was hard not thinking of him as an animal. An elephant. Just as he was strange to me as a living, speaking being, so I must be to Varek and all the other aliens on this planet. They'll stare. It's just something I have to get used to.

Except, it gets so silent in the cab, I become completely aware of nothing else but the alien beside me.

"I saw your tools in the back." I try to start some conversation, but my voice comes out much louder than I intended in the quiet cab. "Do you do these types of jobs often?" As soon as I ask, I realize I'm genuinely curious. "I know you're here to help me with repairs, but what do you do when you're not saving helpless Earth women from their own ignorance?"

He chuckles, the sound rich and warm. It makes his face light up in a way I haven't seen since I met him. The reserved unreadable mask cracks and it's like there's another view of the male beneath it.

"My siblingkin and I, we build and repair structures. Mostly lodges." He pauses, gaze shifting fully to me briefly. "It's more than just work. It's a way to create something meaningful. Something that lasts."

I tilt my head now, intrigued. "What do you mean?"

His lips press into something that looks like a sad smile before the look disappears and he stares ahead. I briefly wonder if the question I asked was a prying one. God knows, I'd probably freeze up too if he asked me about my life back on Earth. But then he responds.

"Many of the beings on this section of Hudo III have lost their homes." Those slitted yellow pits shift to me for a moment and I'm once again struck by the fact that his eyes make him look so dangerous, while his demeanor is so...soothing. "For some, their home is lost and they're endlessly searching for it."

That last line is said almost like a whisper before he turns his attention back to the road ahead. My brow crinkles. "Can't find a home?"

It doesn't sound right. The whole purpose of the New Horizons Initiative, the one I signed up for, is to repopulate this section of the planet that apparently has an abundance of abandoned homes.

"Maybe they can sign up to the Initiative," I suggest. "I think I'm part of the trial run, but I believe it will be successful."

Varek glances my way. His eyes twinkle a little as he agrees with a sharp nod. But something in his gaze makes me think I got it all wrong.

I decide to change the topic. I can sense we're going into

territory filled with hidden memories and thoughts that can be like landmines. Probably because I have so many hidden triggers myself.

"Do you come to town often?" In my periphery, his head tilts slightly and I know he's still watching the road. It's the only reason I let my gaze wander over to him. His jawline is frickin' art.

"Often enough," he replies, his deep voice sending a shiver down my spine as his gaze suddenly shifts to me. "I live there."

I feel like a fool, and maybe the look on my face makes him chuckle again. That same deep, rich sound.

"I used to live there with my siblingkin, but he has…" I'm watching him closely enough to see the flicker of something pass through his eyes. "He's mated now."

I nod. "And you?"

The moment I ask is the moment I wish I'd bit my tongue instead. It had been such a natural lead on from what he said that the words simply slipped past my lips.

"I have no mate."

I try to lighten the sudden load of landmines I've thrown in my path by chuckling. "Well, I guess we have that in common. I don't have a mate either…not that I'm looking for one."

More landmines.

"You aren't?" His question throws me for a loop, flustering the thin foundation I've been walking on between us.

"Well, that part of my life has already passed." There's a crack in the wall I've built around myself. Enough for me to feel it. Emotions I've hidden away threaten to show on my face and I close my eyes briefly just to push them back. "I've put that all behind me."

"Unfortunate."

Not the response I expected. "For me?" I laugh, trying to lighten the mood.

"No. Not for you."

I'm not sure what to say next. The silence returns, but it feels more thoughtful now, like we've each gone deep into our heads. I look out the window again, watching the landscape change as we get closer to town.

Eventually, the buildings become more frequent, and we pass a few small shops and homes. The town is modest but bustling, with beings going about their daily routines. Varek navigates the truck expertly through the narrow streets until we reach a central square where he parks.

He gets out first and comes around to open my door. I smile at the gesture, again surprised by his gentlemanly behavior. Maybe Eleanor's been giving them lessons on what we human females like. As I step down, I take in the surroundings. The market is lively, with stalls set up under colorful awnings, vendors calling out their wares, and townsfolk chatting and bartering. There are so many different types of aliens, it's hard not to stare. Reptilian aliens that look like lizards, some that look like armadillos, even a few that look like snakes. Then there are furry beings; some that look like bipedal canines, others that look like felines, even some that look like human-sized mice people. The sights are staggering, but if I close my eyes, it's almost like being back home. If I close my eyes, I could pretend I'm visiting the farmer's market on a Sunday.

I take a deep breath, letting the familiar yet foreign sounds of the market wrap around me. It's comforting, in a way that I didn't expect and maybe I grow wistful, because when Varek steps up right beside me, close enough I can smell his cologne, I don't even react.

Whatever he's wearing is sweet. Mingles in with the scents all around us while still being distinct. When I pop my eyes open, he's towering over me, blocking the sun. His shadow falls across my face and I tilt my head to look up at him.

The look in his eyes catches me unaware. His gaze shifts over my hair, watching it blow in the slight breeze before moving to my eyes. He holds my gaze there for a moment before it slips down my face. My nose. My lips. All the way to my throat. When I swallow, he watches the movement, too.

As Varek's gaze lingers on my throat, a sudden wave of self-awareness washes over me. His focus is so intense. I don't think he's doing it on purpose. I don't even think he's aware of it.

I clear my throat, breaking the spell between us. "So, where to first?" Even to my ears, my voice is a bit too bright, too cheerful.

Varek blinks, as if coming out of a trance, and his slitted pupils grow slightly narrower for a second. He turns his head, looking toward a far-off section of the town but doesn't move. I realize then that he's standing between me and the bustling foot traffic of the street at his back. He's like a shield between me and the aliens who would be bumping into me as I daydreamed.

He's very...sweet.

"The lodge vendor should have all that we need," he says. His gaze turns back to me, growing slightly larger again across those slitted pupils. "After that, if there is anything you would like to do while we are here..."

How thoughtful...

I want to immediately shake my head. I don't want to take up too much of his time. But who knows when I'll get to come back to the town again. I don't have a truck and I haven't figured out how to use the oogas for transport yet. New Horizons left me a lot of supplies that won't run out soon, but it wouldn't hurt if I got a few things I might need, right? I might as well take the opportunity while it presents itself.

I nod, feeling a flicker of excitement going through me at the prospect of exploring the market with him. "Sounds perfect. Lead the way."

5

———

VAREK

 can see why my brother was drawn to his kahl, even before he knew she was his. Humans are…intriguing. It's busy out here, and yet Catherine pulls my attention from the hustle and bustle of the town. I would say it's this madness threatening my being. The one that makes it almost impossible for me to take my eyes off her, but it isn't. I'm not the only one that's captivated by her.

More than a few males we pass have stopped their dealings to watch her go by. Some even taste the air, trying to get a hint of her scent.

It makes me walk just a bit closer to her. Enough that they know she's not alone, and that she belongs…well, not to me. She made it clear she doesn't belong to anyone nor does she have any plans to. That doesn't stop me from glaring at the males who look at her in interest.

She can do better than every single one of these fools anyway. Better than me, too.

She doesn't even notice their attention. And I'm glad, because even though their forwardness makes me bristle, I've been doing no better. I've been shamelessly staring at her for more than the last few clicks.

She moves with a curious blend of cautiousness and wonder, her eyes darting from stall to stall. There are little movements too, like the way she tucks a stray lock of her mane behind her ear, and the way her lips part slightly as she takes in a particularly interesting display of ripe fruit. Even the way she walks, with a purposeful stride that belies her uncertainty—as if, before all this, she was used to walking with her head high and with a certain poise despite the circumstances around her. It almost fools me. She blends in like a long-time resident, but she only just arrived. This must still be daunting for her.

I don't want to bring it up, but Zynar told me of what happened to my *kahlesta* and, in essence, what happened to all of her kind that have left her planet. Including Catherine. I know the Tasqals traveled across the galaxy and took her from her home. When Zynar and I left Karicek, we'd had no choice. The pain of remaining on that ravaged world had been too great. But we knew of others. We knew other sentient species existed.

Catherine did not.

She's taking this new path the gods have given her incredibly well. I'm impressed as I watch her walk beside me without fear. She doesn't even seem scared of me or the other predator species going about their day around us.

We arrive at the lodge vendor far too quickly. I'd deliberately parked the truck a few leagues down the street just to lengthen this time, but somehow it passed by swiftly all the same. The entire journey here, sitting in the cab of the truck was increasingly torturous. I'd wanted to say something smart. Or perhaps something funny. Anything, but the words did not come. Even on the walk to get the supplies, I'd intended to converse with her, thinking the busy town would distract enough that I could get to know her better without seeming purposeful about it. I've missed that chance, too.

Duty calls, and so I push those thoughts aside and focus on the task before me. The lodge vendor is a grizzled old Kalgonite, with a face like weathered leather and eyes that have seen more than their fair share of hardship. He greets me with a nod of recognition, and we quickly fall into the familiar rhythm of haggling and negotiation.

From the corner of my eye, I'm aware of Catherine watching the exchange with interest, her eyes widening slightly at the array of unfamiliar tools and materials on display. I see her eyes narrow as she tries to make sense of it all. She chooses from the selection of roof material on display, selecting one with a green hue that comes up short to the vibrance in her eyes and even takes over directing the Kalgonite to the type of trim she'd like.

Before long, we have everything we need, with the Kalgonite taking our order of beams and roof material, which he'll have loaded into my truck by the time we're ready to leave town. I turn to Catherine, hoping she doesn't want to return just yet.

"All done," I say, trying to keep my voice light. "We can get supplies for your sustenance stores now, if you like." My suggestion is the safest bet. Surely, she can't reject that offer. Sustenance is always something that's needed and it would give us some more time out here. Some more time for me to… For me to what? Be around her for a bit longer? Ask her about herself? Get her to talk to me? She doesn't even want a mate. That should deter this…*urge* or whatever it is. Instead, it's still there burning like tiny pinpricks on my nerves.

I hold my breath as Catherine gives me a slight smile, her gaze shifting back down the street.

It's that loneliness again, isn't it. It's why I've dragged this poor human into town on an excursion she probably didn't even want to agree to. I grimace, ready to tell her we can head back now if she wants to, when her face suddenly lights up.

Delicate fine lines crinkle at the corners of her eyes as she turns her green gaze up to me.

"If it's not too much," she begins. *Too much? It's not enough.* I frown at my thoughts even as I lean closer to hear her over the noise of new customers who have come beside us. "I saw some things when we were walking up here. They looked like fruits. Like…mangos?"

When I tilt my head, she continues, moving her hands in front of her in a motion as if she is sculpting something invisible.

"They were round with red and orange skin. Smooth."

Realization dawns. "I know just the thing." Giving a nod to the Kalgonite vendor, I guide Catherine back down the street, one arm reaching around her to protect her side from other pedestrians but not daring to actually touch her. When we stop at the exotic fruit stall, her eyes light up.

"This one." She reaches for the fruit she referred to as a mahn-goh. "These look amazing."

She looks up and smiles at me. A genuine one, not those other smiles that don't reach her eyes, and I pause, staring at her for much longer than I have right to.

"How much is it for these?" She directs her focus at the vendor who tells her a price and begins suggesting other things on his stall as well, piling several different fruits in front of her at once. Some quite bitter and others I'd class as inedible. I frown, about to tell him to back down when there's a sound nearby. Someone shouts in alarm and a ripple goes through the crowd.

It happens without conscious thought. I don't realize I've moved till I hear Catherine's soft voice behind me. I've put myself between her and the source of the disturbance, my claw reaching for the blade at my hip.

"What's going on?" she whispers. The heat of her presence behind me spreads across the scales along my spine in a way that makes me want to groan.

"I'm not sure what it is." But as I strain to see through the milling crowd, I realize that the cause of the commotion is nothing more than a pair of drunken Zilox's, their voices raised in a slurred and incoherent argument.

I'm just about to relax my guard when one of the Ziloxs stumbles out of the alley and into the main thoroughfare. He's a big brute of a creature, with a thick, scaly hide and a mouth full of jagged teeth. And he's heading straight for us, his eyes glazed and unfocused.

Someone cries out as he almost tramples them, his staggered steps sending him straight into the stall beside us. The thing topples, sending wares cascading into the street.

Without thinking, I turn and grip Catherine, taking her with me out of the way as the Zilox lurches past. He's so close that I can smell the sour reek of alcohol on his breath, can feel the power in his frame as he bumps into me, sending a growl through my throat. This is no place to stagger around in a drunken stupor. He could have seriously hurt Catherine if I wasn't standing here to block her with my frame.

For a moment, I'm frozen in place, my heart pounding in my chest as I watch the Zilox weave his way unsteadily down the street, irritated sounds and curses from other annoyed shoppers in his wake. But then I feel Catherine's hand on my arm, and I realize just how I'm holding her. I've gripped her to my chest, lifting her from the ground and forcing her to either wrap her thighs around me or hang awkwardly in my arms. And she's chosen the first option.

Now, I freeze for a whole other reason. Still looking over my shoulder, I don't dare to turn my attention to the female in my arms, because the moment I do, I'll have to release her. So I continue watching the Zilox stumble away.

Zynar, that little pile of excrement. He didn't tell me this is how his human mate feels. I've touched her before, even lifted her once, but not like this. It was nothing like this.

Catherine is soft. So incredibly, frakking soft. She's lithe and yet there is flesh there for my claws to grab and sink into. The thought makes lifeblood rush to the wrong place, and I dare not adjust myself.

Catherine's breath hitches as she clings to me, her digits digging into the scales on my arms. I can feel the rapid rise and fall of her chest against mine, the hammering of her core-beat echoing through my body like a vibration that aligns with mine.

I close my eyes for a moment, seeking that thing deep inside me that I want to awaken so much. My core-rhythm. But there is nothing there. It's as silent as it's always been, and a wave of disappointment swells within me.

I'm hoping again. Hoping against reality while the very essence of my being remains dormant. I'm wanting this female in my arms to be something that she isn't. And yet, I can't release her. Despite myself, despite all she's said in the ride to town, that hope still grows.

I know I should let her go. Know that the longer I hold her like this, the harder it will be to pretend that this is just a fleeting moment of protection, a brief lapse in the careful distance I've tried to maintain between us.

But I can't seem to make myself *move*. I don't know what the frakk is wrong with my arms. I can't seem to let go of the feel of her against me, the way her body molds itself to mine like it was always meant to be there.

And so I stay, my arms wrapped around her like a shield against the world, my head dipping slightly into the soft curtain of her mane. I breathe in the scent of her, a heady mix of sweat and cleansing foam and something else. Something uniquely her.

Catherine suddenly stirs in my arms, her muscles tensing as she begins to pull away.

"Varek," she whispers, a strange sound in her voice that cuts through my thoughts. "You can put me down now."

Reluctantly, I loosen my grip, letting her slide down the

length of my body until her feet touch the ground once more. She takes a step back, her cheeks flushed and her eyes wide, and for a moment I think she's going to bolt, to run away from the intensity of what just passed between us.

I'm an idiot. Such a fool. That was too much and far too soon. Far too sudden. If she denies my assistance on her farm now, I would deserve her judgment.

But then she takes a deep breath, and I see a flicker of something in her eyes. Something fierce and determined, a glint of steel beneath the softness.

"Thank you," she says again, her voice steady despite the tremor in her hands as she adjusts the satchel she brought. She's frowning, her brow drawn low and her gaze is on the crowd that's slowly returning to normal. She does not face me. "For getting me out of the way."

I've messed this—whatever it is—up. I've messed it all up.

I jerk my chin to my chest, not trusting myself to speak. Not trusting myself not to say something foolish, something that will shatter this fragile truce between us.

But even as I stand there, tongue-tied and uncertain, I can feel the weight of Catherine's gaze on me the moment I adjust the blade on my hip and look away. Can feel the unspoken questions that hang in the air between us. And behind all that, the stubborn whispers of possibility that tug at the edges of my consciousness.

Frakk.

"We should go, shouldn't we?" She asks, looking away again and adjusting her tunic and satchel as my gaze shifts back to her. "Before any more of those males appear."

"Right. Yes."

Frakkkk.

I know, with a certainty that goes beyond mere instinct, that this moment will change everything. For a terrifying click, I wonder if she felt the hardness lingering in my trouse. I could punch myself if it wouldn't draw more attention to the fact that I am, indeed, what my siblingkin has often called me in jest. A fool.

She walks slightly ahead of me as we head back to the truck and I pause as we go past another stall with the fruits she'd wanted so much. I open my mouth to stop her, but the mood is ruined, so I slam my jaw shut and continue on. She leads the way to the truck, finding it with zero trouble, and I open the door to let her in. Walking around to the other side, I see the Kalgonite is quick. The back is already filled with the beams, bolts, and roof material we purchased. There's no reason to tarry.

Opening the door, I find Catherine sitting with her gaze forward. She offers me a tight smile and I admire her effort of trying to keep the air between us amicable, even as something deep inside me twists.

Sitting at the hover controls, my claws tighten and relax, tighten and relax.

Catherine doesn't say anything. It's almost like she's not even there anymore. Her body is here, but it's suddenly like her presence is guarded away behind some invisible wall. When I look at her, she meets my gaze, doesn't flinch away, but her smile is that same tight thing. A stretch of her lips as her eyebrows lift slightly.

This won't do.

"A moment." It comes out gruff as if all the practicing I've done in the wee hors of dawn was for naught. I can't even apologize, fearing it will come out gruffly too, and as I hop out of the cab, I'm mentally berating myself as I head back down the street.

The fruit vendor's eyes alight the moment he spots me, probably remembering that we'd lingered at his stall once before.

"Greetings good—" The severity of my brow cuts him off,

but all is forgiven the moment I tell him exactly what I want.

6

CATHERINE

The ride back is quiet. Silent even. The only sound being the soft hum of the engine.

I keep my gaze forward, even though I'm completely aware of the alien beside me. He leans back in his seat, a slight frown on his brow as he faces the curved windscreen before us. He hasn't looked at me since he returned to the vehicle. Hasn't said a word. And even though it's what I want, what I *need*, some part of me is disappointed. As if I've been reduced to wanting the attention I've gotten from him so far. As if I crave it even more than I'd like to admit.

I release a slow silent breath, allowing my back to rest on the leather as the hover truck speeds along. It's smooth. Much smoother than riding in a car on a freshly paved highway. Almost like riding on the wind itself, and, I suppose, that's exactly what we're doing. I would ask how it all works—but it just doesn't seem like the right thing to say.

Glancing over my shoulder, something twists deep inside me at the crate of fruits I can see resting there in the trunk. A whole crate. The same fruits I was looking at and wanted to buy. I want to think that he bought them for himself. No way he purchased an entire crate full of the things for me. They were like ten credits each, which is a considerable amount for a single fruit, but I still wonder. He never paid any attention to them when we were on the street. Could he have really...no. Why would he? He's already doing so much for me, that would be going above and beyond for a stranger he's only just met.

One who climbed him like he was a tree.

I want to groan and cover my face with my hands. Possibly scream into the vastness of the plains. But Varek is here. He would see me. Hear me. Stand witness to my mortification.

He lifted me out of the way like I weighed nothing. And my response? Climb him.

It was instinctual.

The moment he lifted me, my body reacted on its own, seeking safety in the strong, solid presence of him. Why in the name of all that is good, did I do that? I haven't—when was the last time I—

I don't even have an excuse. I just did it. And that has me quite unsure of what the hell happened out there. I've always been able to keep my composure. Back on Earth, it was one of my strong points. Can't be a weakling prone to one's emotions when the Richmond name depended on every single thing you did.

That ingrained steel will is what got me through waking up surrounded by aliens and realizing the entire life I lived before was over. It's what got me through the pains and struggles of human existence back on Earth. Yet there I was, clinging to Varek like a lifeline, my heart racing as if my lawyers had discovered a devastating piece of information that could torpedo the entire family name.

Crackers on a stick. His hold on me was steady. He lifted me as if it was so...natural, and I clung to him, images of the war and those horrid aliens that took me from Earth swimming right back into my memory as if it was just yesterday. It's done, it's all finished now, and I thought I was over it. Over the trauma those Tasqals created within me. And yet, the moment that huge alien stumbled our way, all I could see were his teeth and the fact he was coming right at us. I became an object again. Something to be pushed, pulled, beaten, bred, and abused, with no regard for my will or input.

I overreacted.

Now, as we glide over the landscape, I can't stop replaying the moment in my head, over and over again. I didn't have to climb into his arms like that. It wasn't a drastic situation. If I'd just allowed Varek to move me out of the way like he intended, it wouldn't have been a big deal. And Varek? He'd gone like stone. Hard, unmoving, I couldn't even feel him breathing.

I try to ignore the weight of his presence beside me now and the way his scent fills the cab of the truck and makes my head spin. It's even stronger now than before. Colognes fade over time, but this sweet scent only seems to be increasing. He smells good. So good. I want to chide myself for acknowledging even that. It takes everything within me not to berate myself for paying attention to something so simple. Something so masculine it reminds me I'm a woman.

I'm a woman.

One that wants to be touched, even though she says she doesn't. One that wants to be held, even though I push the thought away. One that wants to be loved, even though I know the time for such things has passed. Such thoughts belong where I've hidden them away because they make my chest tighten. My heart ache.

Am I even the same person? The same Catherine Rose Richmond that was living that life on Earth? The one that had a family, a nice home...a husband?

That last one holds me still.

He'd died years before I was even abducted. I've already mourned. Already picked up myself and moved on. It all feels like a distant dream now. And yet, the guilt remains. The sense that having been granted this new life I'm somehow betraying the memory of all those I've left behind.

As if they didn't even exist.

We arrive at the farm just as the sun is reaching its midpoint in the sky. A slight breeze is still blowing, sending the grass swaying as the oogas in the field graze calmly. It's distinctly out of sorts to the turmoil suddenly raging inside me.

Varek hops out of the truck, heading around to my side and I realize he's going to open the door for me. The thought of being so close again makes me try to open the door myself, but there's no lever or button. It opens a short moment later as Varek saves me the embarrassment of fumbling with the thing and I hop out beside him.

"Well then," I start, forcing a smile to chase away the thoughts that feel like dark wisps of smoke threatening to pull me under.

"I'll unload the supplies and get to work." His directness makes my mouth fall shut and I press another smile on my face. Giving him a nod, my gaze shifts to the trunk of the vehicle.

"Need help?"

Varek's expression is unreadable. When he turns to look at my cottage, I realize I'd missed that the Raki had arrived for work and is tending to the roof.

Varek makes a sound in his throat that's awfully close to a growl. One you'd expect something like a lion or bear to make. His gaze could cut steel as he glares at the Raki.

"No, thank you, soft female. That *pilkra* will only hinder me."

I open my mouth to tell him I was referring to *me* helping him, not the Raki, but my mouth slams shut again at how easily he just called me a 'soft' female. At how easily I'm reminded of how hard he was against me. He was like muscle and steel.

He shuts the truck door, still glaring at the Raki as I force my thoughts away.

"Alright, I'll just go change and I'll be right out to help you." I duck away before he can say a thing, and even with my focus forward as I head to my cottage, I can feel his gaze burning into my back. A tense smile at the Raki on my roof and I hurry into the cover my cottage provides. Once inside, I release a breath that had been paused in my chest.

I don't even allow myself to think. To unravel whatever is causing these new emotions. I head to my room and I change. I tie my hair up again, I set down my very empty tote bag, and I square my shoulders.

Taking a deep breath, I step back outside, blinking in the bright sunlight. The Raki is still on the roof, carefully mending the damaged sections, while Varek has already begun unloading the supplies from the truck with an intensity that borders on aggression. His muscles flex with each movement, and I can see the strain in his jaw. Even from a distance, the tension radiates off him like heat from a furnace.

He's angry. Probably because of what happened in the town. I crossed a line, even one of my own lines, clinging on to him like that. He said he doesn't have a mate, but that really is no excuse for what I did. Only, how do I apologize for something we both seem intent on ignoring.

"Where do you want me to start?" I call out, walking towards the truck.

Varek glances over at me, his expression unreadable. For a moment, I think he's going to tell me to go back inside, to leave the heavy lifting to him. But then he nods towards a stack of smaller boards.

"You can start by carrying those over to the perimeter," he says, his voice gruff. "I'll need them to patch up the holes."

I blink at him, but he's already heading to the barn with a massive beam balanced on his shoulders.

The perimeter? As in the perimeter fence? I thought he was only helping with the barn. My focus shifts to the Raki. I'd intended to ask him to do all the repairs, but he's so slow. Maybe it would be better for me to pay Varek to do it instead. That is, if I can smoothen things out between us.

"Look, Varek." His name on my lips seems to make him freeze. Bracing the large beam on his shoulder, he turns to look at me and I'm forced to continue down the track I started on. "About what happened in town—"

"It won't happen again." He heaves the beam, balancing it across his shoulders with an ease that makes my eyebrows rise. "I will not touch you again unless you ask me to, Catherine."

What now?

I'm silenced, his words turning over in my head as he walks toward the barn to set the beam down.

"It was my mistake." It comes out as a whisper I'm not sure he hears because he's almost at the barn now. With a sigh, I take in a deep breath as I reach for the small boards. They're light, easy to carry and I get to work, grateful for the distraction. Grateful for something to do with my hands, something to keep my mind from wandering down dangerous paths.

We work in silence for a while, the only sounds being the grunting of the oogas in the field and the occasional hammer strike from the Raki on the roof. It's hot, sweaty work, and before long I can feel my tunic sticking to my back, my hair plastered to my head. My back aches even though the planks aren't heavy, and

I might be permanently folded at a right angle from my waist. But it feels good, too. Feels good to be doing something physical, something real. Feels good to be working alongside Varek, even if we're not speaking, even if the tension between us is thick enough to cut with a knife.

By the time I finish unloading the planks, he's already done moving the beams and the roof fiber. Only the box of fruit is left and I look at it wistfully, my mouth watering a little before I turn away. The barn roof is about three times as high as the cottage's and Varek uses a black square similar to the Raki's to get on top of it. I watch him work for a bit. Watch as he begins measuring things…or maybe I'm just watching how the sunlight plays on his scales.

I have to pull myself away. There's not much left for me to do out here. I might as well go tidy the house. So I focus on that. I head back inside and I don't allow myself to think. I focus on the house. I wipe. I clean. I make the interior of the little cottage as good as I can make it. It's my home now and, as the only thing I have control of on this farm, I focus on trying to personalize it as much as I can. The New Horizons Representative, Xarion, had been kind enough to ask what color of linen I preferred for my curtains and sheets. So now, the whole place is purple. My favorite color.

As the day wears on, as the sun begins to sink towards the horizon and the shadows lengthen across the grass, I find myself stealing glances out the window. Not at the view. Not at the work going on outside. At him. I find myself watching the alien with the iridescent scales, something strange yet deeply familiar swirling in the depths of my gut. Something I don't want to even acknowledge.

He works fast. Much faster than the Raki, stripping the entire roof in the little time he's been out there. Another lump forms in my throat as I watch the way his body moves, the way his hands grip the tools with sure, steady strength.

Each hammer that he lays down, my body jerks a little with the force of that strength. A man like him could do real damage to a woman like me in bed. I blush at the thought, partially horrified I'm even thinking it. Even more horrified that it's risen in my mind at all.

And when Varek catches me looking, when his gaze meets mine across the yard and holds, I don't have the shame to duck away from the window. Like a deer caught in headlights, I stare back at him, a skitter going straight through the center of my chest like an electric thread. Something hot and hungry and alive, something that makes my breath catch in my throat and my heart stutter in my chest alight.

That stutter in my chest scares me enough that I look away. Force myself to break the moment and shift away from the window. He lifted me and for the first time in a long while, I felt the real strength of a male. The real hardness of one.

That's all this is.

That's all it can be.

Hours later, when he knocks and says that he's leaving, it's long after the Raki had already gone. It's dark, the sun hiding on the other side of the planet, and by the time I reach the door, Varek is already in his hover truck.

I catch his eyes before he leaves. Catch the respectful dip of his head, chin to chest, before he pulls away.

Watching the hover truck go, something tightens in my chest. I pull my shawl closer across my shoulders, frowning at myself as I take a deep breath.

Well, this day was a disaster. I'm about to close the door, lock myself in for the night, when I almost miss the crate of fruit sitting on my doorstep.

That same thing that tightened in my chest grows tenser, as if it's going to strangle my heartstrings.

Lifting the crate, I bring them inside, setting them at the center of the table. I stare at them now and my throat clenches. I swallow hard.

The fruits glisten in the dim light as if calling to me and I lick my lips at the temptation. Because that's what they are. A temptation. Like a tangible manifestation of…something I can't even put into words. It's silly, but it takes great will to turn away.

It feels like the heaviness of the world is on my shoulders as I head to the bedroom, letting my body plop into the bed, facedown, my nose scrunched against the purple linen.

Tomorrow will be better. It always is. It always gets easier.

7

VAREK

I'm despicable.

That doesn't stop me from pumping my fist along my shaft, groaning at the image I've dreamt up in my mind.

Catherine.

She's against me, her soft body tucked underneath mine as she whimpers my name while I plunge into her. The thought makes my eyes roll back, a groan on my lips that vibrates into the still dark room around me. My tongue flicks against my fangs as I lick my lips, my hips shunting forward underneath the sleep coverings right before my entire frame stiffens.

I imagine her body quaking as she reaches her peak while I'm buried deep within her slit. The thought alone is enough to send me over the edge. A pulse goes through me, warm thick seed flowing over my fist and down my arm as I empty my sac.

I really am despicable.

I stay there for a few moments, staring up at the dark roof above me.

She's not looking for a mate. What the frakk is wrong with me?

I'm not looking for a mate. I'm looking for *my* mate. My *kahl.*

Surely, if my *kahl* was right before me, I would know. Somehow, I'd know she is the one I'm searching for.

Twisting, I throw my legs off the sleeping slab and head toward the washroom. There I clean myself without looking at my reflection. I can't. I'm pitiful.

When my comm pings in the other room, I almost stumble over my feet and my still semi-hard cock as I rush back into the room for it. I growl when I see who it is.

"What are you doing awake?" My growl does nothing to rip the grin off my siblingkin's face.

"If you must know, I spent the last few hors pleasuring my mate. What is your reason?"

I sneer at him, feigning disgust. What I'm really feeling is such an onset of pure, raw jealousy that the sneer actually becomes real.

Zynar chuckles. "I had to ping you."

"For what reason, brother?" I head back toward the sleeping slab, scratching my mane as I wonder what else I can do to pass this torturous dark cycle.

"The human called Catherine."

I freeze, my complete focus flying back to the screen.

"Has something happened to her?"

There's a glint in Zynar's eyes. The only indication that makes me realize my tone has changed from one of indifference to being laced with concern.

"No. Eleanor wanted to know how everything went. We simply...got distracted before she was able to ping you. She is resting now."

My shoulders sag, some tension leaving my frame as I collapse on the sleeping slab once more.

"Everything went...well." I grimace, running a claw across my face.

"You are a terrible liar."

I release a breath and drop my arm. The comm lands on the

bedsheets beside me, the dim light from the screen lighting up the immediate area.

Zynar doesn't prod, even though I know he must be curious. When a few clicks pass with only the sound of him adjusting himself on his sleeping slab, I finally release another breath.

"Tell me again, how you knew Eleanor was yours. When your core-rhythm sung, what happened before that."

Zynar grunts and it sounds like he adjusts his body some more. "I told you, brother. We mated and then it happened."

I think about this for a moment. "Do you think if I mate with Catherine, I'd know for sure?"

There's silence on the other line. Silence for so long that I reach for the comm again and bring it above my face. My mirror image stares back at me, only slightly stockier, slightly older. Zynar tilts his head.

"You think the human is your *kahl?*"

The word makes an ache develop in my chest. I shake my head, the motion itself feeling like a proclamation of my failure.

"I think she is beautiful. Captivating in a way I cannot explain."

"That is how I felt with Eleanor."

I groan. "Do not give me false hope, brother."

"It is the truth. There was nothing else to tell me my core-rhythm would sing. If I had known…"

He trails off but he doesn't need to continue. I already know what he was about to say. If he'd known then he wouldn't have put Eleanor in such danger. If he'd known he wouldn't have been so careless as to expose her to his rut.

"I think…" I say after a few moments, shame filling me. That same despicable feeling rising. "I think I want her."

Zynar grins. "What's stopping you then, brother? Even if your core-rhythm doesn't sing, there are other bonds to be had. Humans do not have fated bonds like us. What obstacle—"

"She doesn't want a mate."

He stills, staring at me through the device. "She told you this?"

"Loud and clear."

"Frakk."

"Indeed."

Silence descends on us once more and I can tell Zynar is turning over my dilemma in his mind.

"Well," he says after a few moments, "will you be giving up then?"

I meet his gaze across the comm. "No."

His grin gets wider and I groan, throwing my head back against the slab as I consider ending the communication.

Because I am Kari. We aren't known for giving up when there's something that we want. And I want Catherine.

I just have to make her want me, too.

And then it hits me.

"Zynar." I lift the comm again. He sobers, noting the look in my eyes or probably the way I said his name.

"Yes, brother?"

"Tell me everything you know about humans. Tell me everything a human female likes."

The look on his face morphs to something downright devious, and I wonder for a moment if I'm making the right decision.

"The first thing you need to do, brother, is this…"

CATHERINE

I wake like I usually do every morning nowadays. Alone in my new cottage, the soft glow of the sun reflecting inside my window, and the serene sounds of the plains…

Wait.

I ease up on my elbows, squinting sleep from my eyes.

There's hammering outside. Rhythmic clangs that aren't usually present in my mornings.

I rise from the bed, rubbing sleep from my eyes as I gather my sleeping tunic around me and head to the front door. Opening it, I realize the morning really is very young. The rays of sun that greeted my window were ones that had barely stretched over the horizon. Walking along the porch, I head toward the sound, only to look up and see…him.

Varek is on the barn roof, stripping the rotten beams. He must have been there for a while because he's already stripped a quarter of the roof. I stare open-mouthed, forgetting I'm dressed in nothing but some thin linen and that my hair is a tousled mess.

How does he work so quickly? Where does he get this raw strength from? The Raki took an entire week before he managed to remove the roof fiber from the cottage, which is less than half the size of the barn. Never mind stripping the actual support beams underneath it, which took him another two weeks. Varek is one man, one *male*, and he's already done ten times what the Raki could do and in less than a day.

I must make some sound as I stand there, barefooted and still in nothing but that thin linen gripped against me, because Varek suddenly looks down and across to where I stand.

I don't know why I blush. My cheeks heat as if I've been caught doing or thinking something I shouldn't have been.

"Good dawn, Catherine." That deep voice finds me and sends a tingle from my toes straight up to my center. Goodness. Every pep talk and everything I berated myself about the day before seems all for naught. A shiver goes through me like my inhibitions have been completely reduced to dust.

"Good morning, Varek."

He walks down one of the slanted beams and comes closer.

My heart does a little thud, but this isn't like when the Raki looked clumsy on the roof and I was scared he'd make a mistake and fall off. Varek's body is completely sturdy. His steps are sure and firm.

My hair blows in a soft wind, obscuring my view of him for a moment and plastering the thin linen against me.

"You're awake early," I hear him say. "I didn't mean to disturb your rest."

I brush my hair away from my face, suddenly very aware of what I'm wearing when I find that intense yellow gaze on me. I resist the urge to adjust the linen nightgown and bring attention to it. "Don't worry. You didn't. I'm usually awake at this time anyway."

His gaze shifts to the cottage, then pierces me again. "Will you be drinking your customary heated beverage? I would like to share it with you."

I blink at him, confused. "My customary what now?"

Varek's expression remains stoic, but there's a hint of uncertainty in his eyes as he clarifies. "A brew made with blooms or weeds that you drink every dawn and sometimes at dusk?"

I stare at him for a moment, trying to process his words. "Do you mean tea?"

His face lights up as he places his claws on his narrow hips. My gaze drops and a lump rises in my throat. Much like with human males, there's that dangerous V-shaped cut of muscle that disappears beneath his trousers.

"Yes! Tea!" His exclamation pulls my gaze back to his face and I pray to God he didn't catch me staring. "I would like to share tea with you."

He sounds so excited by the prospect that I smile.

"I don't usually drink tea in the mornings." The moment I say the words is the moment his face falls, making me immediately regretful that I didn't blurt the entire sentence quickly. "But we could share a cup of tea, if you'd like. It's the least—"

I stop short, knowing what I was going to say. That it's the least I could do with him making such good progress. But more than that, it's the least I could do after what happened between us yesterday.

Varek beams again and I swear he stands a bit taller. "I'll be right down."

My eyes widen, awareness of how I'm dressed ringing like a bell in my ears.

I didn't expect him to want that cup of tea immediately.

"Alright! I'll, uh, just come on in." I'm hurrying back into the cottage all flustered. Rushing into the bedroom and closing the door behind me all in one breath. Back pressed against the firm wood, I stare at my tousled bed, wondering what the hell is happening. Tea? I don't even drink tea. But he seems hell-bent on wanting to share a cup with me.

I'm a bit confused and there's a nervous little spark of energy in the center of my chest that I'm trying my damnedest to ignore. I pull on another of the brown tunics and run my hands through my hair, pulling it into a tight ponytail at the back of my head. When I open the door, my breath stops in my throat.

Varek is inside. Inside my house and he fills the entire front room. Sucks the space away so all I can focus on is him. He turns to face me from where he'd been idly staring at the roof with a frown on his brow. The moment he faces me, that frown dissipates as if whatever he'd been thinking about is pushed to the backburner and I'm all that he can see.

Ridiculous. Where's my daily dose of reality that I use to keep me in check? Nowhere to be found apparently. Maybe I have to wait a few more hours before I'm knocked down and imprisoned by the thoughts that haunt me each day.

I smooth a hand down my chest and wish I hadn't. His gaze flicks to the movement, pausing at the gentle lumps of my breasts before he seems to force his gaze back to my eyes.

Oh dear. He doesn't think I'm attractive, does he? His blatant attention is so shocking, I realize I hadn't even considered that before.

What's worse is that there's a light in his eyes that wasn't there yesterday either. He folds his arms at his back, causing those chest muscles to flex like they're waving to me, and gives me his complete attention.

"It's beautiful," he says.

I blink at him, my eyelids fluttering. *He's not talking about you, Catherine.*

"What you've done with the lodge," he continues, gaze flicking around the interior once more.

See.

I could groan. Shaking my head, I try to clear my thoughts as I walk toward the little kitchen.

"Thank you. I've not added many changes, just a few curtains and cleaned up a bit. I'm happy you like it." I stop just inside the door to the kitchen, looking around for the kettle I hardly use.

"I do." Varek's voice makes me jump. He's so close behind me, that a tingle goes right up my spine. I didn't even hear him move. So close, just a breath away, but true to his word, he doesn't touch me.

I clear my throat. "So, tea? What type of tea do you like?" I spot the kettle and rush toward it as if it's a life vest I need in a sea I'm suddenly about to drown in. It puts some distance between me and the alien hunk who leans against the door-frame, watching me now.

He's not even being threatening. Nothing in his demeanor says he's flirting with me either. He simply wants some tea and I'm making a big deal out of it. Poor thing must have been working from the wee hours of dawn and missed breakfast.

"I'll like whatever you like," he replies, his words making my gaze pierce his.

"You've never had tea before, have you?" For the first time since meeting this species, I see Varek's ears move. They sort of flex even though they're planted flat against the sides of his head, their pointed tips disappearing into his—frankly— gorgeous green mane.

He shifts on his feet and I wonder if I've embarrassed him. Turning away, I crank the tap and put the kettle underneath it to fill it up. Back turned to him, I try to salvage the situation.

"I don't usually drink tea but whenever I do, I like mild blends. Something like rose tea or cherry." I glance over my shoulder. "I asked because I wasn't sure if you preferred some- thing more intense."

Something changes in his gaze and I'm not prepared when he says, "Do you like all things mild?"

If I responded immediately, I'd stutter. What does he even mean? "Not all things. Some things I like hard and…" I stop talking, my cheeks heating.

My filthy human brain is doing things it shouldn't.

He's talking about *food*. Just like some people can't take lots of spices in their meals and others absolutely crave it.

"I'm a mixed bag," I finally say, shutting off the tap and putting the kettle on the stove. "Sometimes I don't know what I like until I've had a taste of it, you know?"

The stove isn't like what I'm used to back home. This one is like a funnel that the flame rises through with only a metal plat- form above it to rest the kettle on. It takes me a few tries to get it started before I turn to face Varek again.

His eyes are glued on me.

"About yesterday—" I start. It's heavy on my chest. Some- thing that feels like it will always be in the middle between us if I don't clear the air. But Varek straightens.

"I was out of line," he says. "As promised, Catherine, I will not touch you like that again…unless you ask me to."

I'm silenced not by the fact he's once again taking the blame for the awkward encounter that ruined our trip, but because of the last few words he uttered. *"Unless you ask me to."* That sounds like a damn promise. An oath.

"I'm sorry, too. I shouldn't have climbed on you like that. I was out of line." I turn away, opening my crates of dry goods as I search for the tea flowers New Horizons sent in my pack of supplies. The shuffling sounds as I dig are loud, but not loud enough that I don't catch Varek's murmur.

"You were not out of line, Catherine. Your touch, your closeness…it was not unwelcome."

I pause, my hands stilling in the crate as his words wash over me. There's a gentleness to his tone, a vulnerability there that makes me turn slowly, meeting his gaze across the kitchen.

His eyes are soft, but there's an intensity there that makes my breath catch. "I apologize if my actions made you uncomfortable, but please do not think that your presence in my arms was anything less than a gift."

I swallow hard, my heart pounding in my chest. This is dangerous territory. All my demons come rushing forward, pulling me back from this line we're both tiptoeing around. I don't know this male. His words shouldn't have any effect. Heck, his words shouldn't have been said at all. My touch? A gift?

He speaks as if he really enjoyed it in a way that goes beyond innocent platonic bonds.

But he's not joking. He takes a step forward, his movements slow and deliberate, as if he's trying not to startle me.

Painful memories threaten to rise, yet, somehow, I stand my ground.

"I meant what I said, Catherine. I will not touch you again without your permission. But if you ever find yourself wanting to be held, wanting to feel the warmth of another…I will be here. Always."

8

VAREK

Gods, I really am a fool.

I did too much and far too soon.

AGAIN.

As I watch Catherine hurry past me toward the whistling kettle, I'm not sure if it's what I just proclaimed or the fact the kettle needed to be removed from the fire that made her hurry away.

Zynar said to take it slow. Warned me that if Catherine is anything like his human mate, that she might be hesitant. Skittish even. He said he'd had to let his mate come to him—a test for any Kari. One of the things he told me was that his *kahl* offered to drink this 'tee' beverage with him in the early days and that it brought them closer together. A hot beverage didn't sound like something I'd enjoy, but if Catherine liked it, I'd drink an entire cauldron full if it meant she'd give me some of her time. I was to simply drink this 'tee' with Catherine and then get back to work.

Instead, I all but confessed that I want her pressed against me and that I've been thinking about it. Worse still, she doesn't even enjoy 'tee'.

Frakk me.

If she abandons her tee making and casts me from her lodge, I deserve it.

I grimace, watching her get two drinking receptacles and fill them both with the steaming liquid. She has said nothing since my inadvertent confession. The silence between us is deadly. Her throat moves as she turns to face me again, her gaze flicking to me only briefly, as if she doesn't want to look at me for too long. It makes something ache in my chest. My core-beat. But I deserve the pain.

She holds up two packets of dried blooms. Her voice is so soft, another part of me tightens, and it has nothing to do with chagrin. How much more despicable can I get?

"New Horizons sent these in the welcome pack. I really have no idea what they taste like."

Should I stand still? Should I lean closer?

My brain says to remain where I am, but something tugs me closer to Catherine anyway. As if every muscle within me refuses the distance between us. I lean in, inhaling the packets she's holding. Glancing up, I see her throat bob, a slight almost imperceptible tremor going up her arms. The reaction isn't one I can easily read. Am I scaring her? But when my gaze rises further to her eyes, something trills within me. Catherine doesn't look scared. The look in her eyes isn't one I've seen before, either. Beneath her lashes, those green eyes hold a depth of emotion that almost arrests me.

"This is calla," I point to the tee petals in her left hand. Her throat moves again. "And this one is pargentum." I point to the other packet of tee petals. She nods slightly.

"Any—" Catherine makes a sound in her throat as if the words got stuck and she needed to clear the blockage. "Any, um, any idea what they taste like?"

I lean back, standing normally now, my eyes narrowing

slightly as I take her in. She's affected by something. Was it what I'd said? Or is it…oh gods…

My core-beat skips a note. Could she be affected by *me*?

"Pargentum has a strong scent. I do not know of the taste." I tilt my head, watching her still. She brings the packet of pargentum to her straight little nose, sniffing deeply. Her eyebrows lift. "Calla's scent is mild but sweet."

Her unexpected smile makes my core-beat flutter. Her eyes find mine. "We'll go with calla then."

She turns back to the steaming receptacles, and I lean closer to see what she's doing. Opening the packet of petals, she pulls out a few and drops them into each receptacle before getting a curved utensil and swirling them around in the hot liquid. The steaming water slowly changes color as if dyed by the petals within it.

"We have a flower back on Earth with the same name, so maybe it's a sign."

"Earth?"

There's a subtle pause in her stirring, one that would have gone unnoticed if I wasn't watching her so closely.

"Yes. My, uh, my planet. My home." She glances at me for a moment, that one word seeming to ricochet in the room.

She still thinks of her old planet as her home. Of course, she does. Despite that she'll never be able to return to it, it's all she knew. Everything that occurred the day before comes rushing back. How she'd seemed to shutter when she'd mentioned her homeworld.

This isn't a topic that brings back wistful memories. Just like me and Zynar, all Catherine must feel is pain when she thinks of the world she left behind. I grimace again. I'm supposed to be making her think *good* things, making her *like* me, not reminding her of the trauma she experienced to get here.

Frakk me. I'm failing at this.

"I didn't mean to remind you of—"

"It's okay." She sets down the stirring utensil and places the drink receptacles on separate small trays. "Biscuit?"

I jerk my chin to my chest without even understanding what she's asking. She smiles again and I swear a part of me melts. I'm somewhat confused, not sure where I'm standing but completely convinced I've destroyed this attempt at getting closer to her. But she hasn't cast me out of her dwelling yet. There must be hope.

When she grabs both trays and a pack of flat meal squares she jerks her head toward the main room and I take it as an indication to follow.

The linen she's wearing sways as she walks and my head tilts as I catch the faintest outline of her curved behind underneath the clothing. When she suddenly glances over her shoulder, my fangs could have retracted into my gums and I would welcome the pain. She caught me staring.

"Feel free to have a seat." She jerks her chin at the broad table as she sets both trays down and puts the meal squares in the center. As she pulls out a stool and sits, I hurry to the one on the opposite side.

My gaze drops to the tee and 'biskits', wondering the correct etiquette for such a meal. Zynar didn't go into much detail. He'd hurried off the line because he hadn't wanted to wake his sleeping mate. I'm in unchartered waters here.

My gaze shifts to the crate of senzsi fruit I purchased for Catherine. It sits off to the side on the table and for a moment, my core-beat rises again, hope fueling each beat. But it only takes a click to sink. It's not hard to see she hasn't eaten a single portion of the fruits. I'd thought she'd wanted them. Their untouched presence is not a good sign.

My claws twitch as I rest them on the table, eyes shifting back to Catherine, watching and waiting for her cue. When she takes up her receptacle, I watch her lips as she blows on the hot beverage before taking the smallest of sips. As she sets it back down, my gaze snags on her lips as she takes one of the biskits and takes a bite. Her tongue is the smallest little pink thing as she gathers a few fallen crumbs from the side of her mouth.

When her cheeks begin to change color, turning an intense shade of red, I realize I've been staring again. Grabbing the receptacle in my fist, I ignore the heat as I take a big gulp of the tee.

I freeze. Frakk, it's hot. My face twists as I force it down.

I feel like I've messed up again, my embarrassment growing. But then, to my surprise, Catherine laughs. It's a light, melodic sound that fills the room and makes my ears perk up.

"You don't have to guzzle it like that," she says between giggles. "It's meant to be sipped."

I feel the tension melt away at her laughter, and a sheepish grin tugs at my lips. "Noted," I manage to say, my voice rough from the scalding tea. I can't take my eyes off her, and at the sound of the roughness in my voice, I watch her cover her mouth, trying her darndest to preserve my ego as she tries to stop herself from laughing.

The tee, the biskits, the world fades into the background as I watch her eyes twinkle with her mirth. Something swells within me that I can't explain. Something that makes me feel like I could walk on air. At this moment, I realize I'd do anything to make Catherine laugh again. Her *real* mirth. Not the other times she laughs and it never reflects in her eyes. When she truly laughs, it's like the stars are in those green depths. How much pain and hurt she must have endured for even the stars to stop shining there.

She sobers, taking up a meal square and handing it to me. My claw brushes her thin digits, sending a spark through my arm as I accept the food.

"It's better with the biskit. Gives you something to chew. Back home I always—"

I go still. She does too. My throat tightens, waiting for the shadow of her past to constrict. Waiting for her to shutter and hide herself away from me. Waiting, my core-beat feeling like it's going to fail, for those stars in her eyes to dim again. And they do. Slightly.

"I always would have some sort of biskit or cake on the rare occasions I'd drink some tee. And that was only when my best friend, a woman I met really early on before I got married, visited. God forbid she'd have a glass of wine or anything else. It was always tea."

I release a breath slowly, not daring to engage in case I really do make her shutter. This is the first time she's finished a proper sentence about her life back on her home planet. I'm thankful for just that. But the gods must be looking down this dawn and decided to bless me more because Catherine continues.

"It's...nice." She smiles and her gaze meets mine. "Thank you, Varek."

I pause, the receptacle halfway to my lips. I finish the movement on the pure fact that it will give me more time to figure out what she's thanking me for. I sip the liquid this time, taking a bite of the meal square as Catherine instructed, and chewing them together. It's...surprisingly good.

Catherine's smile softens, but it's real.

I swallow the mixture and set the receptacle down. "For what do you show me gratitude?"

"For reminding me that..." Catherine pauses, her eyes searching mine as if trying to find the right words. "For reminding me that it's okay to remember the good times, too. That even though my life has changed so drastically, there are still small joys to be found in the everyday moments, like sharing a cup of tea with a friend."

Friend? Poor soft little thing has no idea I want to be so *so* much more. But her words have me frozen. She's said a lot. More words than I believe she's ever said to me in one sitting. Is this success? Did this tee meal work? I stare at Catherine, my core-beat picking up in my chest. When Zynar told me to invite her to share a hot beverage, I thought it ludicrous. But maybe he was on to something. After all, he's the one with a *kahl*.

My throat tightens as I swallow another sip of the tee, my gaze shifting to the leaves swirling in the bottom of the receptacle.

We finish the meal in silence, but I do notice one thing. Catherine meets my gaze more and when she stands to clear the items away, I rush to help. She releases a sort of breathless laugh as I set the items down in her meal preparation area. As I wash them, I hear her voice from the main room.

"Oh, you don't have to do that. You're my guest."

I pause in my washing, looking over my shoulder at Catherine. "It is no trouble. You have shown me kindness and shared your meal with me. The least I can do is assist with the cleaning."

Catherine's lips curve into a soft smile, and our gazes lock for a moment before she nods. "That's very thoughtful of you." Her smile doesn't fade. She doesn't look away until I'm forced to in order to complete cleansing the utensils.

I resist punching the air in victory. By the time I'm finished cleaning, I'm buzzing with an unseen energy.

I thank her for the tea as she follows me to the door. "It was my first time. But possibly you will share tee with me again?"

She seems a bit surprised. "Did you really enjoy it?"

I'm at the door when I turn to face her, that note of uncertainty in her voice making my gaze shift over her face.

She was worried I didn't like it? Flurvian gods, if she knew how much I loved it she might not invite me in again.

"I did." The hoarseness in my tone is something I couldn't have removed even if I tried. Catherine pauses there at the door, her gaze directed at my chest. The spot heats under her attention. When her head tilts and she smiles again, I know it's time to say goodbye. At least, for now. I must get back to work and she, well, she will go about her day as she usually did before I arrived.

Except, I wish this moment would never end.

My gaze falls to her lips and a small nest of crumbs at the corner of her mouth. My claw lifts, rising toward her skin where I freeze just a breath away from touching her. I feel the moment her breath stills, the soft feathering no longer brushing over my scales, and a lump forms in my throat, making it even harder to speak.

"May I?" I croak.

I believe she will say no. That she'll shift away from my touch and wipe the crumbs away herself.

She doesn't.

My core-beat leaps, the organ beneath it swelling as Catherine gives the slightest of nods.

As I use a digit to brush across her lips, it's like the world stands still. The softness of her lips underneath my claw, the softness of *her*, only reminds me of all the thoughts that have begun to plague me. Of the thoughts that kept me up for the entire dark cycle as I fisted my shaft and thought of her.

"Thank you," I whisper.

Catherine barely breathes. She's so still, it's like she's frozen too. Those brilliant green eyes search mine. "For what?"

"For reminding me what it feels like, too." Energy crackles between us. "I'll head to work now."

She barely nods. Her eyes are slightly wide, her lips opening slightly as my digit falls away.

I swallow hard, forcing my claw away as I turn and hurry across the porch and to the outbuilding, my mind buzzing and my shaft like a hard cylinder in my trouse.

9

CATHERINE

The day goes by too quickly.

Since I've come to the farm, I've spent most of my days outdoors, trying to wrangle the abandoned homestead into something I can really call home. Those days always went by slowly, as if the days here on Hudo III had double the hours the ones on Earth did.

But today…

I feel heat rise in my cheeks that has nothing to do with the intensity of the sun as I walk among the oogas, pretending I'm checking on the herd. Because I'm not really checking on the gentle animals, am I? Nope. My gaze is on the barn. The slanted roof is much higher than the cottage, looming over it and giving me a clear view of the work going on there even from where I stand in the field.

A lump rises in my throat and I clear it, my cheeks warming even more as I watch Varek work. He's a monster. I've never seen anyone work so fast or so hard. The heavy beams that hold the roof have all been stripped, leaving the barn top completely open now. I don't know how he's done it. How he manages to even lift the heavy timber that looks like it needs someone on the ground assisting him with a crane or something. Even the Raki had brought a machine along at one point to assist him in the much smaller task of my cottage roof.

My gaze shifts to the Raki now, and I notice that even his eyes are on Varek as he glides above the open barn top on one of those little black squares they use for a lift.

My heart thuds in my chest and a strange feeling that's been growing in my belly since this morning increases. A tremor goes through me as Varek turns in my direction and I look away, pretending to pat an ooga that's by my side.

"What am I doing out here, huh girl?"

This jittery strange feeling is so alien, it feels misplaced. I know what it is. I'm completely aware of what's happening... and I'm terrified.

Because it shouldn't be happening.

Is it because he's...nice?

I might just be imagining things because Varek has been nothing but gentlemanly. But this morning, the moment his finger brushed my lips, my lungs ceased to pump air. His touch was barely there, feather-light, and my entire body reacted anyway. Tingles shot up through my spine like electricity moving up through my core straight upward.

The reaction had me breathless. Held me still. The last time I reacted to a male's touch had been so long ago, I might have forgotten what it actually felt like. How *good* it could be. Shifting my gaze back to the barn, I see that Varek's no longer focusing my way.

What *am* I doing? This is silly.

I give myself a mental shake as I pat the ooga on its back and push through the tall grass toward the cottage. I'm just past the gate and heading around the side of the cottage when I hear a sound I've heard before. There's a dull thud as the Raki on the roof loses hold of whatever tool he's using. I look up, just in time to see the thing skating toward me.

But it doesn't snag like the last time.

My eyes widen as I realize it's coming right in my direction. I duck, trying to move out of the way, just before pain rockets through my shoulder.

"Ah!" I hiss, pulling air through my teeth as I grip my shoulder, my legs tangling in my confusion. I almost fall. I would have, if I wasn't suddenly braced up.

A sweet scent floods my nostrils as I hear a growl.

"What the *frakk* are you doing?!"

Varek? How did he…he was just on the roof.

"Curses." His voice sounds different. Dangerous and laced with anger. For a moment, my defenses rise at the fact it seems he's blaming me for what just occurred, but when I look up, his hard yellow pits aren't directed at me. They're focused on the Raki who is standing bewildered at the edge of my roof.

"You could have killed her!" Varek roars. His fangs bare and he snarls at the Raki, who, for a male that's built like a sturdy little elephant, seems to crumple in on himself. His large ears fold over his face and his bushy eyebrows rise high as his small dark eyes widen on me. I'm still wincing, one hand still gripping my shoulder as Varek pulls me away from the cottage.

"I apologize for this," Varek says, his gaze moving over my face as if he's searching for a key to stop the pain rocketing through my arm.

"For what?"

"For touching you. I made a promise I will have to break just this once."

I could laugh. Would have, if the ache wasn't still going through my shoulder. To think he'd still keep that promise even now. If he was a brute, I could push him away so easily. Instead, he's just so nice. For a moment, I wonder if this is what Eleanor experiences every day, living with his brother. Is he nice too? Did she really find a bit of paradise after everything?

When Varek suddenly lifts me, I almost let out a yelp at how easily he does. Just like when he lifted me in town, he does it so easily again, as if I weigh nothing.

With a snarl at the Raki, he heads inside the cottage, moving straight into the bedroom. He fills the space even more here, even worse than he did in the main room. When he sets me down on the bed, I blink up at him. At the concern in his eyes and the heavy breaths making his shoulders rise and fall.

Even with the heavy labor he's been doing, I never saw his chest rise and fall with exertion from lifting those heavy beams.

"Where does it hurt, *sura*?"

Sura? I frown slightly but his voice is so soft, a stark contrast to the anger he showed moments ago. Pointing at my shoulder, I wince as I try to take a peek at it.

"Let me." Varek takes a finger toward me and I watch in complete fascination as one of his claws extends.

"Wow, didn't know you could do that."

His hand—or rather, his claw—pauses. "Does it scare you?"

I shake my head, tongue flicking out to lick my lips as I watch that claw. "No, but I don't want you to rip the tunic. I'll just—"

I shift, sitting more upright on the bed as he hovers both claws over me in universal code for alarm. As if he's afraid I'll shatter to pieces from this one wound. Shifting my weight on one hip, I wince as I pull down the shoulder of the tunic.

Varek hisses and my gaze shoots to him. His face is murderous. Like a predator. Exactly like a predator. The slits in his eyes have widened and his lips have pulled back in a snarl.

"He has hurt you." He stands slowly, easing back and for the first time, I finally look at my shoulder. There's a nasty bruise there from where the tool hit me. Poking it with my finger, I wince again before rolling my shoulder.

"Don't think it's broken. I'll be fine. Was just an accident."

He doesn't respond. When I look at him it appears that he

can't. His fangs have extended and from the looks of it, he's struggling to push them back in. To hide them from me.

"Varek…" I find myself whispering because I'm shocked. Shocked that he's having such a response and…and grateful. My eyelids flutter as the feeling cements. Varek actually cares.

"Don't move." His usual soft tone is hard now, his words an order. Before I can open my mouth, he's gone, his footfalls heavy as he heads out of the cottage. My ears perk as I listen but there's no other sound. I'm trying to sit up straighter when he returns.

"You shouldn't move, sura," he growls. I relax against the bed again. He has a box in his arms that he rests on the bed and flips open. It's clear it's a first-aid kit from all the vials and gauze inside. I frown.

"You don't have to waste all that. I just need to put some ice on it."

Varek shakes his head. "I have never seen such a mark on flesh before," he says. "With Kari, an injury like this could be life-threatening. I do not want to take the chance."

I blink, again surprised, but underneath that surprise is that growing warmth I'm trying my best to ignore. "It's just a bruise, Varek. I'll be okay."

But he's not listening. His claws move quickly, almost frantically, as he prepares a vial and a syringe. "This will help with the pain and prevent any internal damage," he says, his voice firm.

I want to protest, but the look in his eyes stops me. I wouldn't say I'm an expert at reading slitted eyes, but as Varek waits for me to allow him to administer the medicine, it's clear he's genuinely terrified for me. "Okay," I whisper, nodding slightly. "But are you sure that's okay to use on someone like me? A human?"

"My kahlesta was injured. The medic left me with these vials for that reason. In case I needed his expertise, but he was too far away."

"Oh. Eleanor you mean, right?" When he nods, I do too. "Okay, do it."

His light touch on my arm distracts from the pain as he injects the solution near the bruise.

"How did Eleanor get injured?" I whisper, wincing slightly from the pinprick of the needle.

"Got hit down by an ooga. It was an accident."

"Oof," I whisper. "Good thing you were there."

He makes a sound in his throat and pulls the needle away before reaching for a bandage. "It was pure luck. I only found her because I went to protect her from—"

He stops talking abruptly. So abruptly that I look up at him.

He tightens the bandage and wraps up the used needle before closing the first-aid kit.

"Protect her from what?"

Varek doesn't meet my gaze. It actually seems like he won't answer me. But then his throat moves and he lifts the first-aid kit into his arms. "From Zynar."

My frown is warranted. I'm confused. "But...why? Aren't they together? Why would you need to protect Eleanor from her own husband? Her, erm, her mate?"

A heavy breath makes his shoulders rise and fall before his gaze slides to me. It shifts down from my eyes to my lips and goes farther. Down the exposed skin at my shoulders, down my chest, my hips, my legs... Varek seems lost in thought.

"Varek?"

At the sound of his name, his gaze flies right back to my face, and he blinks as if he's just returning from a place far, far away.

"The rut," he finally says.

The word doesn't make much sense to me and I wonder if the translator embedded in the back of my head got hit by the falling tool and is malfunctioning. "I...don't know what that is."

Varek sort of winces as if he'd hoped that one word would have been enough. His shoulders rise and fall in a heavy breath.

"I was there to help Eleanor…because my siblingkin was afraid he would mate her to death."

My eyes widen and I can only blink at him, his words taking a long while to fully settle in my mind. Because what in tarnation…

"I should…I should put this back on the transport," he says before turning, just as there's a sound at the door. The dull thud of someone knocking echoes in the room once more, and my gaze shifts past Varek.

I'm not sure who could be knocking. The moment I shift off the bed, wincing as my shoulder readjusts, is the moment Varek's gaze hardens and I realize that there had been a note of vulnerability there. He watches me as I shift past him and the dull thumps of his boots follow me out to the main room. When I swing the door open, I'm completely aware of Varek's presence at my back.

It's the Raki. His eyes widen again the moment the door opens, his ears folding inward as he cowers. At first, I think it's because he's terrified I might have been critically hurt, but then I hear the growl at my back. When I look over my shoulder, Varek's snarling again. He looks like he'll rip the poor Raki to shreds.

Without thinking, I reach back, placing a steady hand on his arm. The snarl, at least the deep rumbling growl that I'm not quite sure he knew he was doing, cuts off immediately. My own breath hitches. His scales. They're unbelievably soft. Over the muscle that tightens beneath my touch, his scales are like smooth silk.

"Y-yes?" I answer the Raki. In these past few days, I've never been more unsure in my life. The woman who used to be the public face of an entire company suddenly feels reduced to someone who isn't sure quite *who* she is anymore. How could I manage my duties if I'd been like this back on Earth? The Richmond name would have suffered, and I would have suffered more.

"Greetings." The Raki's gaze shifts from Varek to my shoulder and he seems to cower some more. "It was not my intent to harm you."

I smile. "I know that. It's just an accident."

"Your negligence could have killed her." Varek's words could cut through ice. The Raki's ears fold some more and I give Varek a comforting squeeze. I could almost laugh. He seems more upset about the whole thing than I am.

"I will withdraw my services from your lodge," the Raki says.

My brows shoot up. "You don't have to do that," I say. At the same time, Varek speaks as well. "You should."

"I will not accept payment for the work already done," the Raki continues.

My eyes widen on that one. At the same time, Varek growls at my back. "It would do well if you *didn't*."

The Raki bows. "I am at your mercy, female, if you wish to report my negligence."

I stare at him open-mouthed as Varek says, "You should be reported. You're a careless *pilkra*."

Oh goodness. I give Varek's arm a squeeze once more as I lean down and touch the Raki on his shoulder. Varek growls but his annoyance almost makes me smile.

"It's okay, Raki. It really is. It's only a bruise and the accident could have happened to anyone. I'm fine with you still working here."

The Raki looks up. I don't miss the flash of hope in his eyes. But behind me, Varek is like an immovable mountain.

"He should leave."

I stand, glancing over my shoulder at the iridescent wall of scales at my back before my gaze rises to Varek's face. His expression is severe. Not an ounce of mercy in his eyes.

"If the Raki leaves, who is going to finish my roof?"

Varek's gaze shifts to me. "I can."

I swallow hard. Of course, he can. I know he can. But even in my periphery, I can see that the Raki is slowly wilting like a flower without water. I can't just fire him.

"I don't doubt that you could do it." I smile at Varek. "But I won't fire him for his mistake." Varek's eyes narrow, not on me but on the Raki.

"You are too kind, sura," he finally says.

Again, I wonder what that word means, but now is not the time to ask. I face the Raki again, giving him a genuine smile. "Please, if you could finish the roof, I'd appreciate it. No hard feelings."

His large ears flap, his gaze shifting from me to Varek then back. "As you wish. My feelings are also not hard."

I grin, a laugh bubbling in my throat that seems to relax the Raki somewhat. He gives me another nod before hurrying away and disappearing around the side of the house.

I release a heavy breath. "Wow. What a day."

There's a low grunt behind me and I'm reminded that I'm still gripping Varek. Still standing with him at my back. I shift to the side immediately, my hand flying off him as if I was touching him someplace inappropriate.

His gaze as he watches me is unreadable.

"You should rest now, sura," he says, stepping out the door. There, he turns to face me. His whole expression is so unreadable now, it's like the day I first met him and I wish it wasn't so. Wish I could see behind that crack in his exterior that showed me so much of the real him in the time since then.

But maybe that's all gone now.

That along with the opportunity to ask him what he'd meant about his brother killing Eleanor with *sex*. My cheeks heat at the thought even as I tell myself whatever he said must have been lost in translation.

"I will see you on the new dawn…Catherine."

I nod, giving Varek the best smile I can muster as I watch

him walk to his hover truck. But instead of getting in, he pauses, stops, his shoulders rising and falling.

"Varek?"

Turning, he faces me once more.

"I know you said you're fine..." He pauses, studying me in the dying light of the setting sun. "I know you said you're fine, but I would feel better if I could stay for a while. Just to make sure you're truly safe."

I can't even react. His words aren't words I expected him to say.

"I can wait outside by my truck. I will hear you. If anything goes wrong, you only need to call my name."

His words catch me so off guard, that my mouth opens but no words come forth. Instead, I feel warmth bloom in my chest at his thoughtfulness. Part of me wants to decline, to insist that I can take care of myself. But the way he's gripping the first-aid kit tells of his genuine concern. That plus the dull throb of my bruise makes me reconsider.

"I...That would be very kind, Varek. But I wouldn't want to keep you longer than you have to stay."

"I cannot, in good conscience, leave you unwell."

More cursed warmth. I study him. He's like a puzzle.

"Okay," I nod.

Relief washes over his features, and he nods. With that, he turns and walks back to his hover truck. Putting the first-aid kit in, he settles against the side of the vehicle, his gaze fixed on the house. On me.

I watch him for a moment, that warmth rising within me, before I head inside and shut the door. This is all so unexpected. The warmth—and the sense of security knowing he's out there, watching over me.

There's a tingle in my palm where I had touched him, and I find my thoughts drifting to the sensation of his scales as I make my way to the bathroom to run a bath. Even as I sink into the warm water, my mind is filled with images of iridescent scales, strong claws, and piercing eyes.

Hours pass, and every so often, I find myself peeking out the window to see if he's still there. Even long after the Raki left. Each time, I spot him, a steadfast guardian in the fading light. As the night grows darker and the stars begin to shine, I realize just how long he's been out there, ensuring my safety.

Finally, as the moon rises high in the sky, guilt sets in. It's only a bruise. I didn't expect him to wait this long.

"I'm alright, Varek. I really am."

As if he actually heard me, I see him push off from his truck. He tilts his head, a nod to me at the window as he takes one last long look at the house, before getting into the vehicle.

My breath stutters as he drives away, a pang of something I can't quite name going right through me. A mixture of gratitude, longing, and a strange sense of loss.

For the first time in a long while, I find myself looking forward to the new dawn and the possibility of seeing him again.

10

VAREK

The dark cycle was torture. It took everything within me not to hop into my transport and head off to the plains. I'd park just outside Catherine's farm and wait there till dawn came. And I almost did it. If not for the fact that Zynar's words of advice rang in my ears.

Human females are skittish and need convincing.

I don't even know what I want to convince Catherine of.

That I want her? A dangerous game to play when I can't even offer her the joy of having my rhythm sing for her. What am I offering her, exactly? Companionship? She could get that from anyone she chooses. Why would she choose me?

And why do I want it so badly? Why does the thought of her choosing someone else make me feel crippled inside?

Again, I search deep within, closing my eyes as I search for it. My core-rhythm. But it's nowhere to be felt or heard. It doesn't exist. I haven't yet found my mate, even though it feels like Catherine is…

Even though it feels like Catherine is something more than just a potential companion.

By the time dawn lights, I'm already on my way, zooming

toward the plains. I'll finish the outbuilding's roof today and I have plans. Plans based on Zynar's advice. The tee meal was almost a disaster, but against everything, it worked. Now for phase two.

I arrive at Catherine's, gaze shifting to the quiet lodge where she must still be asleep. Just like the day before, there's no indication she's awake and I get to work, trying my hardest to keep the noise low. By the time the star pushes itself over the horizon, I've lined up all the beams and have started hammering them in. Below, the little umus huddle together in their makeshift enclosure, disturbed by the rhythmic bangs.

"Not for long, little ones." One bleats at me as if telling me to hurry up and I grin.

"Who are you talking to?" The sound of her voice makes me freeze, a shiver going through my scales, culminating in the tight sac beneath my shaft.

Catherine.

I turn, looking over my shoulder to find her standing at the edge of her porch. Gods, she really is captivating. She's pulled the strands of her mane back, giving me a full view of her face. The soft lines of her brows, her nose, her lips...

I pause, the float tile I'm balancing on moving closer to the edge of the roof I'm working on. I crouch on it, peering down at her.

"What is wrong with your lips?"

Her eyes widen, her lips pressing into a line as her cheeks grow to match the color her lips now are. They're a warm red that they weren't the sol before or the one before that.

"Is something wrong?" I direct the tile to float down to ground level before hopping off. "Is this because of the injury you received last sol?" My thoughts turn murderous immediately. The image of that Raki in my mind as I growl, leaning closer to the female before me. Before I can stop myself, my claw ventures close to her lips before I pause, a breath away from touching her.

Catherine stops pressing her lips together and a breath huffs from her nose. I'm not sure if it's mirth because she shifts her gaze away from me.

"There's nothing wrong with my lips. I was just…" Her brows furrow now and my focus falls back to her mouth. "I was just a bit silly, I suppose."

Her shoulders rise and fall in a breath and that's when I notice the color on her lips isn't natural. It's artificial. *She* placed the color there.

Easing back, I'm unsure of how to respond to this but clearly I have misstepped because when Catherine's gaze shifts to me, it's lost that twinkle I thought I'd just seen in her eyes.

Curses.

"I was wondering maybe if you wanted another cup of tea this morning," she says, her gaze shifting from me to the outbuilding's in-progress roof. "You've done so much already I suppose you've already had breakfast."

She presses her lips into a line, one that I suppose is meant to be a convincing smile. All it does is turn something to ice deep inside me. What have I done?

"I'll let you get back to work." Then she gestures to the field. "I have things I need to get done too."

She presses her lips into that smile again, and I realize the red stain only accentuates them. She put the stain on to accentuate her lips, and I, like a fool, made it seem like her effort was useless.

It wasn't.

I can't stop staring at her lips now.

As she turns to walk away from me, my core-beat skips.

"Catherine…" She stops at the sound of her name, glancing at me over her shoulder with her eyebrows raised and that strange mirthless smile still on her face. "It's beautiful." My throat bobs. "Your lips."

That red stain shoots across her face again. She dips her gaze. "Thank you."

That wild, panicked fluttering of my core-beat calms down. "I would like to share tee with you."

She blinks, her smile faltering for a split click.

"If you would share it with me again," I add quickly. *Give her the choice. Allow her to pull away, even if it feels like the thought itself is tearing me apart.*

"Alright."

Frakking yes.

As Catherine leads the way inside her lodge, I run my tongue over my fangs, my claw reaching down over the pocket on my trouse to grasp the outline of the item I brought with me this sol. Phase two.

I step into the cool interior of the lodge, my eyes fluttering closed as I breathe in. Her scent is so thick in this space, every fiber touched by her presence. It almost makes me groan.

"—rek?" Her voice makes my eyes fly open to find her peering at me from the meal preparation room.

"Yes, sura?"

She blinks, probably thrown off by the word, her mouth opening slightly before she pulls her gaze away from mine and lifts the tee packets in her hands. "Same tea as yesterday?"

"If it pleases you." If it pleases her, I would drink heated water seasoned with soil. I really don't care about the tee. My fist tightens on the item in my pocket and my core-beat thumps a little harder. I hope Zynar's not wrong about this.

Squaring my shoulders, I move to stand right at the door separating the main room from the meal preparation room as I watch Catherine prepare the beverages.

"I don't think it needs sugar. It was so sweet yesterday." I'm not sure if she's speaking to me or to herself as her voice is so low, I can barely hear it. I hear the tones anyway though. And they're wonderful. Like a smooth caress. How would it feel to hear her speaking to me at first light each dawn? How would it feel to hear her whispering to me exactly what she wants me to do to her while—

"—but we could try cake today. Would you like a slice?"

"Mm?"

Catherine's gaze shoots to me. There's something there in her gaze, so quickly hidden, but not before her cheeks warm. Was I staring again? I'm staring, aren't I?

Prey species are often unnerved by stares from species like mine. It's not like I'm salivating and…no, that's a lie. I *am* salivating, but not because I want Catherine in my mouth.

A dangerous thought that makes me swallow a groan, the sound escaping like a grunt. Because now that I've thought about it, I realize I *do* want her in my mouth. I want my lips on her skin. I want to taste her.

"I have cake." She sets the beverages down and moves over to her storage crate, crouching over it. The thin linen she's wearing does nothing to hide the curve of her soft body away from me and I thank the artisan who made it for his slight. "I'm pretty sure I do. Xarion had mentioned that he'd ordered some for me. Probably because Eleanor had wanted some. It's not exactly like cake from Earth. It's more like bread, but it's pretty good for alien bread."

The moment she finds the item she's searching for is the moment she rises with a slight 'whoop' of victory. But as she unpacks the item, I can only think on one thing.

"Xarion?"

"Hm?"

"Who is Xarion?" I try to keep my tone light, even leaning as nonchalantly against the wall as I can manage while inside there is a riot of emotions.

"Oh? You don't know Xarion? He's the New Horizons representative that brought me here, remember?"

I blink, the male faint in my memory from when he'd visited Eleanor's farm.

"Right." I ease off the wall, suddenly feeling like a fool again. When Catherine's soft little laugh reaches my ears, I find she's looking at me strangely.

"What were you thinking?" She asks. I'm saved from further disgrace when she focuses on using a blade to cut thick slices of the doughy meal block. "I haven't hired someone else to do the job I asked you to do. I actually wish I'd hired you from the start."

I'm happy she seems clueless as to why I asked, and my shoulders straighten at the fact that she seems pleased with my progress so far. But that's not why I asked about this male. "I thought he was courting you."

Catherine laughs in a way that makes her almost choke. "What? No!" Her wide eyes turn to me, but I can see they're no longer shuttered. They're full of life. Perhaps I should continue this line of conversation.

"Why not?" *Because she said she didn't want a mate, you pilkra. She already told you this.*

She finishes cutting the doughy thing, her surprise and mirth sobering somewhat as she places the slices on separate trays. "Well, because he's far too young for me. And, to be honest, a relationship was the last thing on my mind when I grabbed the opportunity to move to these plains. I've already done that. I've already lived that stage of my life."

"What do you mean, sura?" I know I'm pressing. I can't seem to keep my maw shut.

Catherine stops moving and for a moment I think she'll evade my question and shut down again. But then she shrugs and releases a breath as she lifts the trays, balancing them as she heads to the main room.

"I was married once."

It seems like those words should have some significance. Instead, they're lost on me. As she takes a seat and I move to sit in the one facing her, the steaming beverage before me fails to grab my attention. I watch her take a sip of hers before she takes a bite of the doughy thing, almost as if she's purposefully focusing on the meal.

"Married?" *Stop pressing, fool. If she doesn't answer, you're digging a hole you mightn't get out of.*

But Catherine dips her chin in a nod. She finishes chewing before her gaze meets mine. "Yes. For the better part of my life."

I still don't know what she means. "Married?" I ask again and then her eyebrows lift on her head.

"Hmm, you don't know what I mean, do you?" Her eyes are still on mine as she thinks, her digits now tapping a rhythm on the hard table that's attuned to the staggered thumps of my core-beat.

"Mated." She finally says. "I was mated."

My core-beat stutters. "You found your lifemate." Everything I've been dreaming about, everything I've wanted, feels like it's shattering beneath me. "The Tasqals took you from your world...from your mate?"

Catherine shakes her head. "No. He passed away long before that. Cancer." She pauses, her eyes zoning out to memories I cannot see. "Even with our children, I was alone after he left and—"

"Children? Younglings?"

She gives me a slight nod, and the absolute sadness that creeps into her vision makes me immediately regretful that I pressed for this conversation. But a lifemate...Catherine had a lifemate...

"I wouldn't call them younglings." She gives a soft laugh that's so unexpected, I sit up a little straighter. "They're in their forties now. Both married. Kids. I had them young. Far too young, but I wouldn't change that now. My son has a beautiful wife. Really lovely girl who can keep him grounded, and my daughter, well, she's living life out on a farm in Utah. She's happy, though, which is all that matters." She stops suddenly, her eyes widening on me before she presses them closed, a groan in her throat. "I'm sorry. You don't need to hear all this. It's the first time I've talked about…" She trails off. Something compels me to lean forward, because despite everything she's said, about the lifemate and all, something is still rising within me. It's even worse now. I want to hear more about her life. I want to know more about *her*.

"If you wish to talk about them, I'd love to hear it."

Catherine's face loses all emotion, goes completely blank and I fear that I've said the wrong thing. She is nothing like a Kari female who would have either outright rejected me already or made it clear she finds me attractive and wants me in her nest. No. Catherine is nothing like that. I am learning as I go and that might be to the detriment of me. I open my mouth, easing back, my claws rising halfway off the table as I'm about to tell her it's fine if she doesn't want to speak. But that's when I freeze. Because a single drop of water releases from her eye.

It winds a path down her cheek before Catherine sniffles and wipes it away.

"You don't have to be so sweet. It must be so boring for you listening to me yap about my life."

I lean in again, perplexed by her loss of fluids. I've seen it before, with Eleanor. Back then, she'd been stressed by the fact that Zynar was in danger. Right now, I'm not sure exactly why Catherine is leaking.

"On the contrary, I find it…I find *you* fascinating."

She sniffles again, wiping the other eye. "You find me talking about my kids fascinating?"

"They are part of you."

She inhales deeply, before breathing out through her lips but she doesn't continue.

"Even your lifemate…I…" It's strange. I don't know how to put it into words. The fact that she's already found her lifemate is a sure sign that she isn't mine. Right? So why don't I back down?

"He wasn't my lifemate."

I pause. No, I freeze, waiting for her to continue.

"If he was my lifemate, he'd still be here, wouldn't he? *Lifemate* suggests they're with you for life." She sniffles and wipes away another eye leak before it has the chance to reach her cheek. "We humans, we don't…" She stops talking and I realize she's thinking about what she's about to say. "We don't mate for life. It's not like that, though I realize that for some alien cultures, that's the way it's done. Only a few species on Earth do such a thing. And humans," she scoffs, "humans are not it. To find someone to spend the entirety of your life with, only a few humans are lucky enough to find such a soul."

I'm intrigued. Intrigued enough to lean in. "So this married…"

"Marriage," she corrects. "Is like a vow you take to love and care for each other. But vows can be broken. Not everyone stays married. Sometimes it lasts only a week. Sometimes it lasts years." A sadness transcends over her so much that I want to reach out and touch her despite my oath not to without her consent. "Everything always ends," she whispers. One of her hands moves up to her chest, gripping where her life organ must be. "It always does and then you're left with the wounds. Then you're left to pick up the pieces and start again."

My claw itches to reach for her. To pull her into me and take away all this pain. So much pain.

"It isn't the same with Kari." The words tumble from my throat and Catherine lifts her gaze to mine. Her eyes are filled with water and she wipes it away, sniffling underneath her hands.

"What?"

"It isn't the same with Kari," I repeat. "When a Kari finds their true mate, their *kahl*, it is for life. Our core rhythms sync and become one. We live only for our mates, devoted fully to them in every way."

My claw twitches again with the urge to reach for Catherine's claw, but I resist. She's listening to me. Completely focused on my words. "A mated Kari cherishes his *kahl* above all else. He lives to protect her, provide for her, and keep her happy and safe. His greatest joy comes from pleasing her."

I meet Catherine's gaze, hoping she can see the truth of my words reflected there. "He would never intentionally hurt or abandon her. And if she were ever taken from him…" I trail off, old grief rising. Images of the war on Karicek. Of my mor feeling the pain of losing our por. I force it down before continuing. "He would search the universe to find her again. Because for a Kari, the mate bond is eternal. It cannot be broken, not even by death." Our gazes are locked. Our focus completely on each other. "We cannot live without our kahls. We do not take it lightly when we say 'forever mate'."

Catherine is quiet for a moment. When she speaks, her voice is hushed. "That sounds beautiful. But also so sad, if you lose them. I've been through it."

"If you found another mate…" I don't even hide the hope in my voice now. "Would that make you happy?"

She's quiet for a long moment before her eyes meet mine. She shakes her head and my world fades into shadow. "I've been a widow…I know how it feels. What it does to you. Where I am now in life, chances are, I'd cause my partner to become a *widower*. I wouldn't…I can't do that to someone else when I know how it feels."

Her words feel like they echo around me. I don't know why I

press. My core-rhythm is silent. There's a good chance I don't have a mate. A good chance Zynar finding his kahl has just been what we first thought it was: pure luck. A once-in-a-lifetime twist of fate. And yet, I can't let go. There is something that makes me not want to give up.

I want her.

I want Catherine.

"Do you know the fates?" I ask.

Catherine's face is devoid of all emotion once more. Whatever she's feeling has been locked behind a screen I cannot see.

I lean forward, my gaze intense as I try to convey the depth of my conviction. "The fates are not set in stone. They are ever-changing, molding to the choices we make and the paths we take."

The weight of my words dawns on me. Perhaps, that's the same for me too.

Catherine's eyes are on me, guarded now but not entirely closed off. I can't stop now. I have to continue.

"Your past, the one you shared with the male you cared about, that will always be a part of you. But it doesn't dictate your future. Just as your path led you to him, it has now brought you here, to the plains, to..." *To me.* But I dare not utter it. Not yet.

Catherine's breath hitches anyway, her eyes widening. Perhaps I said too much.

Frakk.

I should give her some space. Some time to think.

Reaching into my pocket, I take out the gift I brought her. It's a sleek, oval-shaped device, no bigger than the palm of my claw.

I carefully set it down on the table between us. Catherine's eyes widen as she looks at the device. She picks it up carefully, turning it over in her hands. "What... what is this?" she asks, her voice tinged with confusion and something else I can't quite place.

"A gift for you."

Her delicate hands pause with the item held between them as her eyes shift to mine.

"It's a calming device," I explain, though I can see a flicker of something in her eyes that makes me pause.

A surprising bubble of laughter leaves her lips and warmth floods right through me. Perhaps I have salvaged this after all.

"You think I'm not calm enough?"

Frakk.

I sit up so straight the stool beneath me almost topples. "No. Your spirit sways like a calm wind. This device is only meant to help with relaxation and stress relief."

Catherine releases another small laugh, this one quieter than the last, and I realize she's joking. Toying with me in the nicest way possible. "I'm only joking. This is…this is very thoughtful. Thank you, Varek. But I should be the one giving you gifts. You've already—" Her gaze shifts to the senzsi fruit off to the side before she shifts her gaze away from them.

"I thought you might find it…useful."

In her perusal, she accidentally activates the device and the soothing vibrations begin emanating from the oval.

"It vibrates," she whispers, shock at the edges of her tone. "And people use this to relieve stress?"

"Usually several times each sol. It is especially bought by females across various species."

"I see." After a moment, a look of shocked realization crosses her face. "Oh. OH!" Her cheeks flush a deep pink as she quickly sets the object back down. It vibrates, dancing a path across the table before I reach out and turn it off.

I can't tell if she likes it or not. Her beautiful face is almost as red as the stain she'd placed on her lips.

"Th-thank you, Varek, I—" She lifts her head the moment

there's a sound not far outside the lodge. I can tell it's the Raki who has arrived, despite the fact I wish he wouldn't return, to complete his job. "Oh, the Raki is here!"

She jumps to her feet, gathering the trays. "I should get to work." She gives me a sort of wide-eyed strange panic-filled look but I'm not sure I'm even reading that right. One thing I surely am reading is the fact this conversation is over.

I rise, barely glancing at my untouched tee and dough meal as Catherine disappears into the meal preparation room.

It feels like she's running away from me and I want to reach out and pull her right back in.

I can't.

With a tightness in my chest, I head to the door instead. "I'll get back to work, then…"

I pause, hoping that she'll return and tell me to stay a bit longer. That doesn't happen. Instead, I hear her voice from the other room as she calls out, "Sure thing!"

11

CATHERINE

*H*e bought me a sex toy.

I sit staring at the thing where it remains at the center of my table, untouched.

A sex toy.

My cheeks heat as I stare at the thing. Is this a usual gift among aliens? Goodness, who am I kidding? Of course, it isn't, right? I practically feel as if I'm going to burst into flames as I stare at it. Do I really look like I need an orgasm?

I choke on an incredulous laugh, tears brimming in my eyes from the sudden lack of air, and it takes a few moments before I replace the air in my lungs. He probably thought I needed to orgasm from the mere fact that I've been so rigid with him. Probably thought my expressions meant I was in pain and that I needed to relax.

I laugh but almost choke again.

I've been gifted a vibrator and I have all the time in the world to use it.

My cheeks heat even more.

I'm staring at the thing for whole long minutes when there's suddenly a sound at the door. Grabbing the device, I shove it into my pocket as I jerk to my feet, silently cursing myself for behaving like a teenager who's been caught with marijuana in their bedroom.

Making my way to the door, I pause just before it, straightening my tunic.

"Not that it matters," I murmur. "You tried wearing homemade lipstick this morning as if possessed by some alter being and look where that got you?" Varek's response to my little effort of trying to dress up will make me laugh in a few years when I look back and remember this day. But today, I'll just have to wallow in a bit of embarrassment at the fact that I tried to dress up for him in the first place.

Because why?

Some part of me fears doing that deep dive. A big part of me doesn't want to face the reason why.

As I pull the door open, I plant a smile on my face, my heart already doing a strange unsteady thing instead of beating properly. But there's no purple iridescent muscular hunk of an alien on my doorstep. My gaze drops and it's the Raki there.

His long ears flap the moment my gaze falls on him.

"Oh." Blast it. The disappointment in my tone is so strong I can only pray the Raki doesn't pick up on it.

He dips his head slightly. "Greetings." In his paw, he outstretches something toward me. "This is for you."

Ah, it appears I'm getting a lot of gifts today. First the gift of gab, practically telling Varek my life story. Then his…stress relief instrument. Now this.

My confused gaze drops to the little round wooden canister in the Raki's paw.

"For me?" I ask, confused.

"For the wound you received because of my negligence."

Oh. "It's okay, really you—"

"I must. I did not sleep for the entire dark cycle, worried about you, human female. My mate is in tatters with worry too."

My eyebrows shoot upward. "Oh, you really don't have to worry. It was only an accident. I don't even feel the pain anymore. I'm over it."

He stretches the gift toward me anyway, forcing me to take it in my hands.

"Ointment from my homeworld," he says. "It will heal any mortal wound." He dips his head. "My apologies again."

Releasing a slow breath, I smile a little. "Thank you, Raki."

He dips his head again.

You know, he isn't so bad after all.

I don't know what causes me to look up at the barn roof. Maybe the movement there. The soft glint of sunlight across pink and purple scales. Something within me titters and comes to life even as I stop moving. Varek is there, watching us. His eyes are on the Raki, the look on his face unreadable, except for his eyes. Even with the distance between us and the gap between our species, the look in his eyes is unmistakable.

He's...annoyed.

It's clear he can't stand the poor Raki, and my being injured by him only makes it worse.

As the Raki bids me farewell, telling me he will finish my cottage roof this day, his surprising proclamation doesn't even register. My eyes are on Varek. Not until the Raki leaves does his gaze shift to me and the heat within them is scalding.

The world disappears, my vision becoming a tunnel.

Oh Catherine, you foolish girl. How did you not realize?

I stand there, rooted to the spot, my mind racing. Varek's gaze is intense, filled with an emotion I hadn't dared to hope for. Could he really...? No, it's absurd. I'm sixty, for heaven's sake. Surely he wouldn't be interested in someone my age.

But then I remember the gifts. The way he's been so attentive, offering to help with my roof, buying me the fruits because I showed interest in them *once*, requesting that we share breakfast together. And now, this...device. Could it be that he's been flirting with me all along? That he's been trying to show his intentions in the only way he knows how?

The thought makes my heart race, my cheeks flushing even deeper. I'm not used to this kind of attention anymore. It's been so long since anyone looked at me like that, let alone a handsome alien like Varek.

It's dangerous, I know. Dangerous to hold his gaze. Because the longer I do, the stronger that thing within me. Something rises, like a part of me is slowly lifting her head, the thought both titillating and terrifying for that reason. But I can't seem to help it. Can't seem to tear my eyes away, no matter how hard I try.

And when Varek's gaze heightens on mine, as if he's stripping me bare, as if he's undressing every bit of my clothing and drinking me in, I don't have the shame to break it. Like a deer caught in headlights, I stare back at him, a skitter going straight through the center of my chest like a searing electric thread. Something hot and hungry and alive, something that makes my breath catch in my throat, something that makes my heart stutter alight in my chest.

That does it. That's the thing that scares me enough that I look away. Force myself to break the moment, to shatter the fragile connection before it can grow into something I can't control.

I turn around, heading into the cottage that's suddenly like a safe haven.

My hand rises to grip my chest, a tremor going through my entire body. Because I know what this is. I'd felt it before, a feeling that wants me to lean into this alien. A feeling that makes me...*want*.

An ache goes through my chest, enough that I grip myself harder.

This can't be happening.

I like him.

I like Varek.

And I *can't*. I can't because…because even though he doesn't believe it, I'm right. Things end. Love ends and my heart. My heart…my heart can't take any more loss.

Because love, want, *need*? They can control you. Make you lost in the heat and the hunger of them and once that happens, there will be no coming back. And then, when they eventually end, you're left broken and shattered, a mere shadow of your former self.

And I'm not ready to become even less than who I was before. I've worked hard. Built careful walls. Only kept my children within those walls that protected my heart from the pain of living. From loss. I can't let those walls down now. Or ever. A lifetime as Catherine Richmond, head of the Richmond estate, had cocooned me as a widow for life. And I'd accepted that cocoon, using it as a shield, an excuse to not try to find love again.

I swallow hard, taking deep breaths as I head further into the house. There, I grab my cleaning supplies and begin scrubbing. The surety of each movement is all I have right now to ground me. So I focus on the work. Focus on the simple, repetitive tasks of sweeping and wiping, lifting and carrying, until the room is spotless. I let the physical exertion drive out the thoughts, let the sweat and the strain wash away the longing that is starting in my soul. But even as I work, even as I try to lose myself in the mindless labor, I can't escape the truth. Can't escape the reality of what I'm feeling, of what I'm desperately trying to deny.

Leaning against the counter that I've wiped probably a thousand times, I stare down at the marble-like effect of the stone, my breaths coming heavy from my chest.

I'm waking up.

The woman within me, she's…she's waking up again.

I don't know how he did it. Many men have tried before and gotten nowhere. I just…wouldn't let them in. And somehow, this alien who hasn't even attempted to seduce me, who hasn't made any inappropriate advances or gestures, has me crumbling.

HOW?

The walls I've built up are falling down. The lines I've drawn fading quickly. My body is pushing past the barriers my mind has erected. Those barriers that have kept me standing for so long.

My breaths come harder as I stare at the counter, my thoughts as staggered as the design in the stone.

It's too soon. Too raw, too painful. The wounds of before are still fresh, still bleeding.

Squeezing my eyes shut, I curse underneath my breath. It's stupid and I'm probably getting ahead of myself, but the thought of opening myself up to something new, something that could hurt me all over again—even the very semblance of it—is absolutely terrifying.

If Varek has done anything, he's reminded me I'm still alive. I'm not dead, even though I've been living that way for so long. Existing instead of living. His actions might be completely innocent, but they highlight one thing. I'm so broken inside, I can't even consider letting someone else in. How can I risk the fragile peace I've managed to find, the tentative stability I've fought so hard to achieve?

I...can't do it. I have to be strong. Have to protect myself, even if it means shutting out the possibility of something more.

So I push the rising interest down. I push away whatever it is that has me thinking of him now when I have no right to. I bundle it all and lock it up tight in a corner of my heart and throw away the key. I'll focus on the work, on the simple, tangible tasks that keep my hands busy and my mind occupied.

And when the day is finally done, when the cottage is clean and the animals are fed and the sun is setting over the fields, I'll let myself breathe. Let myself relax, just a little, as I stand alone in the gathering dusk.

Just as it has always been.

My heart clenches, the organ tightening around what feels like a physical manifestation of pain as I force my breaths to even, breathing deeply in and out. When the communication device lights up and makes a sound, I turn my head slowly, eyes falling on it.

"Ping from Eleanor Taylor."

I groan. I don't want her to see me like this. No one knows just how shattered I am inside. All the other humans seem to be adjusting to this new life except me. I am lost. The woman I once was is gone. I am a shell of myself.

I stare at the comm device before forcing another breath through my nose as I reach for it, my arm brushing against the crate of fruit Varek brought me. Something deep inside me clenches again.

"Hiya, Eleanor!" The bright smile I put on my face is hopefully convincing. On the other end of the video feed, Eleanor is grinning back at me.

"Catherine! You look well! Seems like your little problem was sorted?"

My chest tightens. My little problem? I wouldn't call him little. The purple iridescent mountain of a male currently on my barn roof is *not* a little problem. He's turning out to be quite a big problem indeed. But then I realize Eleanor isn't talking about the alien who I can't get out of my mind. She's talking about the initial problem I'd called her about.

"Ah, yes, thank you so much for sending help. The umus are corralled for now."

"Corralled?" Eleanor's eyes widen. "They're dangerous little terrors."

I smile a little. "Varek sorted it. They've been no trouble since."

There's a twinkle in her eyes that I don't miss. "Ah, Varek. He's been helping you, has he?"

I nod, not sure how much I should reveal. She's mated to his brother. I don't want to give her the wrong idea. "He has. He's been working on my barn roof. He's been great."

More than great. He's been…perfect.

I swallow a lump down as Eleanor's eyes light up some more. "That's fantastic. I'm just calling to let you know that there's this festival happening in town tomorrow night. We humans have to attend. I hear there's another human Xarion will be escorting as well. Just for community building and all."

"A festival?" I could groan. I just want to lie in bed for a day and not engage with anyone.

"Yes! For prosperity for the seeds we're sowing. You should come! It would do good for the Initiative."

I bite my lip, thinking about it. It feels like I just lost something. As if I should be mourning. For someone who used to host events, someone who thrived in that space, nothing within me is even excited about the prospect of attending this function.

I give Eleanor a sort of apologetic smile, hoping she will accept my rejection of the offer. "It's nice of you to invite me. I'd love to come but I'm afraid I'll have to skip this one. I don't have any way to get to town on my own. Not yet. I haven't figured out how to use oogas—"

"I can take you." The deep voice by my door makes me freeze. My eyes widen as I turn to find the door opening slowly. Apparently, I'd left it open after taking out the bucket after I'd cleaned the floor.

The dark that dusk brings only highlights the yellow in his eyes as Varek looks at me. I'm speechless, that ache in the center of my chest worsening as I look at him.

"That's great!" Eleanor's voice snaps me back to the present. "Varek will take you." That twinkle in her eye is unmistakable now. "I'll see you there!"

Before I can respond, the comm ends.

I set the device down, a tremor going through my arm, my eyes still on the alien before me.

"Your outbuilding is done, sura." His voice rumbles, electricity crackling in the space between us.

I nod, standing taller and folding my arms across my chest. I need to get a hold of myself. "Does that mean you're done? That you're finished now?" I whisper.

I don't even know why I ask that. Why there's an undertone there that he probably won't even recognize.

Varek doesn't move from where he stands, but when he speaks, it's like he is right before me, not even a breath separating us. His gaze locks with mine, the intensity in his eyes stealing the breath from my lungs. He takes a step forward, the floorboards creaking under his weight, and the sound seems to reverberate right through me.

"No, Catherine," he says, his voice low and filled with a meaning I'm almost afraid to decipher. "I'm not finished. Not even close."

My heart hammers against my ribs, the implication behind his words sending a shiver down my spine. He's not talking about the outbuilding anymore, and we both know it.

"Varek…" I whisper. "What do you want?"

He takes another step, closing the distance between us until I can feel the heat radiating from his body. "I'm saying," he says, "there's still much to be done here. Much to be…explored."

His gaze moves down my face for a brief, searing moment before returning to my eyes. "I find myself drawn to you, Catherine. In ways I can't ignore."

A nervous laugh chokes through me. "I haven't done anything for you to be drawn to me. You hardly know me."

"But I want to." Four simple words that are so powerful they erase the retort on my lips. "And I cannot walk away, not without knowing…without seeing where this path might lead."

I shake my head, stepping away from him, putting some space between us because his proximity is making it hard for me to breathe. "Varek, maybe I've done something to make you think there's potential for something here. But...there isn't. I can't... I'm not on the market for anything."

"Good."

My gaze flies to his. I'm immediately confused. A bit thrown off, to be honest, by that single word. "Good?"

"Yes." His claws clench and unclench as if he's fighting some instinct to do something and when he forces himself to take a step back, I realize he's trying to give me the space I need even though his body is telling him to do the opposite. "Good," he repeats, his voice softer but no less intense. "Because I don't want to share you with anyone, Catherine. I want you all to myself."

The sincerity in his words, the raw honesty, takes my breath away. "Varek, I..." This is all way too soon. I've only just met him. If this was some guy on Earth, I'd have removed myself from the situation. Probably even told security to ensure he never enters the building. But I'm not on Earth. And this isn't just some guy. This isn't even a man. He's male, but he's not human. He's different. Different from anything else I've ever encountered.

He raises a claw, stopping me before I can speak again. "I understand you're hesitant. But know this—I am patient. I will wait. I will prove myself. Because you, Catherine...you are worth it."

I shake my head. "You don't know that."

"Let me find out."

"Varek—" Damn, he's persistent, I'll give him that.

"See where it leads, sura."

I swallow hard, my mouth suddenly dry. "And where do you think it might lead?"

A ghost of a smile plays at the corners of his mouth and I'm struck by just how handsome he is. Not like a human male. Different. There's a raw primal energy that seems to be swirling around him. One that hints at his power. His lust. His potential love.

"I know not," he replies. "Not yet. But I want to find out...if you are willing."

12

CATHERINE

The entire day is filled with a bunch of nerves that seem alight and heightened just underneath my skin. My cottage roof is done, the Raki having been true to his word and completing it the day before. My barn roof is done, too. Varek completed it in record time.

Both things should make me happy. Should have me feeling much more secure and stable. Should reduce some of the stress now that I literally have a roof over my head. But they don't. Because the moment I woke, my heart was beating unnaturally. And when I opened my door and found the bunch of pretty flowers there, that unnatural unsteady beat only increased.

Varek is nowhere to be seen, but his truck is by the gate. And the flowers, well, the flowers didn't just deliver themselves.

I should put them down. I shouldn't accept them. Shouldn't encourage this, whatever it is. I certainly shouldn't bring them to my nose. Certainly shouldn't sniff them.

They're lovely, their sweet scents flowing into my nose along with the morning air. And they're beautiful too. Large petals in pastel hues that make them seem more like a painting than real things. Fighting the twinge of warmth starting in my gut, I head

127

back inside and place the flowers in some water before getting dressed for the day.

I choose a pair of trousers this time—the only one I have. It looks similar to the one Varek wears and I'm pretty certain it was meant for a male twice my size because I have to use a long strip of linen to grab the waist and tie it so it doesn't just slide off my frame.

I tie my hair back into a ponytail too, pausing just in front of my reflection in the mirror as I take myself in. No makeup. Not even a stain of that powder I'd found and mixed with a bit of cooking oil to make the lipstick I'd tried yesterday. Embarrassment fills me again at the thought of it. What was I even doing? Trying to look pretty for him when I know that he and I can never be? Seems counterproductive.

Squaring my shoulders, I remind myself of why I'm here. For peace. I signed up for the Initiative for peace...and this is turning into chaos.

Heading outside, I close the door behind me as I march toward the barn. That's when I hear the undeniable hum of a machine. I halt, turning slowly as I try to figure out where the sound is coming from. Following my ears, they lead me around the cottage and toward the field. I don't need my ears to help me now because I can see. I can see the light reflect off the iridescent scales of the alien riding a massive machine across my field.

I'm dumbstruck as I draw closer.

Half my field has been cleared, great bales of hay rolled and stacked in the center. I can just see the heads of several oogas who are hiding in what's left of the tall grass, probably scared by the noise. My gaze shifts from them and my mouth falls open as I watch Varek clear a large swathe before he spins the machine in my direction, cutting another line as he heads my way.

The moment my gaze shifts upward, I know he's seen me. Even from the distance, those intense eyes eat me up. There's no reason for it—I'm damn well over whatever made me weak—but my cheeks heat anyway.

The sun's rays reflect off his scales like he's signed a contract with the star, the warm glow lighting him up in all the right places, casting shadows across the muscles in his chest, highlighting the contour of his jaw, his prominent brow. I don't know where to look, where to focus. My eyes rove over him even though I'm telling myself I should look away. Because, damn it, purple really is my favorite color.

I watch as he cuts the line he's working on before turning the machine and heading the other way. His back turned to me now, I get a moment to breathe. Goodness, this is going to be harder than I thought. Going to bed the night before, I'd convinced myself that by morning, whatever had come over me —over him—would have washed away and we'd have both come to our senses. Turns out I'm wrong. The machine hums, bumping along, its large wheels rolling over the ground and leaving flat earth in its wake. It's like a huge lawn mower with serrated teeth at the front, each row grabbing the tall grass while some other mechanism turns them into square bales that are left behind.

It looks vaguely familiar. The serrated teeth I'd seen leaning on the back wall of the barn. The arms that set the bales down I recognize as parts I'd seen lying behind the cottage. And I soon realize the machine itself is one I thought was out of service, parked just inside the gate within another small outbuilding.

He put the pieces together in a way I could have never known to do on my own. I watch as he turns the machine once more, heading down the row in my direction. My breath hitches, and I wait for him to complete the row he's mowing before spinning the machine in the other direction again. He doesn't. Instead, he keeps coming down the line.

I blink, my heart stuttering somewhat as he comes closer. Thank God the rumble of the machine drowns out any other sound, because I'm pretty sure I'm screaming loud enough inside for it to be audible.

The machine slows down, the powerful engine vibrating as Varek comes to a stop.

As he leans back in the seat of the machine, one muscular arm draped casually over the steering wheel, his gaze eats me up. Shifting from my face down the loose tunic I'm wearing as a blouse then down to the dark pants I've pulled on this morning.

I'm completely modest. Completely covered. And yet, my skin heats under his roving gaze as if I'm dressed in nothing but my underwear.

But he isn't the only one that's looking. I'd be a liar if I didn't admit I'm looking too. That despite myself, my gaze shifts over him as he sits so casually, so relaxed as if he's meant to be there. As if this is just any other morning, a routine that isn't out of place in our daily lives.

He looks like something out of a fantasy. A warrior god plucked straight from the pages of a romance novel. The sight of him, so strong and capable and undeniably masculine, sends a shiver down my spine that has nothing to do with the morning chill. I push back against it and it remains still. My body betrays me as something within me lights up, pushing back against that barrier I'm so desperately trying to hold in place.

Varek's gaze meets mine, and even from this distance, I can feel the heat of his gaze. It's intense, almost predatory, and yet there's a softness there, too. A tenderness that makes my heart warm in a way I thought I'd forgotten how to feel.

He shifts in his seat, the movement making the muscles in his chest and arms flex beneath his taut, gleaming skin. Doesn't he wear clothes? Shirts I mean. It's distracting and I force myself to blink in an effort to pull myself away. But the effect is hypnotic, and I find myself staring, my mouth going dry as I try to remember how to breathe.

This is ridiculous, Catherine. It really is.

I'm a grown woman, one who was the top of her game back on Earth, not some starry-eyed teenager. I shouldn't be getting weak in the knees over a bit of eye candy, no matter how incredibly attractive that eye candy might be. And especially because I have rules! Rules I've set for myself to follow. Morals I'm set to abide by.

But as Varek continues to watch me, his lips curving into a smile that's equal parts promise and invitation, I can't deny the effect he has on me. The way my pulse races and my stomach flutters, the heat that pools low in my belly and spreads through my veins like wildfire.

It's scary. This...*feeling.* I haven't allowed myself to even contemplate the possibility of desire, of want. Perhaps that's why the force of simply his gaze is so staggering, almost frightening in its intensity.

He tilts his head, his smile widening into an almost rakish grin. "Good dawn, Catherine," he calls out, his deep voice carrying easily over the purr of the machine. "I trust your rest was well?"

There's a knowing glint in his eye, a hint of mischief that tells me he's well aware of the effect he's having on me. And damn him, but it only makes him more attractive.

I clear my throat, trying to regain some semblance of composure. "I did, thank you," I manage, proud of how steady my voice sounds. "And you? I see you've been busy." Even though we haven't even discussed what this contract is between us. Somehow, my tongue doesn't move to bring that up.

Varek chuckles, the sound low and rich and far too seductive for my peace of mind. "Hard work is the best way to start the sol," he says, his gaze never leaving mine. "I couldn't rest, knowing there was so much to be done."

The implication is clear, the subtext unmistakable. He's not just talking about the field, and we both know it.

I swallow hard, my fingers curling into fists at my sides as I fight the urge to close the distance between us. To reach out and touch him, to see if his skin is still as warm and smooth as it looks.

But I can't. I *won't*. Not when I know that this, whatever it is, can only lead to heartache.

So instead, I force a smile, hoping it looks more convincing than it feels. "Well, I appreciate your help, Varek. Truly. But you don't have to do all this. I'm sure you have more important things to attend to."

He frowns, his brow furrowing in a way that shouldn't be nearly as endearing as it is. "There is nothing more important than ensuring your comfort and happiness, Catherine. Surely you must know that by now."

My breath catches, my heart stuttering in my chest at the raw sincerity in his words. The way he looks at me, like I'm the only thing in the universe that matters. The little footing I had feels torn right from under me.

"You..."

"Ah, but you don't know. That's why I promised to show you."

I blink at him, my eyelids fluttering. It's too much. Too intense. Too real. I'm not ready for this, not ready to face the depth of emotion in his eyes.

So I do the only thing I can.

I run.

I give him a slight nod. Waving a hand in the direction of the barn, I mutter something about having things to do, even though my mind goes blank as to what I had planned for this morning. It certainly wasn't this.

Backing away, I catch that same delicious little grin on Varek's lips before he engages the machine again and turns it.

I stop walking when the threat of his gaze is no longer

sending alarm bells all across my being. Watching the machine move down the line, I release a slow breath.

Darn him. He's turning out to be a real problem. But what's worse, what's truly terrifying, is the confidence that bleeds from him. As if he knows his attempts will be fruitful.

A shiver runs down my spine as I realize the truth: I'm scared he will actually succeed. His unwavering confidence, the way he looks at me like he's already won, it all makes me doubt my own resolve. I'm not sure I'm strong enough to keep him away, not sure I have the willpower to resist the definite pull that's growing towards him.

As he makes his way down the line, I watch him go, my thoughts a convoluted mess. As he turns the machine and heads back my way, it's the sound of an ooga baying over the sound of the machine that finally pulls my focus. My gaze flicks to the animals hiding in the tall grass a split second before about seven of them dash out from their hiding spot.

Varek slows down, but the animals keep going, heading straight to the perimeter fence. My eyes are wide as I watch them, expecting them to stop when they get to the other side of the field, but they don't.

As Varek rises from his seat, a shout on his lips that echoes across the plains, I realize just what's happening. The animals are like balls of muscle and hooves as they fight to get away from the machine. And one does. I don't know how it gets out, probably because the creatures targeted the exact spot that ooga had gotten stuck in that first day Varek came to my assistance, but an ooga squeezes through, rushing across the grass on the other side, it's loud squeals piercing over the commotion of the others.

My heart seizes. It's a baby. That's the only reason it managed to squeeze through and the terror of the others has only made it more frightened.

I'm moving without a second thought, even as I hear Varek

cut the engine of the machine. I have to stop the little animal. It's heading this way but I don't think it will stop. That means it will go straight toward a nest of trees a way off. There, a set of animals that have never come close to my farm in the month I've been here are resting.

They're tall, with long necks. Like diplodocus dinosaurs mixed with giraffes. I don't know if they're even friendly. They're wild and the little baby is so panicked, it's heading the wrong way.

Somehow, I hoist myself over the fence. I fall on my ass, hip, and arm all at once, pain shooting through my bum and the wind knocked out of me. All my muscles protest, that little spot of adrenaline fading fast. For a moment, I don't know where is up or down, but I'm on the other side of the fence, at least. That's when something runs straight past me. The baby ooga. Its screams ring in my ears, louder than ever as I crawl to my knees, intent on chasing after it even though my heart is pounding in my chest.

The tall, giraffe-like creatures are only a few meters away now, their eyes wide and alert as they watch the commotion. I have no idea how they'll react to the baby ooga barreling towards them, and I don't want to find out.

"Stop! Please, stop!" I scream, my voice hoarse and desperate. The baby ooga doesn't seem to hear me, or if it does, it's too frightened to stop. It's almost at the trees now, and I push myself to run. I'm not fast by any means. At this rate, I might as well do a power walk, but I push through the tall grass anyway.

I don't think I'll make it. Don't think I'll save the little thing. But then a miracle happens. The little creature changes direction, heading off back toward my right.

My lungs burning with the effort, I dive after it, just a moment before I see one of the dinosaur animals rise from where it was resting.

"Catherine, watch out!" Varek is somewhere behind me, his

voice carrying a note of warning that sends a chill down my spine.

I glance over my shoulder and see him running my way, his powerful legs eating up the distance between us, just as I fall into the grass with a thud. Ouch! My shoulders hurt but there's something underneath my palm. I'm gripping thick hide and I realize it's the little creature's thigh. I've caught the child! But it's wriggling, squealing, intent on rejecting my assistance. I'm going to lose my hold and those dinosaur things are coming. I have to do more. I have to try.

With a burst of strength I didn't know I had in me, I lunge forward, my fingers stretching out, grasping for the ooga's little tail. For a heart-stopping moment, I think I've missed, that my hand will close on empty air.

But then, miraculously, I feel the thrashing appendage beneath my palm. I clench my fist, holding on for dear life as the ooga squeals and kicks up dirt, trying to break free.

I'm dragged on the ground, even as I try to get more of a grip on little thing's midsection. My injured shoulder screams and I bite back the pain as I gain some purchase to wrap my arms around the struggling thing. It's strong for a baby, so much stronger than I anticipated, and for a moment, I'm afraid it will escape my grasp.

But then Varek is there.

"Frakk," he curses. "Catherine, I have to touch you." It's the only warning I get before his large claws join my hands, his muscular arms encircling us both. He holds the ooga tight, pulling the animal against my belly as he pulls me against him.

Staggered breaths leave me as my entire back is enclosed by his thick frame. His grip is firm but gentle, and slowly, gradually, the little creature begins to calm. It begins to calm, but I do not.

I'm panting, my heart racing so fast I'm afraid it might burst. But as I look down at the ooga in my arms, its wide eyes staring up at me with a mix of fear and curiosity, I feel a rush of relief so powerful it makes me dizzy.

"It's okay," I murmur as I try to pull my thoughts from the complete velvety hardness that's pressed against me. "You're safe now. It's okay."

Varek shifts behind me, his chest pressing against my back as he leans down to examine the ooga. "It appears unharmed," he says, his deep voice rumbling through me. "You got to it just in time."

I nod, swallowing hard past the lump in my throat. "I couldn't let it...I had to..." I breathe out, forcing my beating heart to calm. But all seems well with the world again. The oogas on my property no longer seem panicked. The sun is still shining. A soft breeze is blowing. It's paradise again.

"You did well, Catherine," Varek says softly, his breath warm against my ear. I stiffen, completely aware of him once more. "So brave and quick."

His praise washes over me, making me flush with a mix of pride and something else, something warm and fluttery that I wish would not present itself. Not when I'm so acutely aware of his proximity, of the way his body envelops mine, strong and solid and achingly masculine.

I turn my head slightly, meeting his gaze. His pupils are so wide his eyes are almost dark, intense, swirling with emotions I can't quite decipher.

For a long moment, we just stare at each other, my chest still heaving and every breath he takes making those muscles shift against my back. It's like the world suddenly falls away, leaving only him and me and this fragile, precious thing cradled in my arms.

My gaze falls to his lips and Varek goes still. He leans a little closer. So close if I simply moved, our lips would brush. I swallow hard, staring at him. Because I want to. And I shouldn't.

The ooga stirs, letting out a soft grunt, and the spell is

broken. Reality crashes back in, and with it, all the reasons I can't let myself get lost in Varek's eyes, in his touch, in the way he's making me feel.

"We should…we should get this little one back to his mama," I whisper, every word of mine brushing past the alien's lips.

"Yes," he replies, still so so close.

I swallow hard again, finally turning away. As I try to rise, Varek slowly releases me.

"Shh," he makes the sound in his throat as he moves around me to grab the little ooga, his gaze shifting to the long-necked animals not too far from us now.

Rising to my feet, I brush my pants off as I look at them, too. They're large, dwarfing me, even dwarfing Varek, and I take a step back, not sure what to expect.

"Dangerous?" I whisper, gaze shifting to Varek for a moment.

"Not usually," he replies. "They're called tilgrans. Usually friendly, but these are wild. Best to head back to the farm just to be sure."

"Right." I nod, shaking off the tension that feels like it's rising in my blood as I head back toward my perimeter fence. When I look back, I notice Varek standing guard, like a sentinel between me and the tilgrans. When I'm a good distance away, he leaves his post and jogs to catch me up.

"I apologize, sura. This was my fault."

I look up at him, a smile of satisfaction at having caught the little animal on my lips. His gaze falls to my mouth immediately.

"It was the machine. They're not used to it anymore. I should have put them in the outbuilding first."

I shake my head, watching as he places the little animal on the right side of the perimeter fence. "It's okay. Don't worry about it." At once, the little ooga runs off the join the now quietly grazing herd.

I blow a breath through my nose. These animals are going to be a lot of work. But that's what I get for signing up to live on a farm. I'm still smiling when my gaze shifts to Varek again.

His gaze heightens on my lips once more.

"I will lift you."

My eyebrows shoot up and I'm about to tell him it's fine. Fine, because I probably can manage it on my own. But also fine, because the mere idea of his touch on my skin is already sending signals to my brain that are making something tingle in the pit of my gut.

But the fence is high. I'm not sure how I climbed over it in the first place.

"Okay, if you just—" A squeal leaves my lips as Varek lifts me off my feet. My arms wrap around his neck instinctively as he places me on the other side of the fence. My whole body tingles and my cheeks heat. I pretend to turn my attention to the animals as he hops easily over the fence post.

"I will herd them into the outbuilding. But I must prepare it first. It might take the entirety of the rest of the sol."

I nod. "That's a good idea. I will help."

"No."

My eyebrows shoot up, my gaze finally meeting his. "No?"

Varek takes a step closer, close enough that he eats up all the space, and all I can see, all I can smell is him. That sweet scent that makes me want to lean in and inhale deep, pressing my nose into his scales. The thought has my eyes widening slightly. The intensity of it making a feeling buzz between my legs.

I go still. I stop breathing.

"You must get ready," he says simply.

"Get ready?" My voice is almost breathless, but somehow I keep it steady. "Get ready for what?"

"The festival, sura." His gaze is hot. Intense. "We have a date, remember?"

The audacity of this man! He's grinning at me, fangs peeking through and his eyes sparkling with mischief and something else, something heated and provocative that sends a shiver down my spine.

I shake my head, trying to gather my scattered thoughts. "I'm not sure about the festival. I have so much to do and I'm behind."

Varek takes another step closer, and now there's no space left between us. His proximity sends a wave of heat through my body, and I have to fight the urge to lean into him.

"Just one dark cycle," he says softly, his voice a low rumble that sends a shiver down my spine. When no other words of protest spill from my lips, he makes a sound in his throat that sends a delicious tingle up my spine. "I'll take care of the oogas. I will knock when it's time."

I'm…speechless.

With that, he turns and heads toward the outbuilding, his movements sure and confident. I watch him go, my heart pounding in my chest, my mind a whirlwind of emotions I can't seem to control.

13

VAREK

I'm the most nervous that I've ever been since my existence began.

Not even when faced with the hordes of Hedgeruds that descended on my planet did I entertain such nerves. Yet, when faced with the lone female human, I quake deep in my lifeblood.

If she knew how much I fall into this madness sol by sol, she would be even more terrified of me. It has snowballed enough that I don't know what I'm doing anymore. But I know one thing. I want her. I want her more than I've ever wanted anything in my life.

I manage to do the work. To muck out the stalls and reinforce them with fresh barriers. I move the umus and bring in the entire herd of oogas, all while barely focusing on what I'm doing.

I can only think of her.

Her image dances through my mind, my entire being warming with a vision of her that takes my breath away.

I long to run my claw through those silken strands of her mane, to feel them slip through my digits like water. I long to just look into her eyes; long to see deep into her soul.

When she laughs, *truly* laughs, it's a melody I know I could listen to forever.

She is a mystery, a puzzle I long to solve and I *want* to. Never has any female affected me like this. Given me this *urge* to catch them and never let them go. My promise to not touch her unless she asks me to has been torture in itself.

I want to learn everything there is to know about her. I want to listen to her stories, to hear her hopes and dreams, to be the one she turns to in moments of joy and sorrow alike. I must be truly nearing madness because…I think…I think I *need* her.

I pause, staring at the animals as they settle in their new enclosures, my core-beat hard and unsteady.

I need her.

She is mine. She *has* to be.

Catherine is my *kahl*. I'm sure of it. There can be no one else. But as I grip my chest, searching deep inside me for that rhythm that's supposed to rise, I'm disappointed once again. It feels like a part of me breaks in two at the fact there's nothing there. That should mean I haven't found my *kahl*, but how can that be? Catherine is it. I just need to convince my body that's the truth. Because I'm sure of it.

I am hers. Completely and utterly. My core-organ, my soul, my very being…they all belong to her now.

Uncertainty makes me pace, my core-beat still thudding so hard against my chest it sounds percussive, the sound loud in my ears.

I'm losing it. Desperation overtaking me. Because it feels like I have a single chance. A single shot at this before I frustrate Catherine enough and she casts me away for good.

But I *have* to try.

Just the thought that someday she might look at me with the same adoration growing within me for her, that she will see me not as an alien male she should be wary of, but as a male who would move the stars and the planets to make her happy, is all I need to carry on.

Heading to the back of the outbuilding, I turn on the spigot and wash, the fresh pair of trouse and linen placed close by for me to change into. The water is cool and I welcome it as it takes some of the sol's heat away.

It's taken many hors to complete the outbuilding and move the creatures inside, and now, as I complete my preparations, turning off the spigot and getting dressed, the star has almost disappeared on the other side of the horizon. I brush my mane till it settles in waves over my shoulders before taking a deep breath.

It's time to go. The Festival of Abundance is probably my one good shot at this.

Placing my dirty garments in the back of the hover truck, I head back down the path to Catherine's lodge. Since what happened with the oogas earlier, I haven't seen her and I briefly wonder if she'd hidden herself away and will refuse to come out and attend the festival with me.

I stop at her front door, doubt creeping in. Perhaps I should have reminded her about our 'date'. Curses. It was Zynar who told me about such a thing. That Catherine would enjoy it and that it was an integral part of trying to woo her. Perhaps my strategy of keeping busy and out of her way so she wouldn't find another excuse to not attend was not the right tactic.

Core-organ in my throat, I lift my fist and knock.

For a few moments, there's no sound on the other side of the door. My doubt rises. I'm about to knock again when the door suddenly opens.

My fist remains there poised in mid-air as if I'm a fool. I cannot move.

Catherine's eyes widen, her gaze skipping down my frame before she frowns slightly to look down at herself.

"Is this too much? I wasn't sure what the dress code was. Perhaps I should change into—"

"You're...beautiful." The word doesn't seem strong enough to describe the vision I'm seeing. It lacks woefully, failing to describe the goddess before me.

She wears a gown fashioned from the same purple linen that adorns the windows of her home. The fabric drapes over her curves, cinched at her waist and accentuating her figure in such a way that I grow so hard in my trouse my arm finally falls to clasp in front of the tent rising between us.

The neckline of the garment is simple, dipping just low enough to reveal the delicate lines of her collarbone. And the sleeves? Bare. Her soft skin is there for me to drink in.

"Thank you." Heat rises in her cheeks, accentuating the fact that she's stained her lips again. The color only makes them look plumper. Makes me wonder what it would feel like brushing my lips against hers in the way I've seen my siblingkin do to his human mate. "You look really good, too."

I glance down at myself. I'm wearing my best tunic over my trouse but I wonder if she means it. When I turn my attention back to her, her gaze is moving over me in much the same way mine is drinking her in. The fact sends a wonderful tingle through me that shoots right down to my already hard cock.

Turning toward the hover truck, I shift to the side so it won't be so obvious that I'm like a wretched, lifeblood-sucking thing that wants to consume her. "We should—"

"Ah, yes. Let's go. Let me just get my comm."

She heads back in and retrieves the device, placing it into a small linen satchel that hangs by her side before she beams up at me. But it's strained, that smile. As we head toward the hover truck, I can only hope I can bring out her real joy before this sol ends.

Opening the passenger side for her, Catherine hops in and I head to the other side, pausing before I open my door. I don't know what my plan is for this festival. Getting Catherine to relax around me. Getting her to give me a chance. Either of the two would be good, though the latter is more preferable.

I hop in and start the engine and as we zoom across the prairie the cab holds a comfortable silence. I break it by asking her if her planet has any such festivals and, surprisingly, Catherine speaks. She tells me about the various festivals that occur on her home planet regarding the harvest and of others, too. Her world sounds like it's a colorful one filled with beings that enjoy their existence. I can see why she would wish to return and that makes my chest tighten. Because if she could return, I would follow her. Only, she mightn't want that. And that's why this 'date' is so important.

As we near the town, I have to park the transport on the outskirts. Catherine sits up straighter, eyes slightly wide and I can't help but feel a sense of pride at what she sees.

Even from where we are, we can see that the whole town is lit up with colorful lights floating suspended above the streets.

"Wow," she breathes.

I grunt a sound of approval. "It is even more beautiful when you get closer." My gaze skips over her, knowing my words mean something completely different than what she'll assume. Thank the gods she's so entranced with the view she doesn't notice my hunger.

I hop out and open her door for her, extending my free arm in the hopes she'll use me for stability as she steps out of the truck. The moment her soft digits grasp my arm is the moment I almost groan. I manage to hold it back, remaining rigid as she gets on her feet. She's touching me. But her eyes aren't on me. They're on the town ahead. We're walking and she's still holding on to my arm.

Unreasonable pride swells in my chest at the fact she's still on my arm. The sights around us, the other beings heading in the same direction, some with painted faces, others with tall head adornments, I see none of that. My gaze is only on the human by my side.

Catherine walks close beside me, her eyes still wide as she takes it all in. Her body brushes against mine as the crowd grows thicker, and I revel in the sensation. When we reach the heart of the town where the music rises into the air, she finally tilts her head to look up at me.

My core-organ thuds hard in my chest.

"That music. It's beautiful. I've never heard anything so uniquely intoxicating."

I grin. "It's the Raki."

Her eyebrows shoot up higher. "The *Raki?*"

I turn slightly, heading toward where there's a throng of celebrators, their bodies writhing to the rhythm. Just behind them is a group of Raki, instruments in hand.

"Oh my God." Catherine grips me tighter. "They're singing through their trunks."

Her words are somewhat strange, but they make me chuckle softly.

"Oh, that's *my* Raki," she says, pointing to a male off to the side who is playing a stringed instrument. The Raki looks up, giving her a dip of his head in greeting.

My expression drops at the sight of him, my gaze hardening. It's not till Catherine laughs and tugs me closer do I realize I might have been visibly snarling.

"You don't have to protect me from him, you know." She whispers up to me. "He didn't hurt me on purpose."

"He didn't help you either."

She shrugs at that, but I'm happy the smile on her face doesn't fade. It's genuine too, lighting up her eyes. With the star's light quickly fading across the horizon, those lights in her eyes lead me from the darkness.

"May the seeds bring a bountiful harvest." The voice of a

Kalgonite as he thrusts a tray filled with delicacies in Catherine's direction.

"Oh!" She takes a little meal square topped with sweet fruit. "Thank you! May—may the seeds bring a bountiful harvest."

The Kalgonite dips his head in approval before heading to someone else in the crowd as Catherine turns to me. There's a grin on her face now.

"Wow, this is—"

"Not what you expected?"

She laughs. A real laugh. My whole being shivers with delight that flows like a wave through my scales. "Not what I expected at all."

She takes a bite of the treat before her eyes roll back. "Oh, this is so good." But then her face falls, those wide eyes moving to me. "I didn't get one for you."

More warmth swells within me. She's thinking of me.

"We can share." Before she can protest, I lean forward. My mouth closes around the treat still in her hand, my face coming incredibly close to hers. I hear when her breath hitches. See how her gaze drops to my lips. The heat of her digits is right at my mouth. Resisting the urge to wrap my lips around them nearly takes all my strength. I can't help but swipe my tongue over my lips as I pull back. She watches the movement, making me wonder once again about that mouth brushing her kind does. My gaze drops to her lips, too.

I would very much like to try it.

"Catherine!"

My head lifts and I ease back just as my siblingkin and his mate push through the crowd toward us. His mate beams, greeting me before wrapping Catherine in an embrace. Catherine releases me then, the arm she'd been gripping me with since we arrived suddenly gone, and I step back with reluctance, my gaze on her as she converses with her human friend.

I could stand here watching her for eons if she allowed me to, but eyes are boring into my skull. Zynar has an all-fang grin when I look his way.

"Don't." I hiss, low enough that the females can't hear us.

"Don't what?" He grins wider.

"Don't say it."

He stands beside me, crossing his arms as he takes in the revelers around us. "I have never seen you like this before, brother."

"I am no different than any other sol we've spent in each other's company."

He makes a sound in his throat that sounds like he's holding back a laugh. "You've brushed your mane so well, it's shining in the dark."

"You have, too."

"I have a mate. She is radiant. I cannot look like a wandering outcast in her presence."

I clench my jaw, refusing to let him bait me. He continues anyway, slapping an arm across my shoulder. "It's a good thing, brother. When your core-rhythm sings—"

I stiffen. Not because of his words, but because of what they entail and a distinct sensation that I know far too well. Failure. Because my core-rhythm is silent. Still so silent, even though I know the female I'm watching so intently is mine. "There's no guarantee it will ever sing."

And I have made peace with this. If Catherine will accept me even without hearing the song of my soul…if she can see past the silence and embrace the depths of my devotion, then I will dedicate my entire being to her happiness.

I drink her in now, watching that mask slide over her eyes as she converses with Eleanor. It's so evident, it's strange I didn't notice it from the first moment I met her. She plays it off well. The smile she now has isn't her real one. The contentment in her eyes is fake. She is playing a part as if she's been trained to play it for orbits.

This female is like me, needing a salve for her soul.

And I want to soothe her.

"That look in your eyes," Zynar leans closer. "I can see it. Frakk, every male in our proximity is aware you're skimming the edge of sanity."

I look at him then, finally shifting my gaze from Catherine. My hunger for her is that obvious?

Zynar shrugs, bumping my shoulder with his. "I've been there. With Eleanor."

At the sound of her name, his mate looks over her shoulder and grins at him. There's a disgusting rumble in his throat that tells me exactly what he wants to do to her right now. Catherine looks back too, her gaze finding mine and she offers me a gentle sort of smile. Immediately everything around us fades into nothingness. I could melt.

"You must make a plan...in case." Zynar whispers the moment their attention slides from us.

I cringe. "I know. If my core rhythm *does* sing, I will return to my lodge. I will lock myself in. And you...you must tell her what I have become."

Zynar shakes his head. "It won't get to that point. Perhaps you will be able to tell her *before* you descend into insanity."

I stare at Catherine, watching the lights play off her silken strands. Thinking about so far ahead when I haven't even gotten her to like me feels like madness in itself. "I can't tell her about the rut when she's already terrified of even letting me in," I whisper.

"She is tentative?" Zynar whispers back.

"Even more than your *kahl*. I fear I might lose my chance."

Eleanor shoots another glance over her shoulder. "What are you two whispering about?"

We both go still. Neither of us can lie and yet, the truth...

My focus shifts to Catherine. She's watching me closely and I feel a lump rise in my throat.

Eleanor chuckles and Zynar purrs. Gods, take me now.

"Remembering the war," Zynar says. "And how now we have this..." He gestures to the festival around us and then to his mate.

Eleanor's eyes grow warm while a strange look grows in Catherine's gaze.

"The war?" she asks.

I stiffen. I haven't told her about the war. About how we fought for our species. About how we were captured. About—

Alarm goes through me when Eleanor starts explaining, my gaze shifting to Zynar.

"Don't worry, brother. This will help your cause," he murmurs low. "Trust me in this."

I stand there as Eleanor tells Catherine of how we fought. Of how we lost. Of how the Tasqals destroyed our home world. Of how they captured us...did tests on us...of how we broke free and made it here. I can't see how this will help Catherine warm to me, only how it will make her realize how broken I am. Unworthy of something as precious as she is.

As Eleanor recounts the horrors of our past, I stand there waiting. Waiting for the pity. The distance that will come as Catherine puts more space between us. But as the story continues, her gaze shifts to mine.

She looks at me, *really* looks at me, and in that moment, time stills. Zynar disappears...Eleanor...the festival. Catherine takes a step closer, her hand tightening on her little satchel as if she wants to reach out and touch me. "You've lost so much. I knew you did, but..." she whispers. "I suppose I didn't realize just how much. Varek, I'm...I'm so sorry."

"Don't be, sura." In my periphery, Zynar jolts at the name I have given my female. I ignore him and I'm happy Catherine doesn't seem to notice. "I am fine now. I am alive. I am here."

Catherine nods, a small smile tugging at the corners of her lips. Her gaze travels over mine as if reading something in my eyes. "I'm glad."

She holds my gaze for a long moment, and the air crackles between us. Just two simple words and it feels like she's seeing into my very soul, acknowledging the pain I've endured and offering a quiet acceptance that soothes the ache within me. I want to reach out, pull her to me, let the world fade away, but then Eleanor clears her throat, breaking the spell.

"And that's why we all deserve this. This festival is more than just celebrating abundance for our farms. It's about celebrating *life*." She looks up at my siblingkin. "It's about giving thanks for what we now have."

Catherine nods and looks away, a faint warmth staining her cheeks. As Eleanor's words hang in the air, I know she's right, that this festival is a celebration of life and the blessings we have found here on Hudo III. And yet, as I watch Catherine, I can't help but feel that the greatest blessing of all is standing right in front of me.

14

VAREK

"By the way," Eleanor draws Catherine's attention. "Isn't Xarion supposed to be here tonight?"

As if she summoned the Saffion, I spot his tall white ears in the crowd.

"He's there," I say. Catherine's gaze, instead of looking out into the crowd, shifts back to me instead. That small smile is still on her lips and there's still that warmth in her cheeks.

"Xarion!" Eleanor shouts, beckoning the Saffion over. Catherine finally turns to look that way.

"I told you, brother." Zynar leans in with a low whisper. "With these females, you do not have to hide."

His words wash over me as I keep Catherine in my sights.

"Greetings." The Saffion approaches, adjusting his thick outer garment before bowing before us all. Eleanor grips him in an embrace.

"Xarion! So good to see you!"

He nods to us all and does another bow to Catherine. She surprises me by releasing a soft laugh and dipping her body in a strange bow, too, legs crossed as she holds the hem of her garment. "Hello, Xarion."

"I thought you were bringing another human with you," Eleanor says. There's a note of disappointment in her voice and my gaze shifts to Catherine. Is she disappointed as well? There's no indication. Her eyes are unreadable once more.

Around us, I spot a few Kari. Zynar and I are not the only two of our species on this world. But for Catherine and my *kahlesta*, they are the only humans they know on this land.

She's alone. But she doesn't have to be. I want to be there for her.

I almost miss when the Saffion does a flourish and steps to the side, suddenly revealing another female who'd been hidden at his back. Both Catherine and Eleanor go still. Water swells in Eleanor's eyes, and she rushes forward, pulling the new female into a tight embrace.

"Oh my Godddd," the other female's voice sounds strange, and when I catch a look at her face, I notice her eyes are filled with water too. They're both leaking.

Alarm goes through me, and I glance at Zynar. He has a human mate. Surely he can shed some light. But he looks just as lost as I am.

"It's so good to see you," Eleanor sobs.

I glance at Zynar again. "Do you know this female?"

It's Catherine who answers me. "No." She shakes her head, a small smile on her face as she watches the emotional reunion. She takes a step forward, as if to join the embrace, but stops. "It's just…she's human."

She says the words as if that's all the explanation it needs. And I suppose that is right. Because the depth of her meaning transcends through me.

Catherine gives me a sad sort of smile, and I feel the urge to pull her into my arms again. But I made a promise I wouldn't touch her unless she asked. A promise I'm regretting and one I've already broken. I clench my fists instead, watching as Catherine maintains a slight distance from the other two females, her joy at seeing another human tempered by something that makes me ache inside.

"Hello," the new female is finally released by Eleanor and she casts her attention at me and Zynar. "I'm Donna."

"Zynar." I point at my siblingkin. "Varek." I point at myself.

This female is undoubtedly human, but her pigment is darker than Eleanor and Catherine's. Her nose is slightly wider. Her mane a different texture. It's like proof my female has come from a varied, wonderful planet. A planet she's dying to return to and one she would head for the moment it became possible.

It's a lot to give up for someone like me.

"Donna Johnson has accepted the farm provided by the Initiative," the Saffion says, his voice surprisingly distinct despite the revelry around us. "Like you, Eleanor, she has had less than stellar mates back on your home planet and—"

"Boy, if you don't stop exposing all my business." The female called Donna gives the Saffion a stern look, but there's a grin on her face. "We've been through a lot. We can always catch up later." She waves a dismissive hand. "I love music, so if you're up for it..." She does a strange thing with her eyes, closing one for a click while the other remains open. "Let's go dance!"

Eleanor lets out a whoop before reaching for Zynar with one arm and pulling him her way. I take a step back, suddenly unsure of what in the frakk is happening. I'm not the only one, the Saffion ends up at my side, a similar perplexed look causing one of his ears to tilt forward while the other remains straight. He doesn't get to remain there for long though. The new female arrival grabs his arm.

"Xarion, I'm the only one without a mate, so you're with me!" She declares. The Saffion stutters, both ears standing straight before he's tugged into the throng behind Eleanor and Zynar.

That leaves only me and Catherine behind and my stunned expression turns to her. That human...thinks we are mates? A purr starts in my throat that I fight to control. I fail, because Catherine looks up at me with a hesitant smile, but a real smile nonetheless.

"Guess we should follow them." Her tongue appears, barely visible as she licks her lips. "I think I agree with Donna. I need a drink."

I let her walk ahead of me in the direction the others went, my eyes on her back and an insistent surge of want growing within me. We find the others just as they stop a Zalgonite with trays of brew. Reaching for two, I offer one to Catherine. Electricity shoots up my arms at the briefest touch of her digits on my claw as she takes the drink.

A sip and her eyes light up again. "Mm, this tastes like really expensive wine." I am not sure how the drink will make her complain, but she looks surprised by her realization. She takes another sip before turning to the other humans. Their conversation is almost too fast to keep track of as they comment on whining, all swirling the brew in the metallic bulbs before taking more sips.

Catherine smiles, and the mask fades away. She sips the brew, and she speaks to the other humans while I forget I have a drink in my own claw. I am content simply watching her and when they all finish their bulbs and stop another Zalgonite for more, I realize Catherine needed this. She needed to come to the festival. She needed to be around her kind.

As the clicks pass, the straight line of her shoulders sinks as if the tension in her bones drains away. A soft breeze sends tendrils of her hair flying around her soft face, an elegant arm rising to brush them away as she continues speaking to the other two females. I glance at Zynar to find his focus on his *kahl* in the same way my focus is on Catherine. We stand around them like guards, preventing the sway of the crowd from disturbing their conversation. Protecting them from rowdy revelers. Even the Saffion, a bored expression on his face, is standing guard, too.

These females are ours to protect.

Except whatever's growing inside me is telling me to do other things. The longer I watch Catherine, the more I need her. We are standing close enough that should she step back, she will bump into me and the hard thing at the center of my trouse. Gulping back the entire bulb of the drink, I try to calm my nerves. I fail. The brew simply sets my lifeblood on fire.

The Saffion beside us suddenly does another bow, bidding the females goodbye. "I will return Donna to her farm once this revelry is over." He brushes invisible dust from his coat. "Until then." He dips his head in dismissal before his focus suddenly slides to Catherine. "I must say, your integration with Varek is also quite commendable, Catherine Rose Richmond. If you should find companionship with him, the Initiative would be doubly pleased."

Even with the noise around us, it feels like all goes silent. Catherine's eyes have widened and so have Eleanor's. The female called Donna has a strange look on her face, brows lifted as her gaze shifts among us. "I'm no expert on alien customs, but I'm pretty sure that's not how you wingman, buddy."

"I'm...not an avian." The Saffion casts a confused look to her.

"That's not what I meant, Xar." Donna shakes her head, a laugh in her throat. "Ladies." Her eyes widen even more. "Shall we dance?"

"Dance?" Eleanor speaks too loudly, as if trying to distract from what the Saffion said. "Cheese on a string, yes!" She reaches for Zynar again, tugging him along after the new female as they head toward the Raki who have changed their ensemble to a more upbeat melody. The revelers all around us move faster to the beat and Zynar shoots a glance back at me with a grin and a shrug.

The female named Donna has stopped in front of the Raki.

She moves her body in a way that is so natural and fluid with the beat it's like she's heard these melodies before. Laughter peels from Eleanor as she grips Zynar and tugs him against her back as she sways her body, too. She leans back against him as his arms wrap around her and he tugs her tighter against him, her eyes filled with an emotion I've only dreamt of seeing from my own female. My *kahl*.

The hardness that had been growing in my shaft dies as something twists deep inside me—that long-felt loss and loneliness rearing its head. My throat tightens, the shadows chasing me when my gaze finally falls back to Catherine. She's watching me, gaze unreadable again, and I quickly shield her from mine, sliding on that mask that I usually wear. Because I don't want her to see my pain. I don't want her to feel it.

"Would you like to dance?" My voice sounds gruff, as gruff as those other times, and I groan inwardly. I have made little progress. Maybe this is my chance to get closer to her. But my chances are shot when Catherine shakes her head.

"I think I need to sit for a moment," she whispers. "But you can go dance, if you like. Please, don't let me stop you. I just... need a moment."

She tries to look through the crowd, probably to find a place to sit, but if she thinks I am letting her out of my sight for a single moment, she's mistaken. As if I didn't have more of a reason to keep her close, I notice the moment a few other Kari shift closer to the Raki to watch the dancers—or rather, the human, my *kahlesta*, and my siblingkin. Everyone knows who they are, the Kari who has found a mate, and they are interested. They watch Zynar and Eleanor with a wanting, a hunger, that I feel deep in my soul. And they watch the new female, Donna, too. Even as I become aware of this, I lock eyes with a Kari looking my way. Looking *Catherine's* way.

She's mine.

I block his view of her as I gesture off to the side where the crowd is thin. "There are seats over there."

Catherine nods, her eyes grateful as she heads in that direction. I follow at her back, grateful when the Kari watching her loses sight of her in the crowd as she sits on a low bench. I collapse beside her and silence envelopes us both. I'm not sure what to say.

"Enjoying the festival?"

She makes a strange sound that makes her entire body jerk. "Hiccups." She smiles. "But yes, I am enjoying it. I'm glad—" A Kalgonite bearing another tray of brew passes and she gestures at him for one. He obliges, leaning low so she can take her pick. "Thank you." She does another of those hick-ups, another smile coming to her lips.

Does she know how beautiful she is? Right now? As the lights and the shadows play across her face?

"You're glad?"

She dips her head. "I'm glad I came."

I dip my head, chin to chest as I lean back on my arms, my gaze forced on the crowd before us. I can just barely see the top of my siblingkin's head as he dances with his *kahl*.

"You dislike dancing?"

"On the contrary," Catherine chuckles and another shiver goes through my scales at the delicious sound. "I *love* to dance. I just...don't know how to dance like Donna and Eleanor. They have a rhythm I don't have."

Those words pique my interest and my gaze shifts to hers.

"How do you dance?"

Her cheeks grow even redder in the dim light and she shakes her head. "I haven't in a long, long time."

"Show me." I probably shouldn't push but the words tumble from my mouth anyway. Catherine's gaze snags on mine and, for a moment, I think she will reject my request. But then her gaze shifts to a passing Kalgonite and she gestures him over. I'm stunned, somewhat concerned, too, as she takes another bulb of brew.

"Liquid courage," she whispers to me, smiling again. When she abruptly stands, one arm outstretched to me, I resist the urge to grab hold of it and pull her into me. Instead, I look from her arm to her.

She giggles. "Come on."

Standing, I'm not sure what I must do. I'm as stiff as a tree, both my bones and that thing at the center of my groin as Catherine holds my claw and steps into me. I don't move. I don't even breathe.

Catherine begins to guide me, her movements graceful and fluid. She places one of my claws on her waist, and with her other hand, she takes hold of my other claw, positioning it just so. Her touch is gentle but firm, and I can feel the warmth of her skin through the thin fabric of her garment.

"Follow my lead," she whispers, her breath tickling my ear as I lean in. Her voice is a melody, and I am utterly entranced.

She takes a step back, and instinctively, I follow. Her movements are smooth and elegant, and despite my initial stiffness, I find myself moving with her. She glides across the ground, and I am amazed at how effortlessly she moves, like a river flowing over stones. Her grace is mesmerizing, and I am falling harder for her with each step.

Catherine's eyes sparkle with joy as she dances, and I can't take my eyes off her. Her beauty is captivating, her every movement a testament to her elegance and poise. The way she moves, the way she looks at me—it's as if she's casting a spell, and I am powerless to resist.

But as we continue to dance, I become more aware of the attention we are drawing. Every unmated male in the vicinity has their eyes on her, their gazes filled with admiration and longing. But she is mine. The thought ignites a fierce possessiveness within me, and I tighten my hold on her, pulling her closer.

Catherine doesn't seem to notice the attention. Her focus is entirely on me, her eyes locked on mine. She smiles, a radiant smile that takes my breath away, and I know that I am lost. I am falling deeper and deeper into her, and there is no escape.

She twirls, and I spin her effortlessly, the skirts of her garment flaring out like a radiant bloom. She laughs, a sound so pure and joyful that it sends another shiver through me. When she comes back to me, I catch her, holding her close, our bodies pressed together.

"Goodness," she whispers, her eyes shining. "You're a natural."

The only thing natural is the way she fits in my arms. The way this feels.

I can't find the words to respond. I am too caught up in the moment. Too captivated by her. Instead, I pull her even closer, my core-beat pounding in my chest. She rests her head against my shoulder, and we continue to move together, our bodies in perfect harmony.

In this moment, she is mine, and I am hers. The world fades away, and it is just the two of us, lost in the dance. We dance for what feels like hors, lost in the rhythm and each other's arms. And when the music finally fades and we come to a stop, both of us breathless and flushed, I can't help but pull her closer.

Catherine tilts her head back, looking up at me, a strange thing passing in her eyes. I swallow hard, staring back, not wanting to break the moment. Her lips part slightly, and I can see the rapid rise and fall of her chest as she catches her breath. The air between us is charged, crackling again.

"Catherine," I whisper, my voice rough with emotion. Her name on my lips feels like a prayer, a plea for something more. But what?

Everything.

I want everything.

She doesn't respond, but her eyes say it all. They are filled with a longing that mirrors my own, a silent invitation that I can't ignore. My core-beat goes raging in my chest, each beat echoing the urgency of the moment.

The brushing of lips. It's now.

Slowly, hesitantly, I lower my head, my gaze never leaving hers. She doesn't pull away; instead, she leans into me, her digits tightening their grip on my claw as the others tighten on my shoulder. Our breaths mingle, and I can feel the warmth of her skin, the softness of her body pressing against mine.

Our lips are so close now, just a whisper apart. I can feel the heat of her breath on my mouth, and it takes every ounce of my self-control not to close the distance and claim her. But I wait, giving her the chance to pull away if she wants to. Even though each click that passes kills me.

But she doesn't. Instead, she tilts her head slightly, her eyes fluttering closed, and in that moment, I know. I know that she wants this just as much as I do.

Our lips meet, soft and tentative at first, a whisper of a touch that sends sparks dancing across my scales. But then she sighs, a soft, contented sound that sets my lifeblood on fire.

I'm not sure what to do, this intimate act is foreign to me, but Catherine seems to sense my hesitation. She takes the lead, her lips moving gently against mine, guiding me in this dance of passion.

My whole being lights up. I'm dimly aware of those unmated males around us growing more curious but I couldn't give a tarsals ass that they're watching now. I have her and, gods, Zynar was right about this. It isn't simply brushing mouths together. This...this is so much more.

Catherine's hand slides from my shoulder to the back of my neck, her digits tangling in the short hairs there, and I can't suppress the shiver that runs down my spine. She pulls me closer, deepening the movement of our mouths, and I follow her lead, mimicking what she does. Soon, I am lost in the sensation. Her lips are soft and warm, and the way they move against mine is intoxicating. I can taste the sweetness of the brew on her breath, mingling with the unique flavor that is purely her.

When her tongue suddenly brushes lightly against my lips, I jerk, a jolt going through me before I freeze, suddenly aware of my entire being. My breath stills as I expect her to shift away from me now. Because, surely, she can feel it. My shaft is like an unbendable rod poking through my trouse into her belly. I hesitate, unsure of what to do and unable to control the shudder of pleasure that goes through me. But Catherine is patient. She doesn't pull away. Instead, her touch is gentle and encouraging. I dare to open my mouth slightly, allowing her to explore, and the moment her little tongue ventures in, the sensation is like a star exploding in the void.

A groan escapes me as her digits tangle in my mane. She pulls me closer and I respond, my claws tightening around her waist, anchoring her to me. The intensity of our mouths mating grows more urgent, more passionate, and I lose myself in the feel of her against me, the taste of her, the way she makes me feel like I am flying and grounded all at once.

As the Raki start a melody with a slower tempo, it suddenly breaks the magic between us. Catherine pauses, her lips sliding from mine as her chest heaves. There's a panicked look on her face, and I fear I may have pushed too far. But then I catch something else. Another look in her eyes that I've never seen before.

Her eyes close. She squeezes them shut, and that's when I realize she's still holding on to me, because she grips me tight. When her eyes flutter open again, the look she gives me is filled with so much emotion that my lungs seize all over again.

"Varek—"

I stiffen. "No. It was my fault. If you didn't want to brush mouths—"

But then she shifts her arm and two of her digits brush over my lips, quieting me.

"Varek, I…I wanted to."

Her words hold me silent. Gods, I'm imagining things.

"I wanted to," she whispers again. She stares up at me, her chest heaving still.

And then I ask something I'd have been terrified to ask just a few hors ago.

"My lodge is close by here. Would you…would you like to go there with me? Now?"

15

CATHERINE

His words should terrify me. For the simple fact that the implication is the exact thing I've been hiding away from.

I could blame it on Eleanor and the utter way she's smitten with Varek's brother. I could even blame it on Donna's free spirit and the feel of life and fun around us. I could even blame it on the drink, but it's none of those things. I'm completely sober and...I'm tired.

Tired of fighting.

I like this alien. This gentle alien male that's been making me lose my inhibitions hour by hour, day by day. Feeling his lips against mine has only cemented that I have needs and...

And that I don't want to be alone. Not really. I want company.

I want someone to love and someone to love me. Truly love me. My heart has been broken, a part of me ripped open and I've been desperately trying to heal it by pushing everyone else away.

Maybe I will change my mind tomorrow. I'm aware there's a high chance I most definitely will. But Varek is not demanding anything of me. If he just wants to have some fun, I can do that. There's nothing wrong with allowing myself to feel for just a few moments. Nothing wrong with giving myself permission for just one night.

My gaze shifts upward and his entire frame tense as he waits for my response. I notice the way he releases a breath, some tension leaving his shoulders the moment I nod.

Across the crowd of dancing aliens, he motions to his brother who seems to have been watching us. I don't even feel my cheeks warm. Apparently, with this decision, all my shame has gone. Instead, I allow Varek to direct me from the crowd till we're the only two people walking down an empty street. The wind whistles, playing with the skirts of the wrap dress I made from an extra layer of curtain. I tug at it now, other thoughts creeping in.

Thoughts like whether he'll be surprised by the way I look underneath this. I've practically seen him naked. I've even imagined it. Days upon days of staring at his glistening muscles underneath the sun haven't done me any favors, and as we walk in silence down the street, I feel a throb below in a place that hasn't sung a song in a long time.

I bite my lower lip, almost groaning at the intensity of the sensation—at the intense anticipation rising in my blood—but manage to continue walking without showing evidence of just how lost I am.

Varek stops at a building that looks like it has a few floors. As I enter behind him, my gaze shifts down the street again, back in the direction of the festival and I pause. I'm really doing this, aren't I? There's no mistaking what's about to happen once I walk over this threshold.

As I turn away from the festival back to the alien waiting by my side, I find Varek holding the door open. His expression is schooled but his eyes are not. Those slitted yellow pits are filled with what I can only read as hope. Hope...and *need*. My gaze skips down to movement in his throat as he waits there, doing nothing to influence my decision in any way. If I want to turn back right now, I can.

Instead, I step inside.

I swear I hear the pressure of a controlled release of breath through his nostrils as he directs me down the hall. There are multiple doors with symbols written on them that are indecipherable to me.

"This is an apartment building?" My voice comes out with more surety than I feel in this situation. Each step I take, my heart beats harder and harder till I'm quite sure Varek can hear the thundering in my chest.

"Living quarters? Yes," he confirms, his deep voice echoing slightly in the corridor. "We call them 'nestkans.'"

He leads me to a door at the end of the hall and pauses. "This is my dwelling," he breathes. His voice has gone so low it is but a rumble. My tongue swells in my throat as my gaze shifts to the door.

What are you doing, Catherine?

I can feel Varek's gaze on me as he waits for my response.

Just what are you doing?

Taking a deep breath, I nod, giving him a reassuring smile. "I'd like to see it."

Varek's relief is palpable. His shoulders release even more of the tension I didn't realize was there as he places his clawed hand on a smooth panel beside the door. It slides open with a soft hiss, revealing a dimly lit interior.

Varek steps aside, gesturing for me to enter. "Please…"

His growl sends a delicious shudder through me and my focus falls on its own accord, straight to his crotch. *Oh goodness…* The heat rising in my cheeks has nothing to do with embarrassment as my eyes lock on to the definite bulge in his pants.

That's…for me…

Only the sudden increase of warmth in my blood makes me look hurriedly away, stepping into the room before nerves get the best of me. I cross the threshold into his nestkans, my heart pounding with a mixture of anticipation and trepidation. The door slides shut behind us, cocooning us in a world of our own.

Cocooning us in *his* world.

The entire apartment smells like him. That deliciously sweet scent that makes me want to breathe in deep. It's everywhere. My eyelids flutter just from the intensity of it and I brace on a small table nearby the entrance.

"I apologize, sura, for the mess." The apartment isn't small, but Varek swallows the entire space, just like he did in my cottage. It isn't even his size or stature, it's *him*. His existence.

We're standing in what seems to be the sitting room and he pulls out a stool for me to sit on by the large table. I move over, happy to rest my legs because it feels like I will soon collapse from something other than weariness. My entire body is tingling, anticipation stealing my breath.

Varek disappears into another room for a moment and I get a chance to look around. The room is spotless. I'm not sure what mess he's talking about. Just like his truck, it's clean in here. Clean and smells so good. I stand up, walking over to a floating holo-image that gets more distinct the closer I get. It's a picture of Varek and his brother, only much younger. Zynar is grinning, fangs and all, but Varek...Varek is stoic, his face unreadable. I tilt my head, looking at the picture. I've seen so many expressions on his face, I know he's nothing like that stoic mask suggests, and I wonder if he's hiding behind something just like I am.

A sound behind me makes me spin around like I've been caught snooping and I'm immediately reminded of what I'm doing here. My throat goes dry the moment my gaze falls on the alien.

His shirt is gone again, those rippling chest muscles making my eyes fasten on him like glue.

"I...brought you a drink, though you might not be thirsty after—"

Reaching forward, I grab the drink from his claw, downing it with large gulps. *Oh God, I'm about to really do this. It's been so long I...*

But then my thoughts short circuit. Because Varek is so close I can't see anything else. My gaze shifts upward, traveling up those iridescent scales to his throat. My breath hitches as I go higher, gaze traveling up to that chiseled jaw...his lips...

"Catherine..."

I have to do this before I change my mind. I tilt my head back till I meet his gaze and the intensity within those eyes takes my breath away.

"I told you I wouldn't touch you unless..."

"Unless I asked you to," I whisper.

His throat moves. He's just as nervous as I am.

"Varek... Please. Touch me." *I need it.* But that thought isn't one I can say. Not out loud. Not even to myself. By coming here to his quarters, I've already acknowledged what I want, but giving voice to it is another matter entirely.

With a soft growl, Varek dips his head. His lips touch mine again, this time with a newfound intensity that makes my knees weak. His hands—those large, clawed hands—are gentle as they slide up my arms, leaving a trail of heat in their wake. I gasp against his mouth, the sensation overwhelming, and he takes the opportunity to deepen the kiss, his tongue exploring mine with a fervor that sets my blood on fire. His claws come up to cup my face, his touch gentle but firm, as if he's afraid I might disappear if he doesn't hold on tight.

He's a quick learner. At the festival, I was pretty sure he'd been following my lead. Now, he's taking charge. My hands find their way to his chest, tracing the contours of his muscles, feeling the warmth of his skin beneath my fingertips. He shudders under my touch, a low rumble emanating from deep within his chest that vibrates through me and sets me alight. The sound of that rumble is such pure, unadulterated desire, that it makes my knees go weak.

We're just kissing. We haven't even…holy cow. A quiver goes through me that makes me grip Varek tighter. I melt into him, my body molding to his as my hands explore the expanse of his bare chest. He smells even better than before. Just pure, raw masculinity that makes me whimper again despite myself and my inhibitions.

Varek's claws travel lower, the faint sharpness of them tracing the curve of my waist before his palms settle on my hips. He pulls me closer, lifting me slightly so that I'm flush against him. My breath hitches.

It's there. Like a thick, hard metal pole pressing into my belly, I can feel him, and my own desire pulses in response. It's been so long since I've felt this way—since I've *allowed* myself to feel this way—and it's almost too much. But I don't want it to stop. I don't want *him* to stop.

"Catherine," he murmurs against my lips, his voice rough and breathless. "You must stop me now. Otherwise, I can't resist you. You must…" But even as he's telling me to tell him no, there's a plea in his tone that matches the desperation clawing for escape within me.

Just one night.

"If you're not sure," Varek nibbles my upper lip, a low groan leaving his throat. "I can wait. I will wait for as long as you want me to. If you're not sure—"

My hands tighten their grip on his shoulders. "I'm sure," I manage to whisper. "Don't stop."

He doesn't need any more encouragement. With a growl that sends shivers down my spine, Varek scoops me up into his arms, carrying me effortlessly towards what I assume is his bedchamber. The room is dimly lit, the soft glow casting shadows that dance across his scales, making him look even more otherworldly.

Gently, he sets me down on the bed, and for a moment, we just look at each other, the air between us charged with anticipation. His eyes are dark with desire and another thrill goes through me at the sight. Slowly, he crawls onto the bed, hovering over me.

"You're enchanting," he murmurs, almost to himself as his claw traces the line of my jaw, down my neck, to the edge of my wrap dress. "May I?"

I nod, unable to form words.

Slowly, he begins to undress me, his claws surprisingly deft as they work the fastenings of my makeshift dress. Each piece of fabric that falls away leaves me feeling more exposed, more vulnerable, but also more alive than I have in years.

Each layer that falls, each layer that's stripped away, it feels like I'm baring more than my body to this male. As if I'm baring all my past, everything about me, all the trauma and the good, all the fears and the pain, all the laughter and the rain. It's silent when the final layer is removed, my linen panties and my soft linen bra.

I'm finally bare before him and Varek pauses. Goes so still he could be a statue and my breath stills, too. Like a lion pausing to pounce, only his eyes move. They rake over me with an intensity that makes my skin tingle and I realize, in an instant, that no man has ever looked at me like *that*.

"You're bewitching," he whispers, and I release a surprised laugh. But there's no humor in his tone. No humor in his eyes. Varek is looking at me as if he's a forty-niner who's just struck gold in the California hills.

"More beautiful than I've imagined." His voice is so thick with emotion that the stunned humor that had made me laugh seeps away. I stare at him, watching him drink me in and I wonder if this is all a dream. That maybe I wasn't rescued from those horrible Tasqals and I'm in some alien prison of their making being fed drugs that have made me imagine this new world. Imagine *him*.

"How can you be real?" I whisper.

Varek looks up, eyes locking with mine. His pupils are visibly wider, making him look almost intoxicated. "Don't say that, sura. Each sol I wake, I worry that maybe *you're* not real. That I've created you in my head."

"I'm real." My eyes search his for some evidence of deception. But there is none.

My breath hitches as he suddenly leans in, capturing my lips in another searing kiss as his claws start to explore, tracing down the curves of my body, setting my nerve endings alight. He doesn't just touch. He kneads. He squeezes. His claws rove over every inch of me as if he's making a map. Every little hitch of my breath, every little moan or whimper is greeted with a rumble of pleasure that sounds like it comes from the depths of his soul. As if I'm being memorized, my body's responses committed to his mental map. His touch is both possessive and reverent, and it sends shivers down my spine. I arch into his touch, my own hands roaming over the expanse of his back, feeling the shift of his muscles beneath my fingers as he wakes up parts of me that I've ignored for so long.

When his claws find my breasts, I stiffen. I've hated them for years. More when they lost their firmness. Even more when gravity started to take its toll. But Varek doesn't even pause. He cups and kneads the sensitive flesh, causing me to break the kiss with a gasp, my head falling back against the bed. Varek freezes and I catch a glint in his eyes as he inhales deeply. A low moan rumbles in his throat.

He takes the opportunity to trail his lips down my neck, nipping and sucking at the delicate skin, drawing breathy moans from my lips.

When his mouth finally closes around one of my nipples, I arch into him, a soft moan escaping my lips. He answers with one of his own, purring with approval as if my pleasure is intensifying his own. His tongue flicks and swirls, and my hands reach down and tighten in his hair, holding him to me as my body responds in a way it's been yearning to for so so long.

When one of his claws grazes the sensitive skin of my inner thigh, I gasp, my hips bucking involuntarily. Varek rumbles his approval, the sound vibrating through me and making me shudder.

"Sweet sura," he murmurs against my breast, his fangs grazing my delicate skin. "So perfect."

Perfect? I want to respond, to tell him that he's wrong. That I'm nothing but scarred and destroyed within, but my words are stolen by a moan as his claw dips between my legs. I feel the moment he sheathes them as his fingers brush against my center. For a moment, we both pause, caught in the intensity of that single touch.

He brushes his finger again and it travels through my core, the sensitive skin throbbing with the sensation. Varek nibbles on my breast, a deep rumble of a moan making the air vibrate against my nipple. My core swells and throbs in response.

"Show me how to please you, sura," he growls. "Teach me." With a trembling hand, I reach between my legs, fingers closing around his wrist as I guide his claw. Varek rumbles, his head lifting as he buries his face into my neck. His tongue flicks out, licking my skin as he breathes in deep. "Gods, you really are a sura."

"Mm?" A breath shudders from me as my eyes flutter closed, each movement of his fingers sending me higher and higher towards something my body's craving. "Sura? Why do you call me that? What does it mean?"

"Soft." Varek rumbles. "Soft beautiful thing."

A whimper makes me shudder again at his words. My guidance is short-lived. Varek groans as he takes charge, moving his fingers in a pattern that he's learned far too quickly. He strokes and explores with a single-minded focus, each caress winding the coil of tension in my core tighter and tighter. Another moan rumbles from him as he dips his head again to my other breast and I arch, my body demanding more.

I buck against his palm the moment he finds my entrance, sliding two digits within my heat.

"Please," I gasp, my hips lifting to meet his touch. "Varek… I…" I'm not even sure what I'm begging for, only that I need it.

Varek growls against my skin. "Patience, sura," he rumbles. "I want to savor you."

And savor me he does. Varek's touch is sure, his claws and tongue pushing me to the brink. When he suddenly eases off me, the rhythm of the digits buried inside me slowing, I open eyes I didn't realize I'd closed. My vision blurs as I look down a moment before he dips again. Only, he's no longer over me. He's between my legs.

The moment his mouth closes over my center, I peak. My body thrashes. I cry out words that have no meaning but mean everything all at once. A deep rumbling sound comes from his chest as Varek pushes his tongue deep within me. Sucking, slurping, he doesn't let up till he brings me to the brink of ecstasy again and again. Until I'm a trembling, moaning mess beneath him.

I'm boneless as he eases up, the heat of his body disappearing for a moment as I lie there thinking one thing: how will I go back to normal after this? How will I pretend? How will I go back to the solitary, celibate life I'd been leading all the years before?

My vision clears, my chest heaving as I look down, watching this absolute god of a male climb between my legs. He's bare now, the silken scales on his thighs brushing against my legs as he lines himself up.

"Catherine," he groans, and I know he's asking for permission again. Even after all the pleasure he's given me, he's still making sure I want him to take his own.

I nod. "Please." There are tears in my eyes, coming from a place I don't want to face. When he finally enters me, joining our bodies as one, it's with a gentleness and reverence that brings tears to my eyes.

It's too much, the pleasure edging on overwhelming. My hands fist in the bedding, my head tipping back as I surrender to the sensations, to him. He stretches me in a way I don't remember ever being stretched. My mouth opens in a wordless 'O' as I take in a deep, ongoing breath.

I can feel that he's tapered at the tip, getting thicker and thicker the farther he pushes in. And there are ridges and other externalities that I'm not used to. Such a fact should make me pause. Make me stop and rethink this. It doesn't. My core quivers, taking him in, wanting him to sink deeper. Wanting him to fill that aching space inside.

When I catch sight of his face, of the snarl, the clenching of teeth with fangs bared, it should scare me. Again, I don't respond in the way I should.

Varek pulls back and slides in again, his rhythm slowly increasing as the seconds tick by. It's wet and smooth, his own natural lubricant easing the way for us both. I shudder and I shiver, nerve endings waking up in parts of my body I'd forgotten exist. The tension within me builds till I know I can't take it anymore.

"Varek," I manage to gasp out, his name both a plea and a prayer.

Those intoxicated eyes drink me in. "Sweet sura," he rumbles, his voice low and reassuring. "Let go, Catherine. Let me catch you."

Oh God...I'm lost.

Lost in him, lost in this moment, lost in the overwhelming

cascade of sensations and emotions. My body shatters a moment before I feel Varek stiffen, a deep unearthly groan leaving his throat as his shaft throbs deep inside me.

He collapses as do I, bracing himself up on his arms so he doesn't crush me, both our chests rising and falling in quick succession. And as we lie there in the afterglow, our bodies still joined, Varek's arms surround me. He twists, falling on his side and pulling me with him. There, pressed against him in what feels like a world for us alone, his heartbeat is a steady thumping thing beneath my cheek.

For the first time in a long time, I don't feel alone. I feel cherished, perhaps even...

Desired.

Tomorrow will bring what it will. But tonight? Tonight, I have found peace. I have found connection.

This alien...he could break down every wall I've ever built. Could shatter every defense, every carefully constructed barrier around my heart. And maybe that's what terrifies me more than anything else.

VAREK

I collapse beside Catherine, my core-organ pounding, each breath coming in ragged gasps. I can barely believe what just happened, can barely process the overwhelming intensity of the pleasure, the connection, the emotions that consumed us both.

Carefully, I gather Catherine against me, cradling her to my chest as if she's the most precious thing in the universe. Because to me, she is. I still can't quite wrap my head around the fact that this incredible, beautiful, resilient female is here in my arms, that she welcomed me into her body and hopefully into her heart.

I'd dreamed of this moment. Fantasized about it more times than I can count. But the reality was so much more than I ever could have imagined. The feel of her soft skin under my claws, the taste of her on my tongue, the way she moved with me, surrendered to me...it was...*transcendent*.

I know her history, know the horrors she's endured. For her to open herself to me like this, to allow herself to be seen and touched and cherished...it's a gift beyond measure.

My arms tighten around her reflexively, a sudden surge of

protectiveness, of *possessiveness*, welling up within me. I want to shield her from everything, to ensure that nothing and no one ever hurts her again. I want to spend the rest of my days worshiping her, body and soul, showing her just how treasured and adored she is.

Catherine shifts in my arms, her gaze shifting up to mine. Her chest is still heaving, the strain of each breath slowly coming back to normal. Just her eyes meeting mine and my cock throbs where it's still buried deep within her.

Her eyes search mine and I can tell she wants to say something. There's a hesitation there, a conflict. I can almost hear the words she's holding back, the fear that what we just shared might never happen again. The fear that this perfect, life-altering moment might be just that...a moment, never to be repeated.

Part of me wants to reassure her, to promise her forever, to declare my undying love and devotion. But another part of me is painfully aware of one thing Catherine has no clue about.

My core-rhythm. It's still silent.

I've joined with her now. That is unquestionable. But my core-rhythm, the thing that's supposed to sing once I find my mate, remains quiet. I am silent inside.

Pain, the likes of which I didn't expect to feel, consumes me. I grunt, pulling her tighter to my chest as I block out the darkness that threatens to pull me under.

She's mine. I know it. I feel it.

I can't be wrong.

"Varek?" Her question makes me aware that, even with the dim light, she must be watching me, too. But it is difficult to push away the darkness that tears at me from within. The fear of loss before I've even gotten a proper chance to have her echoes within me, but I don't want to face it. Not now. Not when the memory of our shared passion is still so raw and vivid.

And so I don't.

"Are you alright?" Her sweet voice sends a shiver through me as I dip my head, crushing her lips against mine. She grunts before her body suddenly melts, the reaction so soft and sweet that I harden even more, stretching her sweetness as a rumble goes through my chest.

"Oh my, already?" Catherine's eyes are wide with disbelief.

"I will stop if you want me to, sura."

She blinks at me, eyes searching mine once more before she shakes her head from side to side. "No." Her voice drops. "Don't stop."

My growl makes her visibly shiver. But it isn't fear that lights up her eyes but something else. Something that heats my lifeblood in my veins.

"Sura," I growl as I slide out of her. She gasps, looking between us but the dim light hides me. The loss of her heat feels like a crime, but it's not for long. In one easy movement, I flip her in my arms so her back presses into my chest. Here, I lean forward, nuzzling her ear.

"So soft," I whisper and Catherine shivers. "So perfect for me."

She makes a sound in her throat that turns into a soft gasp as I pierce her again.

Frakk.

She is everything. And she is mine. I thrust into her knowing that truth. Once, twice, three times I take her, each time more intense, more consuming than the last.

We move together, a perfect rhythm until we are both spent, collapsing into each other with the fading sounds of the festival in the distance. The dark cycle wraps around us like a cocoon of warmth, but even in this moment of peace, I am painfully aware of one truth: my core-rhythm never awakens.

Pushing a lock of her mane away from her face, I grasp a few of the silver tendrils between my digits. Even in this dim room, they catch the light of the moon. I don't want this moment to end...but...what if I'm wrong? What if Catherine truly is not mine? What if this, as glorious and life-changing as it feels, isn't the eternal bond I so desperately crave?

I tighten my arms around her, burying my face in her mane, breathing in her scent. Willing time to stop. Because what I feel for her, what we just shared...it's real. It's true. It's everything.

My core-rhythm may be silent, but my soul, every instinct within me, screams that she is my mate, my destiny, my forever.

And I choose to trust in that, to have faith in the unshakable rightness of her in my arms.

Core-rhythm or not, Catherine is mine. And I am hers.

I WAKE to the loss of her in my arms. Alarm shoots through me and I sit upright on the bedding immediately.

A soft sound draws my eyes to the far side of the room, air rushing into my lungs the moment I see her.

Catherine stands there, already dressed, the early morning light filtering through the window and casting a radiant glow around her. She looks ethereal. I can't pull my eyes away.

But even as my core-organ swells at the sight of her, a sinking feeling settles in my gut. Because it's clear from her attire, from the way she's standing looking through the window into the town, that she's preparing to leave.

"Catherine?" I call softly, my voice rough with sleep and something more profound.

She turns to me, a soft smile on her lips, but there's a hint of something else in her eyes. Uncertainty, perhaps. Or reluctance.

"Good morning, Varek." Gods, her voice is exactly what I need to hear each dawn. Her digits adjust the strap of her satchel. "I...didn't want to wake you."

"You're leaving." It's not a question, but a statement, a realization that makes my chest tighten. My feet hit the floor, but I force myself not to walk over to her and pull her into my arms.

She nods, her gaze shifting back to the window. "I need to get back to the farm. There's work to be done, and I…" She trails off, and the look in her eyes grows distant.

"Catherine." Her name snaps her back and she shifts her gaze to me. "About the last cycle…"

That vibrant color stains her cheeks, but she doesn't look away. "Last night was…wonderful, Varek. Truly. I don't regret a moment of it."

Relief floods through me at her words, but it's tempered by the unspoken 'but' hanging in the air between us.

"But?" I prompt gently, steeling myself for what I fear is coming.

She sighs, her hand rising to brush her mane away from her face. "But I don't expect anything more from you, Varek. I understand that what we shared…it was a moment out of time, a beautiful interlude. But I know it can't be more than that."

Pain lances through me at her words, at the resignation in her voice. I want to argue, to declare that she's wrong, to beg her to stay with me always. But I bite back the words. Because as much as it hurts, I understand.

The dark cycle has passed and still there is no song within me. My core-rhythm is silent. There is no undeniable biological proof that we are destined mates. I have no claim over Catherine, even though I want her so badly the thought of letting her slip through my claws is ripping a hole right through me.

So instead of arguing, I simply jerk my head, chin to chest. "I understand, sura."

Catherine jerks her head as well, giving me one of those mirthless smiles that tears at me even more before she shifts her gaze back to the view. But not before I see her eyes shine with unshed waters.

"I mean it, Varek," she whispers so low, my ears perk just to pick up her words. "I really did enjoy it. Thank you."

I can't...I can't let her go like this.

Closing the distance between us, I place a digit under her chin, tilting her head back so she's forced to look at me. My throat closes up. There are no words. Only actions.

Leaning down, I press my lips against hers. Soft and lingering. It feels like a promise, like a vow, even if I can't put it into words.

When we part, I rest my forehead against hers for a moment, just breathing her in. "Let me take you back to the farm," I murmur, reluctant to let her go just yet.

She nods, a small smile returning to her lips. "I'd like that."

THE JOURNEY back to Catherine's farm is quiet. It feels like we're both trying to hold on to these last moments, to etch them into our memories before reality intrudes once more.

When we reach the boundary of her property, Catherine turns to me. I brace myself for whatever she will say, knowing fully well that whatever it is will rip me in two or hold me together and that it will be absolutely no fault of hers.

"Thanks for the ride." She's doing that smile again that doesn't reach her eyes and I wish I could fix it. Wish I could give her real joy. "I'm going to head in now."

She reaches for the door and I engage the brakes before hopping out of the vehicle. I'm at her door when she looks up at me through the transparent cab, her lips stretching into that strange smile again once I open the door for her.

"Thanks." She makes a sound in her throat before her gaze shifts to her lodge. "I guess I'll see you."

Something within me dies. This is goodbye, isn't it?

"I still have some more work to do. Your field is infested. I need to treat it."

Catherine's gaze meets mine, something passing behind her eyes before she looks away.

"Hmm," she hums. "Maybe another day? I'm a little tired from the um..." She makes that sound in her throat again. "From the festival. You must be tired too." She meets my gaze again. "You should get some rest."

This is it. A goodbye of sorts. But I can't push it. She needs space even though everything within me is telling me to do the opposite.

It takes all my effort to jerk my chin in acceptance before shutting the door behind her. Leaning on the hover truck, I watch as she heads toward her lodge, my gaze not leaving her until she opens the door and steps inside.

I remain there for a few moments, just watching the lodge, wanting nothing more than to rush after her. But as I grip my chest, the ever-present silence there reminds me that giving her space is the right thing to do. Pushing her now could drive her further away.

Reluctantly, I turn away and head back into my transport.

Claw still gripping my chest, I tell myself this isn't the end of things.

Even if it feels like it is.

17

CATHERINE

The next few days pass by torturously slowly.

The day after our night of passion, Varek doesn't return. My heart drops.

What did I expect? I knew it was only a one-night thing. I agreed to that. I'd been fine with that.

Angrily, I scrub at a spot on the wooden flooring that doesn't seem to want to get rid of the stain I'm working on. A frown so severe on my brow it gives me extra lines.

"Really stupid, Catherine," I scold myself. A grown woman shouldn't be affected by something like this. Varek's absence is for the best. At least, I tell myself it's for the best, that we both need time to process, to reflect on what transpired between us. But the ache of his absence is a constant companion, a dull throb that underlies my every thought, my every action.

"Damnit." I brace on a chair and stand, frowning at the bucket of water and the sponge I was using. Reaching for them, I stomp toward the bathroom, but not before catching sight of the little device Varek had given me as a present.

The little vibrating thing sits unused on the table right beside the crate of equally untouched fruits. A tremor in my core makes a lump rise in my throat before I force my gaze away from the thing and march to the bathroom to empty the bucket.

What is wrong with me?

I'm no virgin but that night…I felt like one.

And now, with him gone, it's like a part of me has been ripped away. I can't focus on anything, can't find solace in the routines that used to comfort me.

I dump the water down the drain and lean against the sink, staring at my reflection in the mirror. My eyes are tired, ringed with dark circles from sleepless nights. My lips press into a thin line as I glare at myself.

"Get it together, Catherine. You're stronger than this."

But the pep talk does little to ease the ache in my chest. I push away from the sink and head back to the main room, determined to find something, anything, to distract myself.

The hours drag on, each one feeling like an eternity. I try to lose myself in work, but my thoughts keep drifting back to Varek. His touch, his voice, the way he made me feel like I was the only person in the universe. I can't shake the feeling that I've pushed him away, that I've made a terrible mistake.

But I haven't!

You don't fall in love at sixty. You get on with the life that God's given you and thank him you're still alive and healthy. I've lived a good life. Taken care of myself so I don't have to visit the doctor every week. The children I have are grown and are hopefully living happy lives back on Earth without me. All in all, my life has been good.

Goddammit. You don't fall in love at my age because—

Because everyone I've ever loved is gone.

The thought hits me like a punch to the gut. They're all gone. And now, I'm terrified that I'll lose Varek too. That I'll let myself love him, only to have him ripped away from me. The fear is a paralyzing, cold, hard knot in my stomach.

I sink into a chair, burying my face in my hands.

"Goodness, girl," I whisper to the silent room. "What have you gotten yourself into?"

I don't know how long I stay like that before I find the strength to rise. To continue on with my day.

I go about my tasks mechanically, tending to the farm, to the animals, but my mind is never fully present. It's always wandering, always drifting back to him. To the feel of his claws on my skin, the heat of his breath against my neck, the overwhelming passion and tenderness in his eyes as he moved within me.

At the end of the fourth day, I catch myself watching the horizon, my heart leaping at every distant sound, hoping against hope to see his transport rumbling down the path. But he doesn't come. And with each day that passes, the weight in my chest grows heavier, the doubts and fears louder.

By the fifth day, I'm a mess of raw nerves and restless energy. I snap at the animals, drop tools with shaking hands, and find myself blinking back tears at the most inopportune moments. I'm torn between the desperate desire to seek him out, even while knowing I can never offer him all of myself.

So I stay put. I focus on my work. I try not to—

My head snaps up the moment I hear the engine. Before me, an umu bleats at me in annoyance, its eyes on the tuft of hay being squeezed tight in my fist. Releasing the food, I hurry from the barn, heart in my throat. I look a mess, my hair damp against my head from sweating all day, my tunic stained with dirt and God knows what. But I can't stop myself from hurrying to the yard.

My heart gives a big, heavy thud the moment I see the light reflect off those beautiful scales.

Varek is just walking past the gate when he stops in his tracks. For a moment, our eyes lock, and the air between us crackles with tension. My breath catches in my throat as I take him in.

He looks tired, his scales less vibrant than usual, and there's a new scar on his jaw, as well as faint darkened spots on his chest that look like bruises underneath his scales. Neither was there before. My heart clenches at the sight, and I have to resist the urge to run to him, to trace the marks with my fingertips and demand to know what happened.

But I don't. I can't. Instead, I force a smile, trying to ignore the way my heart is pounding in my chest.

"Varek," I say, my voice barely above a whisper. "You're back."

"Apologies for the delay, sura." Sura. My entire being warms at the nickname. "There were...complications." He looks like he's been through something, but his eyes—they're as intense and captivating as ever, holding mine with a mix of determination and something else, something that makes my breath catch in my throat.

I swallow hard, my emotions a tangled mess. Relief, anger, longing—they all swirl within me, making it hard to think straight. "Complications?" I manage to say. "You look like you've been through a war."

He gives a small, wry smile that flashes one of his fangs and I stare at his lips, only remembering what they felt like against my own. "Something like that. But I'm here now."

I blink away my lust, scolding myself, as my focus shifts back to his eyes. A moment passes between us, one that feels like the air is charged and heavy with the weight of unsaid words. "Varek...is everything alright?"

For the briefest moment, something passes behind his eyes. And in that moment, it's like I heard every single word he wants to say but doesn't. That he missed me, that he's been through hell, that he's here now and needs this as much as I do.

Instead, he takes a deep breath and nods. "Everything is fine now, Catherine. I promise."

I nod back, not fully believing him but choosing to let it slide for now. "Come inside. You look like you could use a rest."

He follows me into the house, and I can feel his presence behind me, steady and comforting despite the tension that still crackles between us. I motion for him to sit at the table, even as I try to ignore the fact that his sweet scent seems to be chasing out every other scent that had been present in the room. Now he dominates the space in my mind *and* in my home.

"I'll get something for those bruises." My voice is steady but my heart isn't. "And some food. You look like you haven't eaten in days."

He sits, watching me with those intense eyes as I move around the kitchen, gathering supplies. The familiarity of the room helps to calm my racing heart, but I can still feel the weight of his gaze on me, a constant reminder of the unresolved tension between us.

I bring over a bowl of water and a clean cloth, sitting down beside him to tend to his wounds. My hands tremble slightly as I dab at the bruise on his jaw, and he closes his eyes, leaning into my touch.

"Thank you, sura," he murmurs, and the warmth in his voice sends a shiver down my spine.

Fuck.

I rarely curse, but FUCK!

We sit in silence as I clean his wounds, the only sound the gentle splash of water and the soft rustle of fabric. Every now and then, our eyes meet, and the air seems to thicken.

Finally, I finish tending to his injuries and sit back, taking a deep breath. "There," I say. I put on the voice I used to use in meetings with investors. The friendly one that usually puts them at ease all while trying to sound lighthearted. "You'll live."

Varek smiles, and it's like the sun breaking through the clouds. "Thanks to you."

Blast it.

I stand up, moving to prepare some food, needing the distraction. "You should eat something. It'll help you heal faster."

He watches me for a moment longer before nodding. "You're right. I appreciate it, my sura. More than you know."

So I make him food. I watch him eat. All while the crate of fruits and his vibrating toy sit on the table between us. When he finishes, Varek rises, that scorching gaze still on me. I expect him to say something. To bring up what happened between us that night. He doesn't.

He's too polite.

He dips his head in a nod and then he's off, heading off to tend to the very animals that brought us together in the first place.

We fall into a routine over the next few days. Varek helps around the farm, his strong presence a constant source of comfort and distraction. We work side by side, the tension between us simmering just below the surface. Every touch, every glance, feels charged with electricity, and I find myself looking forward to our moments together, even as they leave me feeling breathless and off-balance.

That first night after he returned was the first night I used his gift. And then the night after. And the night after that, too.

Now I wake flushed each day, my cheeks burning from embarrassment all while that nub between my legs throbs and my core clenches for something more. And I know where to get it, too. I know exactly what my body wants. I just...

One afternoon, as we work in my new garden we've started developing at the side of the house, I catch Varek watching me out of the corner of my eye. His gaze is intense, filled with a longing that mirrors my own. My pulse quickens, and I force myself to focus on the task at hand, even as my thoughts drift to the night we shared—and then to the blasted toy he gave me and the fact I will certainly be using it again this night.

Soon it's like I'm walking through an electrically charged field, each stolen glance and lingering touch adding to the growing heat.

One evening, as the sun sets and the sky is painted in hues of orange and pink, we stand together on the porch, watching the horizon. I stare out across the plains, knowing this can't continue for much longer. Soon, there will be no more tasks that require Varek's constant presence on the farm. Soon, there will be no real reason for him to come by.

"Catherine." Varek's soft utterance of my name breaks the silence. "I need you to know something."

My heart immediately slams against my ribs. I force the feeling back, turning to look up at him. "What is it, Varek?"

He takes a deep breath, his eyes locking onto mine. "I know this isn't easy. But…I'm here, sura. I'm not going anywhere."

His words send a flood of emotions crashing through me. My mouth opens before I press it closed. Because what can I say? He's demanding nothing. He's asked nothing of me. But it's like he's read my mind. As if he knows exactly what I'm thinking.

He steps closer, his claw reaching out to cup my cheek. "You don't have to say anything, sura. Just know that I'm here. For as long as you'll have me."

18

CATHERINE

*V*arek's words stay with me.

I almost broke down right there. His words hit a chord within me, playing on the exact thing that plagues me.

By the time he leaves for the night, I'm uncertain of my decisions.

Collapsing in my bed, I stare at the dark ceiling. This dance we're playing is exhausting. Each moment that passes as Varek works alongside me on the farm feels like the tension rises on a nuclear reactor that is bound to meltdown.

The tension in my body makes every nerve ending feel sensitive. Even the brush of my sheets against my skin is making me react.

My eyes slide open, moving to the little device near my bed. The sex toy lies there, a glint of light on its surface.

I groan. Not tonight again. I need to exercise some control.

But as the minutes tick by, it's clear I won't fall asleep. Not like this. I'm a tension-filled mess and I'm *this* close to breaking.

Getting off the bed, I sigh as I head toward the kitchen. Maybe a glass of water will help. Or maybe I should brew myself a cup of tea. I snort at that. I'm passing the dining room

189

table when my gaze snags on the crate of fruit still sitting there. I stare at them, a lump rising in my throat.

Varek's thoughtfulness, his blasted *kindness*, makes me scowl, even as my mouth waters. It would be much easier to hate him, much easier to not be attracted to him, if he was more like an asshole I didn't want to deal with.

Hells bells, what is wrong with you Catherine Rose Richmond? Because let's admit it, even though I don't want to, I am attracted to the tall alien male named Varek. I'm more than attracted to him.

I'm falling. Even though I told myself my heart would never love again.

Standing, I reach for one of the fruits that I'm just going to call a mango until corrected. It feels juicy, and the light in the cottage plays over its skin, creating a soft sheen. I lick my lips, ready to dig in after having tinned bean soup for dinner.

I move to the kitchen, finding my way now without having to look down so I don't trip over anything, and turn on the tap. It's a curved device with a spout and there's a lever I have to crank to get the flow going. Took me ages to figure that out. I crank it a few times now, and there's a soft gurgle in the depths of the pipe that soon dies a moment later. Frowning, my focus shifts from the delicious-looking fruit in my hands to the pipe. I crank it again. Nothing.

Great.

I'm no expert at plumbing, so I have no idea what's the matter. I'll just have to leave it till the morning or ask Varek to look at it. My heart thumps hard at just the thought of seeing him tomorrow.

My cheeks warm before my thoughts go to places I don't want them to as I focus on the fruit again. I don't want to risk eating it without washing it first. If I got sick because I didn't wash a maybe-mango I'd kick myself.

So I slip my feet into the closed-toe shoes we all got as standard wear from the Restitution and I head to the door. I leave it open because, why not. I'm coming back inside just after I wash this thing.

Walking around the cottage, I look up at the dark sky and pause, a soft breath releasing from my chest. I don't know what I'm looking for. A sign?

The well is at the back of the cottage and I reach it without trouble under the light of the stars. As I approach the structure, I squint at it. It's not like wells back home. Instead of a circular stone wall with a bucket and rope, this well is a sleek, cylindrical tower made of a smooth, metallic material that gleams softly in the starlight. I think Xarion had it freshly installed just so I'd have running water in the house, but this was before I arrived. I only found out it was a well because I saw the Raki get water from it. A panel on the side is barely visible as I step up to the thing and I realize I should have brought some kind of light with me. It's not just a simple push-of-a-button I thought it would be.

The panel is adorned with strange symbols and a few buttons that glow faintly. I hesitate, unsure if I should press anything without knowing what they do. For all I know, I could end up activating some kind of alien defense system or worse, break the well and lose access to water altogether.

I tap my foot, staring down at the fruit in my hand. My mouth waters again. Maybe it's the fact the thing looks like food from home. Or maybe it's the fact that Varek gave it to me and it's taken me this long to enjoy it. I could wait until morning and ask him for help, but he's already helping me so much.

No, I'll figure this out on my own. I'm a grown woman, after all, and I've faced far greater challenges than operating an alien well. With renewed determination, I step closer to the panel and study the symbols as best as I can. They look like hieroglyphics and I clench my jaw in concentrated thought. There has to be some kind of logic to them, some pattern that I can decipher.

Five, ten, maybe twenty minutes pass, and no luck. I'm about to admit my defeat when, as I'm turning back toward the house, I notice a small lever on the side of the well. I blink at it squinting in the night even though that doesn't help me to see any better. Reaching for the thing, it's smooth and small, hidden to the side of the panel I was mulling over, but it seems to be separate from the other controls. It's positioned at an odd angle, almost as if it's meant to be pulled rather than pushed. Curiosity gets the better of me, and I reach out to give it a gentle tug.

It's sudden. I don't think I even get to take a breath. The ground beneath my feet gives way, and before I can react, I'm falling. I go down, my head hitting something hard as the fruit tumbles from my hand. I plummet into darkness, a scream lodging in my throat. I brace myself for impact, expecting to hit hard ground, but instead, I plunge into icy water.

The shock of the cold water steals my breath away, and I struggle to orient myself in the dark, watery depths. I kick my legs, desperation pushing me to propel myself upward. I break the surface, the breaths being pulled into my lungs not feeling nearly enough to what I need. Panic surrounds me like the icy water itself as I realize the severity of my situation. I'm trapped in an alien well, with no idea how deep the water is or if there's any way out.

Calm, Catherine. Stay calm. This is not how I want to die! Fear shoots through me. I always thought I'd go in my bed, with those I loved surrounding me. Instead, it might happen here. In the dark. In the cold. *Alone.* The thoughts pull me together. Force me to calm down enough that my breathing becomes a constant deep inhale and exhale that rattles my lungs. Terror fights to rise deep in my gut. I'm not the spring chicken I used to be. I can't tread water forever. Or until morning, when Varek arrives and will probably be able to pull me out.

Varek…

He's going to come and find me here…if I make it…and if I don't.

Dear God, what am I going to do? My breaths hiccup and I go under for a moment, swallowing some water that goes straight into my lungs. I surface again, coughing and choking, the hold on my panic completely gone.

I should have left the fruit and gone to bed!

Blinking, I squeeze my eyes shut, trying to force some of the water away so I can see. My entire body shivers with the extent of the cold quickly seeping into my bones as I turn slowly. It doesn't feel like I'm in a well. It feels like I'm lost in the middle of the ocean at point Nemo in the dead of night.

I reach out, heading for where I know the wall must be. That's when I realize it's not all complete darkness. There's a dim light filtering through the water. My hand hits the wall and I lurch back, almost going under again. There was something soft and slippery against it. Heart thundering in my chest, desperately trying to push blood to warm my extremities, some of that warmth reaches my brain and I finally notice the faint glow emanating from the walls of the well.

Treading the water, I turn in a slow circle, more of the wall becoming visible. It's lined with some kind of bioluminescent algae or fungi, casting an eerie blue-green light through the water. It's not much, but it's enough to give me a sense of my surroundings and a glimmer of hope.

I swim towards the wall again, my fingers brushing against the slimy surface as I search for any kind of handhold or crevice that I can use to pull myself up. But the walls are smooth, not to mention slippery, offering no purchase for my desperate grasp. Not only that, but I'm shivering so much that my fingers keep slipping. The little hope I'm grasping at is slipping too and there's a pain in my head I'm desperately trying to ignore.

"C-come on, come on, come on." My teeth chatter as I move

around the cylinder. "C-come on. S-something. S-something must be there."

Exhaustion begins to set in, my limbs growing heavy and my breathing becoming more labored. I know I can't keep this up forever but I thought I'd last longer. My brain might still feel like I'm in my twenties but my body doesn't hesitate to remind me I'm not. I need help, and I need it soon.

Gathering my remaining strength, I take a deep breath and shout as loudly as I can, my voice echoing in the watery chamber. "H-Help! I'm t-trapped! Trapped in the well! P-p-please, p-please...someone...someone..."

I fight back tears.

No one's out there. No one can hear me. It's a waste of breath. A waste of energy. There's no one out there for miles, and still, I strain my ears for any sign of a response. All I hear is the sound of my own ragged breathing and the gentle lapping of the water against the walls because of my movement.

I'm not...I'm not ready. Not ready to die.

Closing my eyes, my tears mingle with the cold well water as I whisper a silent prayer for rescue. I've always prayed. This is nothing new, but it's different this time.

This time, the prayer feels more desperate, more urgent. It's not just a plea for help, but a bargain with the universe itself.

"God...it...it's me again." I release a deep breath. "I promise to be kinder, to be more open, to embrace the second chance at life that I've been given, if only I can survive this. Please...I... You've given me so much. It seems wrong to ask for more. But please...please...save me from this."

I realize now, in this moment of crisis, just how much I've been holding back, how much I've been denying myself out of fear and self-preservation.

I've been so focused on protecting myself from further hurt that I've forgotten how to live. How to take risks, how to open my heart to the possibility of something new and wonderful.

Now there's the very real possibility of my own demise, and there's nothing…nothing but regret.

I've been such a fool.

I remember everyone I've loved, and a pang of sorrow grips my heart. Their loss is a wound that will never fully heal. But as I try to stay afloat, I remind myself that they would want me to live, not just exist. They would want me to find moments of peace and purpose, even amid chaos.

"P-please," I whisper, my voice barely audible over the sound of the water. "Please, give me another chance. I promise I'll do better. I promise I'll be better."

But as the minutes tick by and the cold seeps deeper into my bones, I begin to lose hope. My limbs feel heavy, my movements sluggish and uncoordinated. I know I can't hold on much longer.

This…

This is it.

Just as I'm about to give in to the darkness, to let myself slip beneath the surface and into oblivion, I hear a sound from above. At first, I think it's just my imagination, a cruel trick of my oxygen-deprived brain. But then I hear it again, louder and clearer this time.

"Catherine?!"

My vision is sluggish as I look up through the well shaft up at the dark sky above. Tears well in my eyes. I remember his voice just like he's here now.

Varek. The male I wanted but was too much of a coward to go for. The patient male who was waiting for me but I was too stubborn to just let myself give in.

"CATHERINE?!!!" The panic in that voice somehow clears some of the fog away and I realize I'm not imagining it. My heart thuds hard.

Varek? But it can't be. He's not supposed to be here.

"CATHERINE?!! Oh Gods. CATHERINE?!"

No, this is real. This isn't my imagination. It *is* Varek. Varek is here!

"V-Varek! I-I'm here!" There's no way he's going to hear me. My voice is so weak it's barely audible. Panic shoots through me, chilling my already frozen bones. He's so close and he might not find me. "Here. In the w-well." My teeth chatter. "I f-fell in."

There's a moment when all above is quiet. As if the world no longer exists. My heart clenches, a deep ache inside me as I lift my eyes to look up at the dark sky above. The stars barely twinkle. Or maybe I just can't see them anymore. Hope fades when something suddenly casts a shadow over the hole.

My breath stills in my throat. All I can see are slitted yellow eyes that widen on mine.

There's no hesitation. No moment where he thinks of the potential danger to himself. One moment, our eyes meet, and the next the water around me is churning and splashing as Varek's large form plunges into the well. For a moment, I'm disoriented, the sudden movement and the ripples obscuring my vision. I choke on water, losing my grasp on things as I go under, but then I feel strong arms wrap around me, pulling me close to a solid, warm chest.

"I have you," Varek murmurs, his deep voice rumbling through me. "Gods, I have you, Catherine."

I cling to him, my numb fingers scrabbling for purchase on his scales. The relief is so overwhelming that a sob escapes my throat, my body shaking not just from the cold but from the sheer force of my emotions.

Varek holds me tighter, one arm securely around my waist while the other strokes my hair. He hums something low in his throat that's like a deep purr. "It's alright now, sura. You're safe. I'm here."

I bury my face in the crook of his neck, breathing in his scent. He smells like home, like comfort, like everything I've been yearning for without even realizing it.

"Wh-what are you doing here? H-how did you f-find me?" I manage to ask, my teeth still chattering.

For some seconds, he doesn't answer. I'm dimly aware of him burying his face into my wet hair and inhaling deeply as his arms tighten around me. His chest shudders with heavy breaths that feel like relief washing through him.

"I...I came because I...I needed to see you again."

I choke on a cough and he presses me even closer to him, giving me no option but to steal his warmth. "You saw me earlier today."

"I know. It doesn't make sense, but...I couldn't rest. I needed to return to you." He breathes out a breath into my hair, the warmth tickling my scalp. "When I got to your lodge, the door was wide open and you weren't there..." He trails off, his chest still heaving with those heavy breaths. "I've never felt such fear in my existence."

"You f-fought in a war..."

"Not even then was I this afraid."

His admission startles me. Varek, scared? The idea seems almost inconceivable. But then I remember the panic in his voice when he was calling my name, the desperation in his eyes when he saw me.

"I'm s-sorry," I whisper. "I didn't mean to worry you. I was only trying to get some water and—"

He pulls back just enough to look at me, his gaze intense and searching in the dim starlight. "Don't apologize, sura. I'm just glad I found you in time."

The sincerity in his words, the depth of emotion in his eyes...it steals my breath away. And suddenly, I realize just how close we are, our bodies pressed together from chest to toe, our faces mere inches apart.

My heart stutters in my chest, my skin tingling with a warmth that has nothing to do with the cold water. Varek seems to feel it too, those luminous eyes of his dropping to my lips.

For a moment, everything else fades away—the chill of the water, the eerie glow of the bioluminescence, the ache in my limbs. There's only him and me, suspended in this timeless, charged moment.

Slowly, tentatively, Varek leans in. His breath ghosts over my lips, making me shiver. I tilt my head up, my eyes fluttering closed as our lips meet.

It's tentative, barely a brush of mouth against mouth, as if we're seeking out each other again, both unsure if the other wants this. But when my fingers dig into his scales, Varek lets out a low moan, his hot lips crushing against mine.

His kiss is like a soothing warmth that eases some of the cold. I cling to him as his lips press into mine, my legs wrapping around him as his tongue dances with mine.

He kisses me as if he's trying to breathe life back into me, as if he's pouring all his fear and relief and longing into this single, searing moment. I melt into him, my fingers tangling in his hair, my body molding to his as if we were always meant to fit together.

But then reality comes crashing back in. A violent shudder wracks my body, my teeth chattering together almost painfully. Varek pulls back with a curse, shaking his head as if to clear away a fog.

"I cannot lose you."

I follow the light of his eyes as he looks around. It's clear just from the way he moves, slowly turning with me in the water, that he can see much better than I can. Even with the bioluminescence, I can hardly see a thing. When he curses under his breath, a sense of guilt and trepidation fills me.

"You can't get out, can you? We're both stuck in here."

There's an answering rumble in his chest, the vibration making me rest my head against him once more. As he continues turning in the water, trying to spot a way out of our predicament, I realize I'm not nearly as frozen as I was before.

His body is so hot, his mere presence is making blood flow through my veins.

When he curses under his breath, I lift my head to look at him.

"I'll find a way out, but there's not much time. Your body is like ice, sura."

I nod. "But I'm much better, now that you're here."

I'm not sure what about my words makes him pause. Those eyes that were searching the walls for some kind of foothold shift to me and I'm transfixed. Under the light of the stars, Varek looks like a god.

Water drips from his hair and scales, each droplet catching the faint glow and shimmering like diamonds against his skin. His eyes, always so intense, seem to burn into me, bright with an emotion I'm almost afraid to name.

"Catherine," he breathes, and the way he says my name, like a prayer and a plea all at once, makes my heart stutter in my chest.

His claw comes up, cupping my cheek with a tenderness that steals my breath. His thumb brushes over my skin, tracing the line of my cheekbone, the curve of my jaw. I lean into his touch, my eyes fluttering closed for a moment as I savor the warmth of his skin against mine.

"I thought I lost you," he whispers, his voice rough with emotion. "When I saw you in this well, so still and pale, I thought…"

He trails off, his throat working as he swallows hard. I reach up, covering his claw with my hand, turning my face to press a kiss to his palm.

"I'm here," I murmur. "Thanks to you, I'm still here."

He pulls me closer, our foreheads touching as we breathe each other in. In this moment, suspended in the starlit water, it feels like we're the only two people in the world. Like nothing else matters but the beat of our hearts, the mingling of our breaths.

"I can't lose you," Varek says again, his voice a low rumble that I feel in my bones. "I won't."

There's a fierce promise in those words, an unshakable resolve. I know, with a sudden, blinding clarity, that he means it. That he would move heaven and earth to keep me safe, to keep me by his side.

The realization is humbling, overwhelming in its intensity. But it's also thrilling, igniting a spark in my chest that grows into a steady, unwavering flame.

Because I feel the same. In this short time, Varek has become essential to me, as vital as the air in my lungs and the blood in my veins. The thought of losing him, of being without him...it's unimaginable.

Unacceptable.

And maybe that's why my throat moves, why my tongue cooperates even before I fully realize what I'm about to do.

"Varek, the other night, at the festival..."

He freezes. Goes so completely still I can feel it.

"Yes, sura?" I can feel the hesitation in his tone. The uncertainty surrounding what I'm about to say. Because after so long, this is the first time we're going to talk about this.

"...would you like to—"

"Yes."

My heart thuds against my chest. "You don't even know what I'm asking." I could chuckle but I'm still a bit too cold and I don't want my teeth to start chattering again.

"When it concerns you, I will always say yes."

I close my eyes for a moment, a shudder going through me. Varek tucks me closer, running his large claw across my spine.

"Even if it means dating someone like me?" He's so silent, that I continue on. "I'm not looking for someone who will be with me for just a few nights. Ideally, I want more. I want a partner. A companion. Someone to—" This time I'm the one that goes silent. I haven't had the chance to gather my thoughts. This must all be confusing to him seeing as it's so sudden. "What I'm trying to say is—"

"I want to be your mate."

My mouth falls open in stunned silence. I blink up at him, my heart pounding so hard I'm sure he can feel it where our chests are pressed together. "You...you want to be my mate?" I whisper, hardly daring to believe it.

Varek nods, his gaze unwavering. "I have for a while now," he admits softly. "From the moment I first saw you. The more time I've spent with you, the deeper it's grown."

He takes a deep breath, as if steeling himself. "I know it might seem sudden, and I understand if you need time. But I need you to know that for me, this is true. I...want you, Catherine. I need you."

His words knock the breath from my lungs. A mate. A lifelong partner. It's everything I've wanted, everything I thought I could no longer have.

And here is Varek, this incredible, amazing male, offering it to me. Offering himself to me, wholly and unreservedly.

"I know you might be concerned there is no confirmation you are my kahl, that my core-rhythm has not sung. I am a brute for wanting to claim you without giving you that confirmation. But believe me when I say I feel you in my soul. Each sol when I leave this place, it's like tearing a part of myself away. I am a brute you should reject and yet..." His eyes search mine. "I am selfish enough to still want you for my own."

His words are a bit confusing. A part of me feels like my heart is floating on a cloud while another part of me is confused. And then I remember what he said that time when referring to Eleanor and Zynar.

When he said he'd been there to protect Eleanor from his brother.

Searching his eyes, I know that right now, we've both laid our hearts open bare. Varek wants me as much as I want him. And after tonight, despite whatever is thrown at me, I won't deny it anymore.

But I need to know.

"Varek...tell me what you mean. What does it mean when you say your core-rhythm has never sung?"

19

VAREK

This isn't nearly the situation in which I wanted to discuss this with her. But Catherine is looking up at me with eyes that are finally showing me her soul. She wants me. She's willing to give me a chance. I have her attention now and despite that I wish I could hide every damning thing about my species away, I owe her this.

In my broken state, she has every right to decide if she wants a male who is silent inside. And one who could potentially harm her if his core-rhythm actually awakened.

I take a deep breath, trying to steady my nerves.

"Here." I take one of her hands and press it to the center of my chest. "Here is where my song should sing."

"Your song?"

"A vibration that awakens when we, Kari, find our true mate."

A flicker of apprehension crosses her face. I hate that I'm the cause of it, but I force myself to continue.

"It is so rare that we believed ourselves the lost ones."

"We?"

"Every displaced Kari."

A shudder goes through her and I'm aware I need to find a way out of this water hole before her health deteriorates more.

"But...Zynar and Eleanor..." Her body shakes slightly and her arms tighten around me.

"His core-rhythm sang."

There's a moment of silence where I can almost see her mind sorting through the information.

"And that was why you had to be there? When it happened?"

I nod slightly. This is the part I didn't want her to hear about. Not like this. She's only just let me in. What I'm about to tell her might just push her away again. And yet, there's an underlying urge to lay everything bare. That if she rejects me now, it will hurt less than if she did it later.

I take another deep breath before continuing. "I had to be there when my brother's core-rhythm awakened, because it put his kahl in danger." I pause, my gaze boring into hers. Maybe I want to see the moment she rejects me. Maybe I want to have the image burned into my brain. "The same way I will have to protect you from me."

Catherine's beautiful eyes are like little gems in the dark. Her brows furrow slightly, but she doesn't say anything. I'm forced to continue.

"When our core-rhythms awaken, it heralds the start of the rut," I begin, my voice low and strained. "It's a primal drive, an ancient instinct that compels us Kari to claim our mates. When it takes hold, it's all-consuming. We lose ourselves to the need to possess, to mark, to ensure that our bond is unbreakable."

Her brow rises this time. "You have the urge to take your partner to bed?"

A strange laugh escapes my throat. "No, sura. It is much worse than that."

"Tell me." Her voice falls so low it whispers across the water's surface.

"When it happens, I will mate with you repeatedly, each time more fiercely than the last. I'll be relentless, almost feral. I won't stop until your scent is intertwined with mine, until there's no doubt that you belong to me and I to you completely."

This time, she's the one that does a strange laugh. "You say that as if you think I'm this person for you. How can I be when...when I've already lived a life and—"

I shudder at the vulnerability in her voice, at the pain that laces through her words. Gently, I cradle her face in my claws, tilting her chin up until our gazes meet.

"Catherine," I breathe, pouring every ounce of my conviction into her name. "I've told you. I don't care about your past, about the life you've lived before. All I care about is the future we can build together."

Her eyes shimmer with unshed tears, and it takes everything in me not to press my lips to hers and take them all away. "How can you know that I'm meant for you, when we're so...different?"

When my core-rhythm hasn't sung...

Her unsaid words send a lance through me.

"I feel it," I tell her, my thumbs brushing over the delicate skin of her cheeks. It's the only thing I can say. The only thing I'm going on. "In my core-beat, you are there. In my soul, in every fiber of my being. You're a part of me, Catherine. You always have been, and you always will be."

Her throat moves and a shudder goes through her frame, her body stealing some of my heat, but not fast enough. "What about the fact that I was married before? Had children? A life."

"I'm not here to replace them." I study her beautiful face. "You don't have to let go to move on, Catherine."

She blinks and a single tear escapes, tracing a silvery path down her face. I catch it with my claw, marveling at the precious drop.

"My heart..." she whispers, hand shifting over her chest and I know she must be referring to her core-organ.

"Let me heal your heart."

More water escapes her eyes and I'm not sure that is a good sign. But she grips me tighter. She leans into me as her shoulders rise and fall with heavy sobs.

"I'm sorry, my sura," I murmur, my chest aching with the weight of her pain. "I'm sorry you had to go through so much to find your way to me. But I believe it was all for a reason. Every hardship, every heartbreak...it led you here, to this moment. To us."

Catherine's breath hitches, her hands coming up to cover mine where they cradle her face. "You really believe that?" she asks, hope warring with disbelief in her eyes.

"With each core-beat that calls your name," I vow. "This is fate, Catherine. You and me, here and now...it's what was always meant to be."

A shaky laugh bubbles up from her throat, half-sob and half-joy. "I never thought I'd have this again," she confesses. "Love, a future, a...a mate."

The word sends a thrill down my spine, a primal satisfaction that settles deep in my bones. "Say it again," I rumble, my cock rising in my trouse despite the cold water around us.

Her eyes sparkle up at me, a slow smile curving her lips. "Mate," she repeats, stronger this time. "My mate."

A growl rumbles up from my chest, and I crush her to me, sealing my mouth over hers. Catherine responds with equal fervor, her digits tangling in my mane as she arches into me.

"When it happens, it's not gentle, sura," I warn, my voice dropping to a near whisper when we take a moment to breathe. "There will be biting, scratching, a level of force you've never experienced. When I take you, truly take you, the rut strips away all civility, leaving only the basest of instincts. It's about domination, my sura, about leaving a mark that can never be erased."

I can hear Catherine's heart pounding, can smell the mix of

fear and…excitement rolling off her skin. She moans into my mouth as I take her lips again, the sound sending all my lifeblood rushing to a singular place. It takes every ounce of my control not to pull her against me, to claim her right here and now.

"I want to have every ounce of you, Catherine. I will."

I've said a lot. Enough to scare my little human away certainly now. To my surprise, she breaks the seal of our lips, deep breaths wracking her frame as she pierces me with those gemstone eyes.

"Varek." The way she says my name, full of tenderness and understanding, nearly undoes me. "I'm not afraid. Not of the rut, not of any part of you."

I search her gaze, hardly daring to believe what I'm hearing. "You must understand. Once the rut takes hold, I won't be able to control myself. I could hurt you, I—"

She silences me with a digit pressed to my lips. "You could never hurt me," she says with a conviction that rocks me to my core. "I trust you, Varek. With my body, with my heart…with everything I am."

Emotion clogs my throat, rendering me speechless. I pull her close, burying my face in her damp mane as I try to compose myself.

"I don't deserve you," I manage after a moment. "But gods help me, I want you. I need you, Catherine. More than I've ever needed anything in my life."

"Then I'm yours," she whispers, her breath warm against my throat.

Joy, pure and incandescent, explodes in my chest.

I have to get her out of here. Have to get her to safety.

"Catherine." I push away from her so she can look at me. "I know a way out of this. At least, to get you out of the cold water. But…"

"But what?" Her body shivers again and I know it's the only option.

"But it will mean getting rid of all the water stored in this well. I can direct it to your field, but with no crops there, it will simply be wasted to the earth. And you...you will be without water for several sols."

Her body shivers again. "I can do without water, Varek. Do it."

I study her. She won't be without water. I could never allow that. I will personally use my truck to bring her enough, so she has water to drink and wash herself. But the animals and the rest of the farm will suffer. Not to mention, the protective algae in the water hole will all die. Getting them regrown will take several moons. Her farm, this farm she's been working so hard on, will be useless for some time.

"There is more. Your farm...this water hole is important. Your farm will be crippled without it."

Catherine shakes her head. "It doesn't matter, Varek. We'll deal with it when the time comes. Just as we will with every-thing else." The double meaning in her words makes something warm swell inside of me. "If you can save us, do it."

It pains me to put her at such a disadvantage, but there is no other choice. I hold her for a few more moments before slowly releasing her. She treads the water as I take a deep breath.

"I must go to the bottom. I won't be long."

She nods, her throat moving as I dip beneath the surface.

There, I turn to look up at her.

The shimmering moonlight filters through the water, casting an ethereal glow on Catherine's face. Even from this depth, I can see the trust in her eyes, the unwavering faith she has in me. It steels my resolve, driving me to do whatever it takes to get her out of here safely.

I dive to the bottom of the well, navigating the murky depths with ease. It doesn't take long to find what I'm looking for—a small, circular grate set into the floor. This is the water hole's drainage system, designed to prevent overflow during heavy rains.

With a twist, I wrench the grate free, sending a cloud of sediment billowing up around me. Immediately, I feel the water begin to rush out, the current tugging at my limbs as it's sucked down into the underground channels.

I kick back up to the surface, bursting through with a gasp. Catherine is already swimming towards me, her face etched with concern.

"Are you alright?" she asks, running her hands over my shoulders as if checking for injury.

I nod, pulling her close. "I'm fine. The water is draining out now. We just need to hold on until the level drops enough for us to stand."

She shivers in my arms, her teeth beginning to chatter again. The cold is getting to her, seeping into her bones. I curse myself for not being able to get us out of this sooner.

"Here." I guide her arms around my neck, letting her cling to me. "I'll keep you warm."

Catherine presses her face into my shoulder, her breath hot against my skin. "Thank you," she murmurs, her words slightly slurred. "For everything."

I tighten my grip on her, silently vowing to never let her go. "Anything for you, my sura. Anything at all."

As the water drains, soon my feet hit the ground, the surface of the water hole now far above us.

"What now?" Catherine whispers. Her concern echoes my own.

"We wait." I stare at the stars above, knowing that I won't leave this place without the female in my arms. I will stay here until someone finds us.

"Do you think someone will come by?" Catherine settles

against me as the last of the water drains and I slide to the floor with her in my arms.

"Zynar. If he pings me and I don't respond, he might come looking for me."

Catherine nods, her damp mane brushing against my jaw. "And if he doesn't?"

I release a slow breath. "Then I only have one other option. But that will mean destroying your water hole completely."

"If that's the only choice…"

"No." I ease away somewhat, brushing damp tendrils from her face as I force her to look at me. "You need it and this farm…it's important to you."

Catherine studies my eyes, her focus strong and sure.

"Wait with me here. When dawn lights, if no one comes, I will do what I must."

She studies me for a moment before giving me a soft nod. I pull her into me again, reveling in the feel of her against me and the fact that despite the circumstances, this is our first time together as mates.

Catherine has accepted me. And I will turn the world over to ensure her faith in me is not misplaced.

20

CATHERINE

I must drift off to sleep at some point because when Varek stirs beneath me, I open my eyes with a weariness that suggests I'd been resting. In a well. My body draped across his as I straddle him.

I'm supposed to be cold and worried. Instead, I feel warm and…safe.

My eyes flutter to meet his and he grimaces.

"Apologies, sura. I did not mean to wake you."

Stifling a yawn, I run a hand through my hair, wincing as I disrupt the skin at my temple where I must have hit my head in the fall.

Varek notices immediately, his arm a blur as he reaches forward, his claw tightening around my wrist. "You're in pain."

I can't help the soft smile that graces my lips. "Not really. I hit my head—"

"Where?" He tugs me closer, his scent enveloping me as he leans in, his face so close to mine that I can feel the warmth of his breath fanning across my cheek as he examines the wound hidden just behind my hairline. His brow furrows, a rumbling growl building in his chest.

"You're hurt," he growls, but somehow I know his anger isn't directed at me. "I should have protected you better." And I'm right. It's directed at himself.

Before I can reassure him, he leans in closer, his tongue darting out to gently lap at the cut. I gasp at the sensation, my fingers instinctively curling into his shoulders. His saliva is warm and slightly tingling, soothing away the sting.

"Varek, what…?"

He pulls back just enough to meet my gaze, his eyes glowing faintly in the dim light. "To help you heal." He says it as if it's just another usual thing, but the way he's looking at me sends a tingle to the base of my spine. There's a rumble in his chest that makes his scales feel like they shift against me.

"What is it?" My whisper is barely there, as if I'm almost afraid of what he'll respond with.

"I can taste your lifeblood." Without hesitation, he leans forward, swiping his tongue over the wound again. Another rumble starts in his chest. One that should concern me. All it does is send that tingle from my spine to my center. "Sweet," he growls.

A nervous little giggle rises from my throat. "Should I be concerned that you like it so much?"

For the first time since I've known him, I see the corners of his eyes crinkle.

"Maybe, sura. Maybe you should worry that after a taste of your lifeblood, I will want to consume you now." Those yellow pits warm as they regard me and I finally realize that I can see much more of him than I could before. The sun is rising. We made it through the night.

I breathe a laugh through my nose. "Consume me, huh?" I tease, trying to lighten the suddenly charged atmosphere between us. "I thought you were supposed to be my protector, not my predator."

Varek's eyes flash with a heat that makes my breath catch.

"Can't I be both?" he rumbles, his voice a low, seductive purr. "I would consume you in the most pleasurable of ways. Devour every inch of your sweetness until you're trembling and crying out for more."

My core clenches, my thighs tightening on either side where I'm straddling him and his eyes darken at the same time. I've never seen this side of him before, this raw, sensual creature who looks at me like he wants to feast on my body for hours.

Varek's claws slide down my back, the sharp tips lightly grazing my spine through the thin fabric of my shirt. I shiver at the sensation, heat pooling low in my gut.

"I want to take my time with you," he murmurs, his lips brushing the shell of my ear. "Worship every inch of your body until you're drunk on pleasure. Until the only word you remember is my name."

It's only then that I realize the hard thing between my thighs isn't his leg. It's *him*. That the entire time I'd been sleeping on him, he'd been nursing the most massive hard-on I've ever encountered. It feels even bigger now than the last time. As if he's so engorged his shaft has swollen to the size of my arm.

A whimper escapes me as he rocks his hips up, pressing the hard length of him against my center. Even through our clothes, I can feel how much he wants me, how much he's straining to keep control.

"Goodness, you're big."

The rumble of approval makes me release a laugh through my nose.

"Better than your human mates?"

I laugh again as he shifts his hips once more, forcing my core to grind against his hardness. The sensation almost makes my eyes roll over in my head.

"Bigger than any human male." I pant.

He rumbles something in his chest again. "But not better."

I huff out a laugh. "I didn't mean that you're not—"

Varek presses his lips against my ear. "Not to matter. I intend to be the best you've ever had. I won't stop until I am." His voice is a sinful growl that vibrates through my core. "I have a lifetime to prove it to you, my sura. A lifetime to learn every secret place that makes you moan, every touch that makes you tremble."

He punctuates his declaration with a slow, deliberate roll of his hips, grinding the thick length of his arousal against my aching center. I gasp, my head falling back as pleasure sparks through my veins.

"Mm, I've got you," he soothes, one claw coming up to cup the back of my head, angling me for a deep, drugging kiss that leaves me breathless and aching. "I'll give you everything, my Catherine. Everything you need, everything you want."

He seals that promise with another soul-searing kiss before trailing his lips down the column of my throat. I let my head fall back, surrendering to the bliss of his mouth on my skin. He finds my pulse point, lavishing it with attention, licking and suckling until I'm sure he'll leave a mark.

A small, distant part of me knows we shouldn't be doing this here, not when rescue could arrive at any moment. But the rest of me, the part that's been craving Varek's touch for longer than I care to admit, can't bring myself to care.

Let them find us like this, I think hazily as Varek's claws slice through the fabric of my tunic, baring my breasts to his hungry gaze. Let the whole world see that I'm his. That this powerful, magnificent male has claimed me, body and soul.

"Gods, I missed this," Varek rasps, reverence in his eyes as he drinks in the sight of me. "So many sols the memory of you has haunted me."

Then he's cupping my breasts in his massive fists, his rough palms igniting sparks across my sensitive flesh as he sheathes his claws. I cry out as he takes one aching peak into the wet heat of his mouth, swirling his tongue around the tight bud.

He lavishes first one breast, then the other with devastating attention, until I'm mindless with need, my hips rolling shamelessly against the thick ridge of his hardness.

"Oh," I gasp out, my nails digging into his shoulders. "Oh my. I don't think…I don't think I can wait. I need you inside me…"

I've never been one to beg, especially for something like this. But my shame has gone. I can only feel. And I *need*. I need him.

A deep, approving growl rumbles through his chest. In a move almost too fast to follow, he lifts me so I'm standing over him. For a split second, I'm confused as I look down at him. With a wicked glint in his eye, Varek slides his claws up my legs, the tips of his fingers hooking into the waistband of my panties a second before he rips them away. He shifts the tunic up, leaving me bare and open to his scorching gaze.

"I'm going to feast on you now," he tells me, his voice a sinful caress against my overheated skin. "I'm going to taste your sweet honey until you scream for me. And then, when you're wet and ready and begging, I'm going to bury myself so deep inside you, you'll never want me to leave."

My mouth falls open in both a gasp and shock. Before I can do more than whimper my enthusiasm for this plan, he's shouldering my thighs apart and tilting his head back as he pulls me down on his face.

The first hot swipe of his tongue through my folds has me arching. I reach for the walls of the well as a strangled moan tears from my throat. I miss. The only other thing to hold on to is his green mane. As soon as my fingers slide through the strands to grip on to his skull, he groans in appreciation. The vibrations echo through my core as he licks me again, more firmly this time.

"Delicious," he praises, his eyes flashing up to meet mine. "You taste divine, my sura."

Then he seals his mouth over the throbbing pearl at the apex of my thighs and proceeds to make good on every filthy, electrifying promise.

Varek's talented tongue works me mercilessly, licking and suckling at my most sensitive flesh until I'm writhing beneath him, my hands fisted in his hair. He traces obscene patterns through my slick folds, dipping inside to tease at my entrance before returning to the bundle of nerves that has me seeing stars.

"Varek," I pant, my hips undulating shamelessly against his face. "Oh, don't stop…"

He growls more approval. Spearing me with his tongue, he reaches up to grip one of my breasts, kneading it in his palm as another rumble of pleasure goes through him. The dual assault ratchets my pleasure impossibly higher.

I can feel the tension coiling tighter and tighter at the base of my spine, my inner muscles fluttering around his invading tongue. I'm close, so close, I just need a little more…

As if reading my mind, Varek moves his claw from my breast, trailing it down the quivering plane of my stomach to where I'm spread open for him. Still licking my center, he presses one long, thick digit inside me.

The added sensation is my undoing. With a hoarse cry of his name, I shatter, my body arching backward as ecstasy crashes through me in violent, cresting waves. Varek growls in male satisfaction, continuing to stroke me through the aftershocks until I collapse back against him. He catches me, pulling me back down into his arms as my entire body heaves with the aftereffects of my peak. I'm boneless and spent.

When I open my eyes and my gaze meets his, his eyes are like molten gold in the growing light. I can see the barely leashed hunger in his expression, the raw, primal need to claim me, to make me his in every way.

"I need you now," he rasps, his voice guttural and strained. "I burn for you, my Catherine."

"Then take me," I breathe, reaching for him with trembling hands. "I'm yours, Varek. Now and always."

I reach for him, but he catches my hand. His hips roll underneath me as he forces me upward, bracing me above him with one arm as he undoes the clasp of his trousers with the other. A deep, reverberating groan tears from his throat the moment his shaft is released. Even without touching him, I can feel the heat of it between us. With a sinuous roll of his hips, he notches himself at my entrance and thrusts forward, sheathing himself to the hilt in one powerful stroke.

I cry out at the sudden fullness, my body stretching to accommodate his girth. He stills beneath me, his massive frame trembling with restraint as he gives me a moment to adjust.

"You feel..." He shakes his head, seeming to struggle for words. "There are no words. You consume me, my sura. Body and soul."

Overwhelmed by the depth of emotion shining in his eyes, I dip my head to capture his lips in a searing kiss, trying to pour everything I feel for him into that one point of connection.

He drinks me in like a man dying of thirst, his tongue plundering my mouth in a drugging slide. Slowly, carefully, he begins to move, withdrawing almost completely before surging forward again, starting a rhythm as old as time itself.

I meet him thrust for thrust, drawing him impossibly deeper. Our bodies move in perfect sync, our gasps and moans mingling in the charged air between us.

Varek buries his face in the crook of my neck, his sharp teeth grazing the sensitive skin almost as if he wishes to pierce my flesh with his fangs. He keeps them there as he drives into me again and again, stoking the embers of my desire back into an inferno.

"Let go, my sura," he commands, his dark voice seductive silk against my ear. "Let me feel you come undone around me."

His words ignite something primal inside me, an urge to

obey, to surrender myself completely to the ecstasy he's offering. Throwing my head back, I give myself over to the sensations, letting them build and build until I'm teetering on the knife's edge of release.

"That's it," Varek encourages, his thrusts becoming erratic as he chases his own end. "Give yourself to me, Catherine. You're mine. The gods know it. The fates know it. *I* know it. And you will, too."

With a keening wail, I do just that, my inner muscles clamping down on him like a vice as rapture floods my veins. Varek roars his own completion, his shaft throbbing with each pump of his release as he fills me up.

I'm a boneless mess as I collapse against him once again.

In this moment, cradled in the strength of his arms with desire thrumming through my blood, I know he'll be true to his word. He won't rest until every cell within me belongs to him. Until the mere brush of his fingers is enough to set me aflame.

He will ruin me. And oh, what a sweet, exquisite ruin it will be.

21

CATHERINE

Maybe an hour or two passes and I'm still wrapped in Varek's arms. I'm cramped—probably can't move without someone helping me up—but Varek has made no indication of wanting to stand and stretch. I remain content with his arms around me.

My gaze shifts to his face. The faint scar from the wound he'd appeared with that day.

"Varek," I whisper.

"Mm, sura?" His yellow eyes shift up at me, warmth making them look more vibrant than ever.

"That day…the day you returned to the farm. You were hurt. I didn't want to ask but I guess…I want to know. What happened? Why were you bruised? Why did it look like you hadn't eaten in days?"

He studies me for a moment, his gaze searching mine. Lifting a hand, I brush his hair back from his handsome face, marveling at the fact that he's mine.

"I went to the fighting pits," he finally says.

My hand stills.

"You were gone. I thought…I thought I'd lost you." His gaze

shifts away to stare at the wall at my back. "I needed to feel pain. Physical pain."

"Oh, Varek..."

His gaze shifts back to me. "But the pain didn't help. Didn't erase the pain in here." He touches his chest. "Long after, I realized the only way to heal it was to come to you—even if you didn't want me the way I wanted you. Just seeing you that sol made it a little better."

My heart aches and I pull him into me.

"I'm sorry," I whisper, holding him tight.

It feels like a dream. As if everything is finally as it should be. It all feels...perfect.

At my age, I should know better than to believe in perfection. Life has a way of correcting us about such naive notions, of reminding us that every moment of joy is fleeting, destined to be chased by the inevitable shadows.

I look up the moment something blocks the light of the rising sun. Varek does too, just as two white furry ears appear over the entrance of the well.

"The Saffion," Varek growls.

My heart thuds and I ease up a bit, ignoring Varek's pout of disapproval at the loss of my heat against him. "Xarion?"

The New Horizon's representative leans over the well, his red eyes displaying shock at seeing us there. His expression would have otherwise made me laugh if I wasn't stuck in a hole.

"What in the gods of Hudo..." Xarion's wide eyes look down at us. "What sort of human-Kari mating ritual is *this*?"

This time I do choke on a laugh. "Xarion, can you get us out? We're...kind of...we're kind of stuck here."

Xarion tilts his head, and even with his rabbit-like features I can see his clear mortification.

"Stuck," he repeats flatly, his long ears twitching. "In a well. Together." His gaze darts between Varek and me, taking in our rumpled clothing and the intimate way we're still tangled around each other.

A knowing glint enters his red eyes, and I feel my cheeks heat under his scrutiny. Beside me, Varek doesn't help the situation as he wraps his arms around my middle, pulling me against him once more.

"Yes, stuck," I confirm, trying to keep my voice level. The heat of Varek's scales against me seems even hotter now without the cool water around us. I hadn't realized he emitted so much heat. But then again, I've never been pressed against him like this for extended periods. "It's a long story, but we could really use some help getting out of here. Please."

Xarion blinks, then shakes his head as if to clear it. "Right. Of course. Hold on a moment."

He disappears from view, and I hear him calling out to someone else. The responding voice sounds like a female and it takes me a moment to recognize that it's the new human settler, Donna's voice.

"Oh no," I groan. It's bad enough for Xarion to see me like this. But Donna is going to also witness my less-than-graceful appearance from this hole.

Sensing my distress, Varek growls, the sound rumbling between us. "You do not trust this male, sura?"

I shake my head, turning my gaze back to him. The way his gaze travels over my face as if he's taking every moment to catalog my features makes a warm thrill go through me. "It's not that. Don't worry about it. I can't be modest in this predicament."

Varek is silent, but I can see the thoughtful look that goes through his eyes as he watches me. Reads me.

A few tense moments pass before Xarion reappears, a coil of sturdy-looking rope looped over one shoulder. He tosses one end down to us, bracing himself in the dirt.

"Grab on," he instructs. "I'll pull you up one at a time."

Varek looks like he wants to argue. "Tie it to the base of the water shaft, Saffion. I will not risk you making my mate fall."

Xarion's ears straighten. "Your mate?"

My cheeks heat at the same moment that Donna pops her head over the hole, her brown eyes widening comically as she takes in the scene below. A delighted grin spreads across her face, and I just know she's never going to let me live this down.

Before I can realize what she's doing, she's humming a tune that becomes immediately clear once the words ring from her lips. It's *Hoochie Coochie Man* by Muddy Waters. Her voice is rich, as if she's grown up singing the blues, and right now, it only highlights the mischief in her eyes as she waggles her eyebrows at us.

"Well, well, well," she drawls, her voice practically dripping with mirth. "When I heard Xarion shouting about needing rope to get something from the well, I never imagined it would be you two lovebirds!"

My blush deepens at her teasing tone, and Varek's growl of annoyance kicks up a notch. Donna, however, seems entirely unperturbed by his display of aggression, her grin only widening.

"Looks like you guys have been getting up to some fun down there," she continues, grinning unashamedly. "Guess that explains why you weren't answering your comm all night. You've been busy…exploring each other's depths, hmm?"

"Donna!" I splutter, torn between embarrassment and reluctant amusement at her audacity. I've only known her for what, a whole day, and it already feels like one of my old girlfriends from Earth.

She grins wider, looking like the Cheshire Cat before Xarion clears his throat.

"I've secured the rope to the well shaft, Kari. I will still attempt to pull your mate up."

"I'll help too," Donna eases back and the rope sways as if she grabs hold of it with Xarion. "Whenever you're ready, big guy, send your sweetheart up."

Varek's eyes narrow as if he doesn't trust either of them with my wellbeing. Grumbling under his breath, he boosts me up to grab the rope, making sure I have a secure hold before reluctantly letting me go.

With a grunt of effort, Xarion and Donna start hauling me up. I try to help as much as I can, walking my feet up the slick walls, but my limbs are stiff and uncooperative after so long in one position.

Finally, after what feels like an eternity, I'm heaved over the lip of the hole, collapsing onto the sun-warmed grass with a gasp of relief. Xarion offers me a hand up, which I accept gratefully, wincing as my cramped muscles protest the sudden movement.

No sooner have I gained my feet than Varek is surging up out of the well under his own power, using only the rope and no one else's help.

"Well, damn. Color me tickled," Donna breathes as Varek lands in a predatory crouch, his eyes immediately seeking me out, assessing me for any sign of injury or distress.

Seeing that I'm unharmed, he rises to his full, imposing height, turning to face Xarion. The two males regard each other warily, the air between them practically crackling with tension.

"Thank you for your assistance," Varek says stiffly, the words sounding like they're being dragged out of him. A slight frown creases my brow. He isn't usually like this. But then, he was a bit annoyed with the Raki, too. Only, Xarion hasn't done anything to harm me. "We are in your debt."

Xarion adjust his collar. "It's not the first time I've had to come to you and your siblingkin's assistance. You Kari and these humans..." He shakes his head before turning away. He moves over to the lever I'd pulled that opened the hole in the first place, and activates it. Once more the covering slides over the hole, the tufted grass above it making it blend in like it's not even there.

"Remind me not to touch this thing again." I shake myself, a shudder going through me until I feel eyes on me. My gaze shifts to Donna and I hold back a laugh at her expression, feigning annoyance instead.

Donna's eyes are practically sparkling with mischief as she looks me over, her gaze zeroing in on my torn clothing and my overall 'freshly-bedded' look. She sidles up to me, throwing an arm around my shoulders and giving me a conspiratorial squeeze. "You know, at this age, I thought I was past being scandalized by anything. But you two young'uns are giving me a run for my money!"

"It really isn't what it looks like."

Donna laughs. It's a full head-thrown-back belly laugh that puts me to shame. Because it is exactly what it looks like. I just had sex with an alien in a well and it was the best time of my life.

"Come, Catherine Richmond. You look like you need a rest." Xarion reaches for my other arm, ready to assist me inside when a growl cuts through the air causing both Donna and Xarion to freeze. Xarion's long ears twitch nervously as he quickly withdraws his hand from my arm. Even Donna looks momentarily startled, her eyes going wide as she glances between me and my glowering mate.

Confused, I pause walking toward the lodge to look back at Varek. What I see has my heart giving a heavy thump in my chest. He doesn't...he doesn't look right.

Varek is snarling, his brow drawn, and his complete focus is on Xarion, even after I call his name.

"Varek?" He doesn't budge. His claws form fists at his side even as he squeezes his eyes shut and shakes his head. I step toward him even as Xarion moves to block my path.

"Tell me, Catherine Richmond. How long has he been like this?"

I shake my head, not really seeing Xarion as I look around him and attempt to move toward Varek again. Xarion doesn't let me, using an arm to block me.

"Like what?"

But even as I ask, I can see that Varek looks different. Pinker than usual. As if his scales are changing color.

"Kari, are you…"

"No," Varek growls, shaking his head again. He opens his eyes and his gaze finds me immediately. "It's not that."

Xarion's shoulders sag as he removes his arm from where he'd been blocking me. "Well, let us get the females inside. They both need to rest. Donna Johnson from the journey here and Catherine for having spent the dark cycle in such conditions."

Varek nods, his gaze still on me and my eyes linger on his as Xarion directs me and Donna to the house.

Once we get inside, I collapse on a stool by the table.

"You've done great with the place," Donna breathes. "Mine is still barebones. I can't wait till I can get it like this."

I huff a laugh of appreciation through my nose, but I'm distracted. My gaze shifts back to the door. Varek hasn't come inside yet. When more minutes pass and he still doesn't appear, my fear grows. I rise from the stool, barely aware of Xarion and Donna in the kitchen preparing tea—with Xarion instructing that he'd ordered tea flasks to be sent in the packages for all new arrivals. Apparently, water isn't needed for those as they're premade. Meanwhile, Donna waves off Xarion's explanation, her eyes twinkling with mirth. "Honey, I've been making tea since before you were a twinkle in your daddy's eye," she drawls. "I think I can handle a little pre-packaged brew without supervision."

Xarion bristles, his ears twitching indignantly. "I was merely trying to be helpful," he sniffs. "Forgive me for assuming you might appreciate some guidance in navigating unfamiliar provisions."

Their banter fades into the background as I walk silently to the door. There's a ball of something sour settling in the base of my gut. That feeling you get when you know you're about to see or hear something that will set your world on fire.

I reach the door, my gaze shifting to the spot where I last saw Varek before we headed inside. He's not there.

"Varek?"

I take a step outside the door, more trepidation rising along my spine. That's when I see him.

On all fours. His claws dig into the dirt, his muscles rippling beneath his scales that are definitely taking on a pinkish hue now.

"Varek?" I call out again, moving to go to him despite the sour feeling of dread growing in my stomach.

Before I can take more than a couple steps, a strong hand grabs my arm, yanking me back. I whirl to see Xarion, his red eyes wide with alarm.

"Don't. You mustn't go near him right now." He may look like a tall white rabbit person, but he's stronger than he looks. With little effort, Xarion tugs me back towards the house.

I struggle against his grip. "Something is wrong with him! Something's happening—"

"It's the rut." Xarion's voice is tight as he all but drags me inside. "Neither of us are safe here."

My heart stops, my gaze sliding back to Varek a moment before Xarion pulls the door closed. He releases me then, pressing his back against it, his chest heaving and his eyes wide. "I didn't think I would be dealing with this so soon again," he murmurs.

His words fall on almost deaf ears as I rush to the window. Varek is still on all fours, his head hanging low as he visibly trembles. It looks like he's struggling to maintain control, to keep his wits about him.

"Oh no…" I whisper. Or, oh yes? I'm not sure what I'm supposed to feel right now. All I know is that Varek is in trouble. Varek needs me.

"Let me out." I turn back to the door but Xarion has plastered his body against it, his communicator in one hand as he desperately types out a message.

"Negative, human. I cannot put you at risk of death. The Initiative forbids it."

"I don't care about the blasted Initiative. Varek is in trouble! He's in pain."

"On the contrary, you're the one who will be in pain if I let him in here." His ears fall flat behind his head. "And me. Gods. I'm the only male here. That Kari will rip me to shreds to get to you."

My hands form fists at my sides, my patience growing thin. "Xarion…*move*."

"As much as I would *not* like to be a meat shield between you and your fated, I must." He stands taller, resolute, blocking my only exit. "You are not aware of what this bond means. Of what can happen if I let that Kari inside."

I grit my teeth. "I do. He explained it to me."

Xarion seems mildly taken aback, but his shoulders straighten anyway. "Did he tell you that Kari females sometimes die from the pressure of this mating ritual?"

"Say what now?" Donna steps out of the kitchen, mouth and eyes open wide.

I blink at Xarion. I didn't know that. "We didn't have the time to discuss it all." But even hearing the words, I know deep down my decision is the same. I'm done keeping myself from moving on. From living.

"Let me go." I walk up to him.

"Unfortunately, human—"

I grunt, trying to moving his stiff body. "Blast it!"

It's no use. Xarion is like a solid block. I hurry back to the window at the same time that Donna comes up at my side. I hear her soft exclamation underneath her breath.

After a long, tense moment, Varek staggers to his feet. He sways unsteadily, shaking his head as if to clear it. Then, with what looks like a herculean effort, he turns and looks directly at me. My heart clenches. I need to go to him. And I know he will come to me. Only...he doesn't. With one last lingering look, as if he wants to tell me the world in that one glance, Varek turns in the other direction, stumbling as he heads toward his hover truck parked by the gate. The two oogas that Xarion and Donna must have ridden to my farm shift a few feet away from the drunk-looking Kari, giving Varek enough room to head around to the driver's side of his vehicle.

I watch, my heart in my throat, as he fumbles with the door, finally managing to haul himself inside. The engine roars to life and within seconds, the truck is speeding away, kicking up a cloud of dust in its wake.

I stand there stunned. My heart breaking. For a few moments, I can only stare at the cloud of dust left in his wake, the entirety of my world seeming to freeze and come to a standstill around me.

"Yes, this is Xarion. I need to speak with your mate, Eleanor Taylor."

I hear Eleanor's response to Xarion, her voice so happy on the line that the sound is distinctly at odds with the dark gray cloud suddenly moving over me.

"Zynar?" she asks on the line. "Why do you need Zynar?"

"It's his siblingkin," Xarion says. "His core-rhythm. It has sung."

There is silence on the other line before there is a screech as Eleanor screams in delight. Xarion stretches the device away from him as my head slowly turns in his direction.

"Where is he?" the gruff voice on the line is no doubt Varek's brother. I can just barely make out his image on the screen because it feels like I'm still in a trance. As if none of this is really happening. And then my brain picks up the strings, the pieces, the coincidences, the way how one thing relates to another, and my heart clenches some more.

Because this feels like I'm being left again. As if I've opened my heart and made myself vulnerable, only to have it shattered once more. Except this is nothing like when my previous partner died. This is worse. As if a part of me that I never knew is being ripped out by the root.

"I need to go to him," I whisper.

"He has gone in his hover truck. Possibly to his quarters to lock himself away," Xarion relays.

"Frakk," Zynar curses. "He's done it to protect her. Like I did for Eleanor. She doesn't know, does she? She doesn't know about the rut."

Xarion's gaze shifts to me.

"I need to go to him." My head lifts slowly, the certainty of that one statement all I can rely on.

"You can't let her. There's no telling how this will turn out. I must inform her of the dangers first. If you let her leave and she doesn't—"

I grip the device, facing Zynar. "I know."

His throat moves. Yellow eyes that look so much like the ones I love look back at me and I can see the fear within them. "Catherine—" Zynar starts.

"He told me. Varek told me everything."

Zynar regards me for a long moment. "And you're sure?" The big alien male on the other end of the line seems to plead with me, his eyes giving everything away. "You're sure you want this? That you want my brother?" He pauses.

"Of course. He's everything—" My heart clenches. "He's everything I've ever wanted. Everything I've ever needed."

Behind me, Donna makes a soft sound while Zynar studies me from the other side of the screen. Then I hear a female voice; Eleanor's voice. "She loves him."

Zynar's throat moves. "Then I will do my best to assist you, my *kahlesta*." He says the word with complete reverence, bowing his head to me on the vid feed. "Together, we will save my siblingkin and your matehood."

From the corner of my eye, Xarion steps toward me. "Unfortunately, I cannot let that happen."

I wouldn't call myself a physical person. I've never put my hands on a stranger. Never thrown a fit in public. Never assaulted anyone.

But in this moment, I could move a mountain. "I'm going to Varek, and that's final."

"That's my girl," Donna praises at my back like the sidekick I never knew I needed.

Xarion holds up his hands in a placating gesture, his long ears folding backward again. "Catherine Richmond, please. My duty is to ensure your safety. I cannot in good conscience allow you to put yourself at risk. The rut could *kill* you."

But I'm done listening. Done waiting. Every fiber of my being is screaming at me to go to Varek, to be with him, no matter the consequences.

In one swift motion, I lunge forward and tug the door with all my strength. Caught off guard, he stumbles forward, his red eyes wide with shock.

"I've faced death many times. This time isn't any different."

I don't wait for him to recover. Seizing my chance, I yank open the door and burst out of the house, my feet pounding against the packed earth as I hurry toward the waiting ooga. If they rode them here, I can ride them away. They can't be that different from riding horses.

"Catherine Richmond!" Xarion's desperate shout follows me, but I don't look back. Can't look back.

"You go, girl!" Donna's voice echoes across the plains.

Xarion rushes after me, his long strides quickly eating up the distance between us. "You don't understand!" he calls, his voice strained with distress. "The Kari is a predator species. They are not like us. The rut…it's not safe for you! Varek wouldn't want you to endanger yourself like this! That is why he left. He knows the damage he could do."

I shake my head, my hair whipping around my face as I push my body to move. "He won't hurt me." I manage to gasp out. "Varek needs me. And I need him. I'm not afraid."

And it's true. The fear that had gripped me so tightly earlier has melted away, replaced by a fierce determination, an unshakable certainty that this is right. That Varek and I belong together, come what may.

Xarion makes one last grab for my arm, but I twist away, my chest heaving with exertion. He stands there helplessly as I race towards the oogas, his expression a mix of frustration and deep concern. "You face death on both sides, human. Eleanor Taylor was lucky."

I don't know how I manage to heave myself on top of the ooga. The gentle animal doesn't protest and I'm happy. But Xarion's words stop me in my tracks. "What do you mean by that?"

The Saffion sighs before straightening and adjusting the cuff of his coat. "We do not want to lose you, Catherine. Your welfare is of great importance. But…"

"But?" My jaw tightens, impatience rising high in my blood.

"If you don't accept the Kari's mate bond, he will certainly die."

I got still. "What?"

Xarion releases a breath before walking slowly toward the remaining ooga. "He will go insane with the need to claim you. It will lead to his demise."

I glare at Xarion. "And you think that's a good reason for me to *not* go to him?"

Xarion releases a defeated sigh. In a graceful movement, he launches himself on top of the free ooga. "I said no such thing." His gaze shifts to me. "I am simply concerned. I meant it when I said your welfare is important."

My brows furrow as I turn the ooga, guiding it with cues from my legs. "You're not changing my mind. You're not stopping me."

"I am no longer attempting to." The defeated tone makes my gaze shift back to the Saffion.

"Then what are you doing?"

He sighs again. "I am accompanying you. The least I can do is get you there safely...despite my reservations."

I blink in surprise, not expecting this turn of events. But I'm not about to look a gift horse—or in this case, a gift Saffion—in the mouth. If Xarion's presence means a swifter, safer journey to Varek, then I'll take it.

I nod curtly, adjusting my grip on the ooga. "Fine. But we need to hurry. Every second counts."

Xarion inclines his head in agreement, his own mount shifting restlessly beneath him. Together, we turn our steeds towards the path Varek took, ready to race after him.

Just as we're about to kick our oogas into a gallop, Donna's voice rings out from the porch behind us. "You two be careful now," she calls, her usually jovial tone undercut with genuine worry. "And Catherine, honey, you give that male of yours a good wallop upside the head for runnin' off like that! Then a big ol' smooch to make it better!"

She winks at me, letting me know she means I should give him so much more than a smooch and the action releases some of the tension from my veins. I smile at her. "Sorry for running off like this!"

Donna shakes her head. "It's fine. I'll be waiting here." Her face grows serious. "Go get your man."

I push back the intensity of emotion swelling within me as I give her a nod and face the road again.

I'm going to go get my man.

My love.

My everything.

22

CATHERINE

The oogas move much faster than I expected, their powerful legs eating up the distance with every stride. The wind whips through my hair as we race across the Hudoian landscape, the morning sun rising high over the horizon and warming my back as we go.

Beside me, Xarion has been peppering me with questions about Varek's rut for the entire ride, his brow furrowed in contemplation. But I can barely focus on his words, my mind consumed with thoughts of Varek. Is he okay? Will I reach him in time? Will our love be enough to see us through this?

I'm jolted out of my thoughts by Xarion's next question, his tone unusually hesitant. "Catherine, I must ask…has Varek ever been in contact with your lifeblood?"

I blink, mildly surprised by the unexpected query. "No. Why would…" But then my memory twinges. Memory of Varek soothing the wound on my forehead comes back clear as day. The sensation of his tongue on my skin. How he rumbled with pleasure and teased me about consuming me. It all comes back. Something hurts deep inside me. I want to see him like that again. I want to see him well.

"Yes, actually. He has. Why?"

Xarion's ears twitch, his expression turning pensive. "I have a theory," he says. But he doesn't continue and I'm too distracted to push him to. Because the town is just ahead.

I lean forward, pushing the ooga to go faster as it barrels down the road. Beings already on their way to whatever task they have for the day, step out of our way as we hurry into the town square.

"Do you know where—" Xarion begins, but I'm already nudging the ooga toward Varek's dwelling. The ooga responds to my urgent commands, veering down the narrow street that leads to Varek's home. My heart pounds in my chest as we draw closer, a mixture of fear and desperate hope swirling in my gut.

Please let him be okay, I pray silently. Please let me not be too late.

We skid to a halt outside Varek's dwelling, the oogas snorting and stomping their feet as I leap to the ground. I barely register Xarion's startled shout behind me as I race towards the door, my entire being focused on one thing and one thing only.

Varek.

"Catherine Richmond," Xarion calls, and I turn to find him watching me with a sort of resigned respect. "I can go no further."

I nod, my throat tightening.

"May the gods be with you."

I nod again, holding those words close as I push the door open and head into the building.

I remember my way. After all, I spent one of the best nights of my life within these walls. Heading to the end of the corridor, I stand before Varek's door, my heart beating hard in my chest.

I take a deep breath, my hand hovering over the door. A part of me is terrified of what I might find on the other side, of what state Varek might be in. But a larger part, the part that loves him with every fiber of my being, knows that there's nowhere else I'd rather be.

Gathering my courage, I pound my fist, my knock echoing on the other side.

There is silence, and for a moment, I wonder if I've come to the wrong place. What if he ran off somewhere else?

The potential of that makes me unsettled and I knock again, calling his name this time. "Varek? Are you in there?"

That's when I hear a sound behind the door. Directly behind it, as if he's right up against the surface, listening to me.

I press my forehead to the strange material, my breaths coming hard from the intense journey or probably from the swell of emotions within me.

"It's me...Catherine. Will you? Will you open the door for me?"

I can't hear much, but I swear I hear a rustle on the other side. He's in there. I'm sure of it. But he's not opening the door.

"I'm not afraid, Varek. I...I want this. I want us. I want to try."

Another rustle, but he still does not open. Is he really that afraid of hurting me? Eleanor has a Kari mate. She's as happy as ever. The rut can't be *that* bad. Varek must just be overly concerned that I'll break or something. But I'm stronger than that.

I pound my fist on the door again. My voice rises a little higher than before. "Open up or I'll find a way in."

When there's a sound behind me and another door down the corridor opens, my fist pauses midway in the air.

For a moment, I think I'm seeing double. But the Kari that steps out from about three doors down is not my Varek. He has similar green hair, similar yellow eyes, but his hair is shaved at the sides, and he is tall, but not as tall as Varek.

"Need some help, little female?" he purrs, his gaze heightening on mine the moment he seems to recognize me. "You are one of the new females who has found a mate with my kind." Something rises in his gaze that makes me completely aware he is male and of the fact I'm wearing ripped clothing. "I am Tovan of the line Kamesh, and I would be happy to assist—"

A deep growl chills the air as the door before me opens. I only have a moment to gasp before I'm pulled inside Varek's room and the door slides shut once more. He bolts the door and I only get a moment where his sweet scent almost overwhelms me before he's gone. He disappears from beside me, his absolutely scorching touch leaving my arm. Only the brush of air and movement tells me he's put himself on the other side of the room.

I'm left with my heart in my throat, my breaths coming hard as my back presses against the door and my eyes try desperately to adjust to the absolute darkness in the room.

The next thing that hits me is the heat. It's like walking into a furnace, the air thick and heavy with a primal, masculine energy that makes my skin prickle and my blood sing.

I blink, eyelids fluttering as I try to make out Varek's form in the pitch-black room. The only sound is my heavy breathing and the pounding of my heart in my ears.

"Varek?" I whisper, taking a slow step forward.

A low, pained groan echoes from far away, making me freeze in place.

"Stay back," Varek rasps, his voice rough and strained. "Please, Catherine. You shouldn't be here. It's not safe."

I shake my head, even though he probably can't see me in the darkness. "I'm not afraid," I inch further into the room. "I trust you, Varek. Completely."

There's a rustling sound, like he's shifting restlessly, followed by a dull thud as if he slams his fist into the wall. "You don't understand," he grits out, and I can hear the agony in his tone. "I can barely control myself. And this is just the start. You're so precious. Too precious." More rustling. "Leave now."

"No." Cautiously, I keep moving forward, navigating by sound and memory until my shin bumps against what I think is the bed. I pause, not realizing I'd made it that far in his quarters. "I'm not going anywhere." I try my best to parse the darkness as I sink down onto the mattress. "This...rut. It means your core-rhythm has sung, doesn't it?"

There's a scraping sound like his claws are digging into the flooring.

"That I'm your mate?" The words make my heart swell. I can hardly believe it. But my disbelief will have to be enjoyed another time. Not now. Not when this is a matter of life and death.

"You're *mine*," he snarls, his voice sounding inhuman in a way that makes something flutter inside me.

"And you're mine."

A shuddering breath escapes him, and I feel the bed dip as he presses down on the far edge, keeping a careful distance between us.

"Leave, Catherine. Leave now." It isn't a normal whisper, his voice. It holds a threat beneath it that should make me run. Instead, I remain where I am, against all my instincts of self-preservation. "I could never forgive myself if I..." He trails off.

But if what Xarion said is true... "I won't leave you here to die."

There's silence. Tense silence before Varek curses. "They told you."

"Yes," I whisper, inching closer ever so slowly, giving him time to pull away if he needs to. "And I still choose you." I reach out through the darkness until my fingers brush against his arm. He flinches at the contact but doesn't move away.

"I don't want to hurt you." His voice is so distorted now, as if he's fighting something primal and dangerous all at once. As if he's fighting a beast within him.

"You won't." I trail my hand up to cup his jaw. Because I

know about living with pain. About being hurt and broken in ways that feel like they'll never heal. And I know this male, this wonderful, gentle, patient male, would never do the same to me, mentally or physically, despite his own fears.

I can feel the tension thrumming through him, the way he's fighting to hold himself back. "I know you, Varek. I trust you."

He leans into my touch for just a moment, a soft, wounded sound catching in his throat. I feel the exact moment his resolve crumbles, his body shuddering against mine as he lets out a ragged groan.

"Catherine," he rasps, my name a desperate, reverent prayer on his lips.

"Shh, I know," I whisper. Slowly, giving him time to adjust, I slide my hand from his jaw to the back of his neck, my fingers tangling in the sweat-dampened strands of his hair. "I'm here."

A broken sound escapes him and then he's moving, his large claws gripping my hips as he hauls me fully across the bed. I barely have time to gasp before he's hovering over me, his powerful body caging me in, surrounding me with his heat and scent.

But he doesn't touch me, not yet. I can feel the tension vibrating through him, the barely leashed control as he fights his baser instincts.

"Catherine," he says again, his voice guttural, on the edge of human and completely beastlike. "If we do this...if I claim you... there's no going back." His claws flex against my hips, pricking my skin through the thin fabric of my dress. "You'll be mine, utterly and completely. My mate. Forever."

All I feel is a bone-deep rightness at his warning, a soul-deep certainty that this is exactly where I'm meant to be—beneath him, bound to him, in heart, body and spirit. Maybe he was right about fate and the paths we take. Here, right now, I believe I was always meant to be here at this exact place, this exact moment.

I reach up, framing his face in my hands as I stare into the glowing embers of his eyes. "I already am," I tell him softly. "This is just making it official."

He shudders violently, a low growl rumbling up from his chest. "I won't be able to be gentle. The rut...it will demand I take you, hard and fierce and thorough. I'll scratch you. I'll bite you. I might..."

A thrill runs through me at his words, heat pooling low in my belly. "You won't hurt me. Not in the way you're thinking." I know he won't.

A tremor goes through him, like a beast underneath his scales is writhing for release. I half expect him to transform into a creature like those old films I used to watch.

"There's one more thing." His body does that rippling thing, as if his bones are about to crack, his flesh rippling and distorting. I lean closer, one hand stretching toward him. He jerks back. "There's one more thing you should know."

I pause. "What?" My voice is barely a whisper now. Barely there.

Through the shadows, I watch as Varek strips down his pants, and for the first time since we've been together, I get full sight of what he's working with.

"Good God." My eyes widen as it springs forward, bobbing in the air like a thick plank. There's no way that thing has ever fit inside me. But even as I lean closer and more heat pools within me, I know that I'm not deterred.

Pink and purple scales, more pink than purple now, splatter across his base. The rest of the shaft is a dark purple that almost looks black as my eyes adjust to the dim light. He's ridged, both on the upper and underside. I lean closer, unable to stop myself, my eyes widening at the small frills that decorate the upper shaft. They alternate between raised bumps that form a line straight to his slightly curved tip.

I move a little closer and Varek steps back. Looking up, he's hidden in the shadows, the little light available highlighting this thing he's showing me. He's magnificent. I don't know why this is so important to him. Frankly, if he's scared I'll be turned off by his alien dick, it's a little late for that. But then I realize what he's showing me. I see them then.

I see the scars.

"Varek—" My breath hitches as I reach for him. He steps back again, just out of reach. All over his shaft and his lower abdomen the scars crisscross, telling a story of cruelty. Of pain. "Who did this to you?"

I look up at him once more, blinking through my suddenly blurry vision. I can hardly see his face in the shadows.

"The Tasqals. Their tests. A story from my past," he growls. "One I cannot let go. But with you…I can move on."

His words strike something deep within me. They're the same words he said to me. Just like that night at the festival and now as I gaze upon the scarred evidence of his pain, I realize we are more alike than I ever knew. Both of us bearing the marks of old wounds, both of us seeking healing and wholeness in the shelter of each other's souls.

"Come to me."

Varek hesitates but his will is weak. Like a prowling cat, he slowly leans down. I shift back as he crawls on all fours, his breaths ragged things as they force through his nose.

"Take me," I breathe, arching up to nip at his throat. I suck at his pulse point, reveling in his answering groan. "Claim me. I need it. I need this, too."

That seems to shatter the last threads of his control. With a roar that shakes the very walls, he surges against me, his mouth crashing over mine in a bruising, passionate kiss.

I moan into it, opening for him, welcoming the thrust of his tongue as he licks into my mouth, staking his claim. My hands scrabble at his back, my nails digging into his heated skin as I give myself over to the utter rush of sensation.

Clothes tear, seams popping as he rips the fabric from my body, too far gone to bother with niceties.

"Mine," he snarls against my lips, his claws tracing possessive lines down my sides.

"Yes," I gasp, my head tipping back as he blazes a trail of open-mouthed kisses down the column of my throat. "Yours, always."

He makes a rough sound of agreement, his body moving over mine. With a throaty growl, he claims my mouth once again, his tongue delving deep as he presses me into the mattress with the weight of his body. I can feel the hard, thick length of him nestled against my thigh, pulsing with heat, and I moan into his mouth, my hips arching instinctively to meet his.

When his head dips, his mouth blazing a hot trail down my throat to my breasts, he nuzzles into the soft swells of my breasts before drawing one aching peak between his lips, sucking hard.

I cry out sharply, my back bowing as pleasure jolts through me like lightning. He lavishes attention on my breasts, licking, sucking, grazing my sensitized flesh with his fangs until I'm writhing beneath him, whimpering with need.

"Varek, please..." The teasing makes me ache for him so badly, but he's not done yet. He makes a trail down the center of my chest till he's between my legs. I barely get a breath before his mouth is pressed against my core, his tongue speaking a language the little bud at the center of my folds reacts to. Varek lathers me with saliva, making me ready for him as he brings me to a peak that crashes through me out of nowhere.

With a low snarl, he licks his lips as if the taste of me is like sugar and surges up to cover my body fully with his own. I feel the broad head of his shaft notch against my entrance a moment before he drives forward, sheathing himself to the hilt in one powerful thrust.

I scream, my nails digging into his shoulders as I'm stretched and filled almost beyond bearing. He's so big, so hot and hard inside me, the fit so tight it's nearly painful.

But it's a pain edged with the most exquisite pleasure, a feeling of utter rightness and completion, as if I was made solely for him, to accept and welcome all that he is.

He stills for a moment, his breath gusting harshly against my neck, letting me adjust to his girth. Beside my head, his claws dig into the bedding and I know that even now, he's exercising control.

"Let go," I whisper, reaching up to thread my fingers through the hair at his nape. "Give me your all."

With a deep growl, he moves, withdrawing almost completely before slamming back in, driving a rhythm that has me seeing stars.

"Catherine," he groans, his hips churning relentlessly into mine. "My Catherine..." His thrusts grow harder, faster, spurred by the rut and my pleasured cries. "Going to fill you..."

The words send a dark thrill through me. The "yes" that pants past my lips makes him roar, the sound primal and triumphant. His body practically blurs with the force of his thrusts, every stroke reaching that secret place inside me that makes me see white. I feel the tension coiling tighter and tighter at the base of my spine, my inner muscles fluttering wildly around his plunging length.

Then one broad claw snakes between our straining bodies, his fingers finding the swollen pearl at the apex of my thighs. He rubs the sensitive nub in tight, knowing circles and that's all it takes to send me hurtling over the edge into ecstasy.

I scream his name as I shatter, my release crashing over me in wave after wave of searing bliss. I clamp down on him like a vise, rippling along his shaft, trying to milk his own climax from him.

With a harsh shout, he buries himself to the root, forcing that impossibly wide bit at the base of his shaft inside me. It swells, becomes so engorged I feel my core stretch to its limit. There, he stills, his hips jerking as his scorching seed pulses deep inside me. He's so swollen, it locks us together as he marks me from the inside out, staking his claim.

For long moments, we simply cling to each other, shuddering through the aftershocks, lost in the haze.

A little giggle rises in my throat. Chest heaving with heavy breaths, I gaze down up at him. "That…that wasn't so bad."

But as Varek eases up enough so he can look at me, the look in his eyes sends a deep thrill through me. As if I'm looking in the eyes of something I shouldn't face head-on. Like a rabbit caught in the hypnotic stare of a wolf. There's something so raw and untamed in those molten depths, a wildness that sends a thrill of both fear and exhilaration racing down my spine.

"Again," he rumbles, his claws kneading my hips as he nips at my shoulder. "Going to take you again and again, until the whole nestkans knows you've been well and thoroughly claimed."

With a growl, he flips me onto my stomach, blanketing my back with his muscular torso, his still-hard shaft nestled along the cleft of my bottom.

I moan at the dark promise in his words, my body already stirring back to life, empty and aching despite the seed running down my thighs. With a ravenous snarl, he sheathes himself to the hilt once more.

THE MOMENT VAREK surrenders to the rut, it's as if a switch is flipped inside him, turning him from a rational being into a creature of pure instinct and primal need.

One large claw fists in my hair, holding me still for his taking, while the other roams feverishly over me, his claws leaving stinging trails in their wake. There's no art or finesse to his touch, only a blind need to map and mark every inch of me, to imprint himself on my very skin.

I can do nothing but surrender to the onslaught, my own hands scrabbling desperately at his back, my nails raking down the corded planes of muscle as I give myself over to him. Time doesn't seem to matter anymore. We move from the bed to the floor. The floor to the wall. At one point, I'm even sure we switch rooms. Things crash and shatter. Things are ripped and torn. And all the while, Varek takes me.

There's an edge of pain to the pleasure, a sharpness that only serves to wind me higher, tighter, until I'm writhing mindlessly beneath him, mewling into his mouth, his neck, his skin.

He tears himself away from the kiss with a ragged growl, his chest heaving as he stares down at me with those wild, glowing eyes.

He doesn't give me time to adjust, just pulls back and then surges forward again, setting a punishing pace that has the bed slamming against the wall with every jarring thrust. He's so deep, I swear I can feel him in my throat.

I've never been loved like this and I know I never will be again. And even then, I know this is what I needed. This. Him.

There's no tenderness here, no gentle lovemaking. This is raw and rough and almost brutal, a carnal claiming in the truest sense of the word. Hours pass. Days I suppose. I keep track of the passing time by little changes of light my consciousness picks up. And though some distant part of me knows I'll be sore, aching, bruised after this…I can't bring myself to care.

Because there's something profoundly, primitively satisfying about being taken like this, about being the sole focus of all that strength, all that fierce, wild need.

So I give myself over to it, my body going soft and pliant even as my inner muscles clench greedily around his pistoning length. Let him wring cries and moans and broken pleas from my lips, the sounds muffled by the ripped bedding my face is pressed into as he ruts into me with single-minded purpose. Let him use me, fill me, flood me with his seed, until there can be no doubt that I belong to him, that I was made for him and him alone.

The thought has me clenching even tighter around him, my nails scrabbling uselessly against whatever I can grasp as I hurtle toward the edge of some great, looming precipice. I can feel it building at the base of my spine, in the uncontrollable flutters of my core around his driving hardness.

"Oh!" I keen, the sound thin and thready and desperate. "I don't know if I can again…I'm going to…"

He snarls in response, his pace growing even more frantic, more relentless. He leans down over me, his chest pressing me into the pillow on the floor as his fangs find the curve where my neck meets my shoulder. He bites down hard, the bright burst of pain, the final spark that sends me into oblivion.

I scream as I shatter, my body convulsing almost violently as wave after wave of ecstasy crashes over me. I feel him crash into his own release, but the moment is not done.

I'm lifted and spun as he settles over me again, his lips lapping at my core to soothe me for the next round and I am lost…so lost…lost without him.

23

VAREK

I wake in a haze.

Consciousness returns to me slowly, like swimming up through murky depths toward a distant light. The first thing I notice is the feel of soft skin beneath my claws, the scent of something sweet and familiar filling my airways.

My eyes flutter open and I blink rapidly, trying to focus my blurred vision. Gradually, the world resolves into the dim interior of my quarters, and the small, still form curled against my chest.

Catherine.

Memory crashes over me like a tidal wave and I jerk fully awake, a litany of curses in a dozen languages spilling past my lips. Stars above, what have I done?

She's here, bare in my arms, her skin mottled with bruises and bite marks, her mane a wild tangle around her pale face. Even in the low light, I can see the claw-shaped impressions on her hips, the scratches marring the creamy expanse of her back.

Bile rises and I swallow hard against the sudden urge to be violently sick. *I* did this. I hurt her, used her, *ravaged her like a beast*, with no care for her comfort or enjoyment.

Disgust and self-loathing churn in my gut. The most precious thing in existence to me and look what I have done. How can I...how can I ever fix this?

Taking a deep, shuddering breath, I try to steady myself. The urge to hide, to turn away from the evidence of my savagery, is strong. Shame, hot and bitter, rises like fire in my throat.

But I force it down. No. I cannot hide from this. From what I've done. I cannot pretend it didn't happen, cannot absolve myself of the responsibility. I am many things—a warrior, a killer, a monster in the eyes of many. But I am not a coward.

Slowly, gingerly, I ease away from her. But as I start to pull away, her brow furrows and she makes a small, distressed sound, her hands clutching weakly at my arms. My core-beat stutters. Even now, even after what I've done, she reaches for me, seeks my comfort and protection.

The organ in my chest aches with a pain I've never known before...and behind it...behind its strangled beats, there is something else. Something I never thought I would ever hear. Ever feel.

The rhythm that sings beneath every beat is sure and strong. My core-rhythm. My song for the very female clutching at me, seeking my comfort.

Catherine is my *kahl*. My whole being sings for her.

A strangled sound comes from my lips. She really is mine. This soft, beautiful female is mine. And I have harmed her.

My throat tightens with a swell of emotion I can't name. Despite my disgust with myself, I can't help but gather her close again, cradling her gently against my chest. She yearns for comfort after what I have done and when she wakes, she might not want me to touch her anymore.

At this moment, I am taking a liberty, and my core-beat stutters some more.

Catherine stirs slightly, her lashes fluttering as she struggles towards wakefulness and I go still. I am not ready to face this. To face her with my shame.

"Varek?" Her voice is a thready rasp, hoarse from overuse.

"I'm here, sura." I smooth her tangled mane back from her face with a trembling hand, marveling at the softness of the strands despite everything. "Don't move. You need rest."

Her eyes finally blink open, hazy and unfocused but so very green in the dim light. She frowns up at me for a moment, confusion creasing her brow. Then memory seems to surface and her expression clears, a weak but genuine smile curving her lips.

My core-beat stills.

"You're back," she whispers, lifting a trembling hand to cup my jaw. "Really back."

I turn my face into her palm, breathing in the scent of her skin, letting it ground me. "I'm so sorry, sura," I rasp, the words tearing at my throat. "Catherine, I never meant to hurt you. I tried to keep control and still… What I did…it's unforgivable."

To my shock, she shakes her head, her thumb stroking gently over my cheekbone. "No. You didn't hurt me. I mean, yes, I'm sore but…" Another genuine smile creases her face. "It was incredible, Varek. Being with you like that, so raw and…and real…it was…it was everything I needed."

I stare at her, searching her face for any hint of fear or revulsion and finding only tired satisfaction, affection, and wonder. "You…enjoyed it?" I hardly dare to believe what I'm hearing.

Her smile widens and she nods, curling herself more snugly into my embrace with a contented little sigh. "Mmm, very much. Though I may need a day or two before we do anything like that again." A light, shy laugh escapes her. "I'm going to need time to recover."

Relief crashes through me, so intense it's nearly dizzying. She doesn't hate me. She doesn't fear me. Incredibly, impossibly, she seems...happy. Content, even after the brutality of my rutting.

But I can't let myself forget the marks I've left on her, the evidence of my violence written across her skin. I may not have hurt her heart or her spirit, but I have wounded her body. And that is something I must atone for.

"Let me tend to you," I murmur, pressing my lips to her forehead. "A warm wash to soothe your aches, something nourishing to eat and drink."

She hums in sleepy approval, nuzzling into my throat. "That sounds perfect."

Carefully, so carefully, I gather her into my arms and rise from the bedding, carrying her like the precious treasure she is. Pieces of the bedding material become displaced and I get a view of the beast I was. I've destroyed the sleeping material, evidence of my claws ripping through the fibers clear as they scatter with my movement. And that's not all.

I swallow hard against the lump in my throat as I take in the destruction surrounding us. It's not just the bedding that bears the marks of my savagery. The walls are gouged with deep claw marks, the metal table beside the bed is dented and twisted out of shape, as if struck by a powerful blow. Shattered remnants from other fixtures crunch underfoot, and even the flooring bears damage.

Everywhere I look, there is evidence of the violence that transpired here, the uncontrolled fury of my rutting. It's like a scene from a nightmare, a testament to the monster that lurks beneath my skin. What's worse? I recall none of this.

Catherine makes a soft sound, drawing my attention back to her. She loops her arms around my neck, resting her head against my shoulder. Carefully adjusting my hold on her, I use my body to shield her from the worst of the destruction as I carry her towards the bathing room.

But I can't shield myself from the knowledge of what I've done. The room looks like a battlefield, like a place where a vicious, brutal struggle took place. I clench my jaw against the wave of self-recrimination that crashes over me. I did this. I let the animal inside me run rampant. I let it loose on the one person in the universe I should protect above all others.

The bathing room, thankfully, seems to have escaped the worst of my rampage. There are a few cracks in the tiled walls, a shattered mirror, but it's largely intact.

Setting my mate gently on a bench, I move to fill the sunken tub, making sure the water is the perfect temperature before adding soothing oils and salts I'd shamelessly bought and left here sols ago just for this purpose. Just in case. I don't know whether to thank the old me or be disgusted in my yearning, but I can't deny that despite my shame, there's an undercurrent of warmth going through me. I have a mate. I have found my *kahl*. And within me, a song sings.

The fragrant steam rises, filling the room with a calming scent as I turn to face my female. Moving over to her, I lift her once again, taking care to hold her gently so I don't upset any of her bruises.

Slowly, I lower her into the warm, scented water. She sighs in bliss as it envelops her, her eyes fluttering shut.

With utmost gentleness, I bathe her, cleansing her skin of the evidence of our joining. I stroke reverent digits over every bruise, every mark, silently vowing to replace each one with the tender brush of my lips as soon as she's healed.

She is pliant and trusting beneath my hands, a precious gift I will never take for granted. I wash and condition her mane, gently combing out the tangles until it floats on the water like strands of liquid silk.

When she is clean and relaxed, languorous in the steaming water, I leave her for a moment. Hurrying to the sleeping quarters, I strip the bedding material and replace it with fresh clean sheets. Hurrying back to the bathing room, I stop in the doorway.

She looks like a goddess, reclining in the steaming water, her skin flushed pink from the heat, her damp mane clinging to her shoulders and floating around her. Creeping closer, I am silent. I don't want to wake this delicate human female who has become the center of my universe.

I watch her for a few moments before she stirs, her low lids opening to find me. She smiles again and my core-beat stops. But I am no longer silent. My core-rhythm vibrates with a strength I could have only imagined. Catherine smiles up at me and I know this is all I ever wanted. *She* is all I ever wanted.

Lifting her out, I wrap her in a clean swathe of fabric, patting her dry. Then I carry her back to our sleeping quarters. I settle her on the fresh bedding and Catherine releases a contented sigh.

The meal preparation area is thankfully untouched. I head to that room and begin preparing something to eat. Retrieving a tray I fill it with fruits, meal squares, fresh, dried meat, and sweet, pulpy juice. Settling beside her, I hand-feed her morsels, coaxing her to eat and drink her fill. She accepts each bite from my claw, taking everything except the dried meat with gusto, her eyes soft and trusting. And as I tend to her, caring for her as she deserves, I feel the tight knot of self-loathing in my chest begin to ease. I cannot change what I've done…but I can work every day to be the male she deserves, to cherish and protect her as my *kahl*.

Satiated at last, she curls into my side with a contented sigh, her eyes already heavy with impending sleep. I gather her close, marveling at the way she fits so perfectly against me. She has always been the other half of me. Always. And in this perfect, tranquil moment, with my love safe in my arms, I finally allow myself to believe that, just maybe, the ancestors knew what they were on about.

That two broken creatures can find completion—and absolution—in each other.

For I have found my kahl. I have found my mate.

I am finally whole.

EPILOGUE

CATHERINE

We spend a few days at Varek's place. During those precious days, we exist in a bubble of peaceful intimacy, learning each other anew. Varek is attentive and tender, his every touch a wordless apology, a silent pledge. He bathes me, feeds me, holds me as if I am the most precious thing in his universe. And in those moments, cocooned in his fierce, gentle love, I feel cherished down to my very bones.

But reality can only be held at bay for so long.

When there's a hard knock at his door, coupled with frantic muffled voices, I know our time of peace in our little world is over.

Varek groans as he heads to the door, fastening the pants he's hastily pulled on before he disengages the lock.

"For frakk's sake, you live?!" Zynar's voice booms both into the room and down the corridor.

"Zynar," I hear Eleanor's calming voice. "Look. He looks okay." Then her voice dips. "Does that mean…"

Varek lets out a groan as he shifts to the side, gaze meeting mine as he lets them in. Immediately, Eleanor grabs on to Zynar for support. "Whoo, it's dark in here."

I chuckle. "I guess we forgot to open the curtains." Sitting on Varek's couch, I adjust his large shirt that I'm wearing.

Eleanor's eyes widen as they land on me and I can tell her first instinct is to rush over and give me a hug. I grin. She's always been trying to be my friend and I'd been so resistant to it. Resistant to everything because I was so afraid.

"What have you done to her?" Zynar growls, a frown on his brow as he regards me.

"Careful, brother. That's my mate you're talking about." Varek closes the door and heads back to my side, shamelessly sitting on the floor between my legs and throwing his head back into my lap as he levels his gaze on his brother.

Both Zynar and Eleanor have identical looks of surprise.

"You completed the rut." There's a strange note of something in Zynar's voice that I can't quite place. But from the look in Eleanor's eyes, it's clear they had surmised that fact before they arrived. After all, Varek might not still be here if I hadn't accepted his call.

With a suddenness that makes me jump, Zynar falls to one knee before me. Varek growls, but his bark has no bite.

"I am honored," Zynar says, "to accept you as my kahlesta." He lifts his head, his gaze meeting mine. "Thank you."

My heart clenches, because I know exactly what he's thanking me for. Thanking me for choosing his brother. Thanking me for accepting his love. For saving his life. If only he knew, it was no sacrifice on my part. Loving Varek is easy. I would do it all again, only for him.

Eleanor does a curtsy and a happy laugh bubbles in my throat.

"Oh stop it, you two." I tangle my hands into Varek's hair and he groans in unadulterated pleasure that makes my cheeks heat.

"We were worried," Eleanor says quietly, clearly unperturbed by the groaning male between my legs. "When we couldn't reach you...we feared the worst."

Of course. A sense of guilt twinges within me. "I forgot all about my comm."

"We tried Varek's too." Her gaze shifts to my mate.

My mate. It still feels so strange saying that. Strange but so right.

"I don't know where it is," Varek murmurs, his eyes rolled back as he accepts my gentle scalp massage like a content kitty cat.

At his words, their gazes shift around the room and I'm immediately glad we're not in the bedroom for them to see the destruction there. I don't even remember half of it happening. When I finally was able to look around, I couldn't believe it. It's no wonder Varek has been treating me like an egg he's afraid will break. Ever so gentle. But what I see when I look at that room is the fact that even in the throes of the rut, he didn't once harm me. Even mindless, he tried to be gentle with me. The room evidences it. Evidences what he *could* have done.

"I apologize kahlesta...Zynar." Varek pops one eye open. "I should have contacted you."

"You should have," Zynar growls.

Eleanor beams. "It's all forgiven. You had other things on your mind." Her gaze shifts back to me, full-on glee on her face.

As Zynar stands, he moves over to the table and pulls out a stool for Eleanor to sit on. She does so gracefully, a grin on her face as she looks at me. Zynar makes a sound in his throat then, one that's almost like he clears it but not. Varek's head pops up and he releases a heavy breath.

"Fine, brother."

"Hmm?" Some kind of unsaid communication passed between them that I can't parse.

"He wants to talk." Varek rises then leans in to brush his lips against mine. "I'll just be a moment, sura."

I nod, immediately missing his warmth as he heads out the door, leaving me and Eleanor alone.

"So," she begins.

"I know. This is…"

"Amazing!" She hops off the stool and plops on the couch beside me. "We're like…sisters or something now."

I laugh. "I guess we are. I never thought…"

Eleanor sobers a little and for a moment, I see behind her good mood. I see scars of a lifetime before. The same fears I faced. The same loss.

"Oh Eleanor…"

She takes my hand. "Listen. I never thought either. But they are good men, Catherine. The best."

A slow smile washes over my features as I stare into her eyes. Because I know it's the truth. Even before she told me.

"How was the rut?" Eleanor whispers. "I brought an ointment…" She dips a hand in the pocket of her tunic and pulls out an ointment that looks exactly like the one the Raki gave me how long ago. "Got it from an elephant alien. Says it heals all wounds. I used it after…" Her cheeks grow warm. "Well, all I have to say is it's good after the rut."

She grins at me then and I laugh as I accept her gift. "Thank you. That's really…that's really thoughtful."

I stare at the little canister for a few moments, my mind a whirlwind of thoughts.

"Eleanor, I'd like to apologize."

Her eyes widen. "Whatever for?!"

I release a soft breath. "When I first came here, I didn't even try to make friends with you. As a matter of fact, I was terrified of becoming your friend. I didn't want to get close to anyone. Too scared of it all being taken away from me again, I suppose." I pause. "Back on Earth, I had it all, as some would say. Money. Family. A thriving career. I was at the top of my game. I was strong. Until suddenly, I wasn't anymore."

"Oh dearie, you were abducted from the only planet you knew. We all were, and thrust into this world where we had no place. It's only natural."

I shake my head, my brow crinkling. "I know."

"Listen." Eleanor smiles. "Don't be so hard on yourself. If coming here, finding Zynar, finding this—" She waves around herself. "It's taught me that I don't have to be strong all the time. I just have to keep on going."

I nod, a genuine smile coming to my lips as I lean in and she accepts my hug. "Thank you."

"No need to thank me. Thank them. These men that have come into our lives are...*everything*."

I sniffle, still holding on to her. "They are. He is."

"And now that there's evidence that mating with a Kari will slow our aging I'm—"

I release her, easing back. "What?"

Eleanor giggles. "Sorry, you don't know yet, do you? Xarion has been doing research, carrying out tests. I've been his loyal guinea pig, so to say."

I blink, my eyelids fluttering. "What do you mean?"

Eleanor takes a deep breath before taking my hands in hers. "We're not aging."

My eyelids flutter again. "That's...not possible. Is it?"

She shrugs. "At least I'm not, and it's purely because of Zynar. Well...his...his uh..." her cheeks warm. "Let's just say a regular exchange of a certain fluid is extending our lifespan to meet theirs."

My eyebrows shoot up. "Are you saying..."

"They are very virile." Eleanor grins. "Don't resist it. Doctor's orders."

My expression must be so shocked that she bursts out with a

laugh. "Oh goodness me. If your expression is like this, I can't imagine what Donna's will be like when she hears."

My mouth falls open. "Oh dear. I left her at my farm when I ran after Varek. Is she okay?"

Eleanor waves a hand in dismissal. "Trust me, Donna's great. She's actually started a shop here in town."

My eyebrows fly higher. "Wow, already?"

Eleanor shrugs. "What can I say, the lady is resourceful."

I breathe out a surprised breath, nodding my head as I let everything Eleanor told me settle in my brain.

"There's something else too," she suddenly says, the tentativeness in her voice making my gaze slide back to her.

When she doesn't immediately continue, I get the feeling it's something serious.

"What is it?" I prod.

She releases a breath before tugging down the neck of her tunic to reveal...

I startle, eyes going wide before I lean in, probably invading her personal space as I stare at the marks on her chest.

Delicate swirls in an intricate pattern disappear deep below her neckline.

"What are those?"

Eleanor adjusts her clothing, her gaze boring into mine. "I guess that means you don't have them yet."

"Why would I...it's not a tattoo?"

She shakes her head. "They're kahl sigils."

I blink at her, eyelids fluttering again.

"They appeared soon after Zynar's rut. Kind of like evidence that I'm his mate."

I unconsciously grip my own chest, my fingers searching for any raised markings, any unfamiliar patterns. But I feel nothing but smooth skin beneath Varek's shirt. A strange mix of disappointment and uncertainty washes through me.

Eleanor must read something in my expression because she

reaches out, squeezing my hand reassuringly. "Hey, don't worry about it. Zynar says they're rare. Even rarer than finding a *kahl*. And even if they never do appear, it doesn't change what you and Varek have."

I nod slowly, trying to absorb this new information. The idea of physical marks tying me to Varek is thrilling. Tangible proof of our bond, but also an indelible claim on my body.

"What do they mean?" I whisper. "The sigils, what do they represent?"

Eleanor shrugs, a slight frown creasing her brow. "From what I've gathered, each pattern is unique to the mated pair. Some kind of symbolism that reflects the nature of their bond."

She traces a finger over her chest, following the invisible lines of her markings. "I like to think mine represent the way Zynar and I balance each other. His strength and this resilience I've had to find, woven together into something unbreakable."

There's a soft, almost reverent look on her face.

"Xarion's looking into it. The Initiative is greatly interested in the fact we've, um, settled in so well." She gives me a devious little wink that has me chuckling. "Turns out that proximity and emotional connection are what kick the mating bond into gear."

"Hmm," I muse. "So it's not just about physical attraction?"

Eleanor shakes her head. ""No. Xarion's tests point to the fact that, for example, I've always been Zynar's fated. But because I'm human and not Kari, it took time for Zynar's body to recognize who I am."

I clear my throat. "Varek and I, we spent time together, got to know each other before his core-rhythm awakened."

"It's a process." Eleanor smiles. "For me, it happened during an...intense moment. Nothing like adrenaline to speed things up."

I nod, taking it all in. "To think I had to nearly get myself killed for this all to come to be."

Eleanor barks out a surprised laugh. "Me too! Well, not

exactly, but let's just say it wasn't your typical engagement party."

"These men and their dramatic timing."

"Tell me about it. But hey, at least they keep things interesting."

I grin. I never thought I'd find a female friend here, but I can already feel a connection with Eleanor. "And they're not bad to look at either."

"Luckily, they know how to use those good looks." Eleanor winks.

We're both laughing when the door opens slightly and Varek pops his head in. His gaze finds me immediately and warmth fills my soul. I'm about to ask if he's finished when I hear another voice, not his brother's, out in the corridor.

My brow furrows as I stand and head to the door, peeking out to see the Kari I'd seen that day. The one who apparently lives a few doors down. The moment I appear, his gaze shifts to me.

"A successful rut," he says.

I'm momentarily surprised by his greeting. It's not exactly the thing I expected him to say. Varek steps before me, partially blocking the stranger—what was his name again? Tovan?—from view.

"Yes, successful," Varek growls. "The females here are mated. They are not looking for a suitor."

Zynar growls in agreement. With him and Varek standing together, I'm suddenly given the image of them both fighting side by side.

They look impressive even now. Even here.

The other Kari male lifts his arms in a placating gesture, a wry smile on his face. "Peace, friends. I mean no disrespect. After hearing the extent of that rut, I simply wished to offer my congratulations."

Heat fills my cheeks. He *heard* us?!

Varek remains tense, his stance still protective, but he gives a curt nod. "Gratitude. Your well-wishes are appreciated."

The male's gaze flicks to me, curious but not invasive. "You are a lucky female," he says. His yellow eyes pierce me but his voice is sincere. "To be the kahl of a warrior as fierce and loyal as Varek…may your bond be blessed with strength and joy."

I'm a bit taken aback, but I incline my head in acknowledgment. "Thank you. I am indeed fortunate."

Varek's posture relaxes slightly at my words, and he reaches back to take my hand, twining our fingers together. The gesture is both possessive and comforting.

The other Kari's grin widens, becoming more genuine. "I will not keep you any longer. I simply wanted to pay my respects, and to let you know that if you ever require assistance, my door is open to you."

Varek's brow furrows, a hint of suspicion in his eyes. "Why would we need your assistance?"

The male shrugs, his expression turning serious. "These are uncertain times, my friend. With you two finding your *kahls*…it is wise to have allies. Even unexpected ones."

His gaze meets mine again, and there's a depth of understanding there that surprises me. As if he knows, better than most, the challenges that come with being an outsider in this world.

"Thank you," I say again, meaning it this time. "We will keep that in mind."

He nods, satisfied, and with a final respectful bow, he takes his leave. Varek watches him go, his jaw tight, before turning to me with a sigh.

"I don't like him," he mutters.

"Me neither," Zynar agrees.

I squeeze his claw, leaning into his side. "I don't think he meant any harm. He was just being neighborly."

Varek and Zynar snort.

"He wants his own kahl, but you are mine." He pulls me against him.

"We could always introduce him to Donna," Eleanor says as we step back into the room.

"Donna?" I turn to her. "Do you think she'd be open to it?"

Eleanor shrugs. "Can't know till we find out, can we."

The thought fills my mind as the door closes and Varek heads to the kitchen for food for our guests. As we settle back into the comfort of Varek's quarters, the idea of introducing Donna to the neighboring Kari takes root in my mind. It's a tantalizing possibility—a chance for her to find the same kind of life-altering connection that Eleanor and I have discovered.

But even as the thought excites me, a flicker of uncertainty follows close behind. Donna is my friend, and I want nothing more than her happiness. But is pushing her towards an alien mate really the answer?

I think back to my own journey—the fear, the confusion, the exhilarating rush of finding a love I never dreamed possible. It wasn't an easy path, but I wouldn't trade a single step of it. Because it led me here, to this moment, surrounded by the warmth of Varek's presence and the steadfast support of newfound friends. Family.

Donna seems secure and happy already. But I know better than most that it's easy to hide the pain we bear. Displaced from our home, perhaps this is what she needs most right now. Not necessarily a mate, but a family. A place to belong, to heal, to discover her own strength.

A new home.

As I watch Varek and Zynar move about the kitchen, their easy camaraderie a balm to my soul, I realize that's exactly what we've found here. Not just within these walls, but within the unbreakable bonds we've forged with each other.

Eleanor catches my eye from across the room, a knowing smile playing on her lips. She understands, I think. The enormity of what we've been given, and the responsibility that comes with it.

We are the pioneers of a new world, the first to bridge the gap between our species. And while that role is daunting, it's also incredibly precious.

As Varek returns to my side, his arm slipping around my waist with effortless affection, I lean into his strength and allow myself a moment of perfect contentment.

Whatever the future holds, whatever challenges we may face, I know one thing for certain.

We will face them together.

Humans and Kari, mates and friends, an unshakable unit bound by love, loyalty, and the endless possibilities of a universe that brought us together.

And that, I realize with a brilliant surge of hope and joy, is the greatest gift of all.

EPILOGUE 2

VAREK

Two moons after the rut and we've moved back to Catherine's farm. We've settled in. All the buildings are operational. All the tools.

The little farm has truly blossomed. The little garden by the side of the lodge is lush and vibrant, thanks to Catherine's tireless dedication and the rich soil. I have treated the field too, getting rid of the pests in the soil, and fed it with fertilizers, ready for the new planting season.

The grasses have been cleared and the samplings of great trees planted along the perimeter. I have never seen a farm with such a thing before, but it was my mate's idea. She drew in the soft earth, explaining her vision with a light in her eyes that made me pledge to do anything to see that line continue to shine.

Each dawn I wake, I head to the fields with a song in my throat the same melody as my core-rhythm. I have found happiness and it shows. Even the animals know.

The wild tilgran have begun to venture close. Catherine has

even named a few. And the umus, those little puffballs that were the reason I ventured out to this farm in the first place, have settled into their new home with ease.

Each morning, I wake to the sight of Catherine tending to them, her face alight with a pure, uncomplicated joy as she runs her hands through their soft fur. She's experimented by shaving one and twisting the fibers into a thick string she calls 'wool'. She's confident she can make clothing from the string and even though I am happy about her joy and excitement, I'd rather she not put too much effort into something I will simply rip off her at the earliest opportunity.

"Clothes to sell in the town, silly!" She chuckles, setting down the umu she's been petting. The creatures have taken to her as if she were one of their own, nuzzling into her touch and trilling soft melodies that seem to wrap around her like an ethereal embrace.

The oogas, too, have flourished under her care. Their enclosures now ring with the sounds of contented bays and playful yips, a far cry from the frightened creatures I first encountered. Catherine has even begun to train them, teaching them to come when called and to perform simple tasks.

She is…my mate is just magnificent.

As for me, I've thrown myself into the role of being everything she needs. I've reinforced the perimeter fencing, set up surveillance systems to monitor for any potential threats, and even constructed a small workshop where I can mend the equipment that breaks around the farm.

But my proudest achievement by far is the fail-safe lock on that thrice-damned water hole. The mere thought of Catherine falling in again sends icy shards of fear through my veins. Never again. Never again will I let carelessness put her at risk.

She teased me about it at first, calling me her fierce, over-protective mate. But I could see the warmth in her eyes, the unspoken gratitude for my efforts. She understands, I think, the depth of my devotion. The lengths I will go to ensure her safety and happiness.

Which reminds me. I chuckle as I look at the relaxation device I'd gifted my kahl. Catherine admitted to using it to pleasure herself—a task it was not meant for.

"It vibrates, and you told me it's to help me relax!" She's laughing, but her cheeks are a vibrant red.

"Yes. You were to place it at pressure points to relieve tension." Nonetheless, I'm shocked and intrigued as to how it brought her to her peak.

Catherine grins, her eyes sparkling with humor. "Well, I *did* use it on a pressure point that was really tense. You know, the one down south that needed some extra attention."

A growl rises in my throat as I grip the device. "I want to try."

Her eyes widen and she yelps as I go after her. She runs and I let her. I will catch her, but I like watching her try to get away from me.

"No, Varek! We just got out of bed!"

"And we can go in again." I purr, tackling her into the soft cushions.

I pull her into my arms, our laughter echoing through the room.

In the evenings, we sit together on the porch, watching star's rays paint the sky orange and pink as it sinks below the horizon. Catherine leans into my side, her head on my shoulder, and I marvel at the perfect fit of her body against mine.

We talk about everything and nothing, sharing stories of our pasts and dreams for our future. She tells me of her childhood on Earth, of the family she left behind, and the ache in her voice makes me hold her just a little bit tighter.

I tell her of my own family, of the brother who stands at my side and the parents who raised us to be strong, honorable males. I speak of my fears, too—the worry that I will somehow fail her, that I won't be the mate she deserves.

But she silences those doubts with what I now know is called a kiss, her lips soft and sure against mine. "You are everything I could ever want," she whispers. "Everything I never knew I needed. Never doubt that."

And so, I don't. Because here, in this moment, with my mate in my arms and our future stretching out before us like an endless sea of stars, I am whole.

I am home.

But one day, when I return from checking the perimeter, I hear a sound that sends a child down my spine. A deep groan of pain. And it's coming from the lodge.

I rush inside to find Catherine on the floor, her skin as hot as the star and her hands clutching her chest.

I drop to my knees beside her, my heart pounding with fear. "Catherine!"

She looks up at me, her eyes glassy with pain. "It hurts," she gasps. "My chest…I thought I was having a heart attack, but that's not it. My chest feels like it's on fire."

I scoop her into my arms, cradling her against my chest as I carry her to our bed. Her skin is scorching to the touch, and I can feel the rapid flutter of her heartbeat beneath my palm.

"I have you," I murmur, brushing the sweat-dampened strands of her mane from her forehead. "I have you."

She nods, her digits clutching at my chest as another wave of pain washes over her. I hold her close, whispering soothing words in her ear as I try to quell the rising panic in my chest.

And then I see it. Just above the neckline of her tunic, a faint glow begins to emanate from her skin. It starts as a soft shimmer, barely noticeable, but as I watch, it grows darker and more distinct.

The lines of a *kahl* sigil.

I let out a shaky breath, relief and wonder warring for dominance in my heart. She's not dying. She's not ill.

She's becoming mine in the most profound way possible.

I press a gentle kiss to her forehead, my lips lingering against her fevered skin. "It's the sigil," I tell her softly. "It's appearing on your chest. That's what's causing the pain."

Her eyes widen, a mix of fear and awe in their depths. "The sigil? But…it's been months."

"I don't know why it's just appearing now," I admit. "But it's a sacred thing, a symbol of our bond. It means you're truly my *kahl*, in every way that matters."

She nods, a small smile curving her lips despite the pain. "I like the sound of that. But is it supposed to hurt this much?"

I hold her closer. "I was there when my siblignkin's mate received her kahl sigils."

"Eleanor?"

I nod.

"Did it hurt like this?"

"Unfortunately."

She grits her teeth, gripping me tighter.

For the next few hours, I hold her as the sigil slowly takes shape, the intricate lines etching themselves into her skin. She whimpers and cries out as the pain crests and ebbs, but I never let her go.

Finally, as the last rays of the star fade from the sky, the last lines of the sigil take shape. Catherine sags against me, exhausted but smiling.

I tug her tunic down, baring her skin.

"It's beautiful," she whispers, tracing the lines with a single digit.

"*You're* beautiful," I correct her, pressing a kiss to the top of her head. "My brave, strong, incredible mate."

She tilts her face up to mine, brushing my lips with her. "I'm glad it was you," she says softly. "So glad the universe brought me to you."

I swallow past the lump in my throat, my core-organ too full for words. Instead, I lower my head and capture her lips with mine, pouring every ounce of my love and devotion into the kiss.

She responds with equal fervor, her arms twining around my neck as she presses herself closer. We lose ourselves in each other, the rest of the world falling away as I fill her with my love, my length, my seed.

When we finally slow, I rest my forehead against hers, marveling at the perfect rightness of this moment. I gather her close, my arms banded tight around her and my face buried in the wild tousle of her mane. There is an utter sense of peace and belonging.

This is where I was always meant to be. Not just in this moment, but in this life, on this path that had led me to her. All the tragedies and triumphs, the pain and the joy...it was all so I could find my way here. To my home, my haven.

To the other half of my soul.

"I love you," she whispers, the words ringing with unshakable certainty.

A low rumble of contentment vibrates through me. "I love you, my kahl. My Catherine. Now and always."

The words wrap around me like a vow, like an unbreakable cord binding us together for all eternity.

And in that perfect, shining moment, I know nothing will ever be the same.

And I have never been more grateful for it.

AFTERWORD

Whew! What a ride, right? I hope you enjoyed Catherine and Varek's story as much as I loved writing it. I mean, who doesn't love a sweet farm girl and a persistent alien hunk?

This story is kind of an ode to all of us who've faced those unexpected twists in life. Maybe you've lost someone, or found yourself suddenly single, or just realized life isn't going the way you planned. It's scary, isn't it? Putting yourself out there again, opening your heart to new possibilities.

I remember when my father passed, my mother didn't find a new partner. She was still so full of life and had so much love to give. I always hoped she'd find someone new, but I think she was a bit afraid. And...I don't blame her. You think your life is going one way and then boom, you're hit with a curveball. It's terrifying to even think about dating again. (And do I need to mention these dating apps can give you whole other trauma!)

That's' why I wrote this book. It's for those of us who dream of second chances and unexpected love, but maybe aren't quite ready to take that leap ourselves.

With Catherine and Varek, we get to imagine what it might be like to open our hearts again, to trust, to love... and yes, to be loved by a hunky alien who thinks we're the center of the universe!

So whether you're happily single, cautiously considering dipping your toes back into the dating pool, or just looking for a fun escape, I hope this story gave you a little taste of that romantic adventure we all secretly crave.

Up next is Donna and Tovan's story. She's stubborn and suspicious of males, but who knows, maybe Tovan's charm will win her over in the end. (No spoilers, I promise!)

Until next time, happy reading and may your life be filled with love – alien or otherwise!

 AG

NEXT IN THE SERIES

An Alien for the Future

Donna

I've been burned too many times to believe in fairy tales. So when this golden-eyed alien, Tovan, shows up claiming I'm his destined mate, I'm not buying it. Sure, he's gorgeous and infuriatingly persistent, but I've got a farm to run and a life to live. I don't need some whirlwind romance complicating things. So, why does my heart race every time he's near?

Tovan

From the moment I saw her, I knew. Donna Johnson is my kahl, my destined mate. She's everything I've ever wanted: strong, passionate, and beautifully stubborn. But she denies our connection, pushes me away at every turn. I must prove to her that our love is real, that we belong together. For without her, my life, my existence, will never be complete.

Xul

Series Title: Captured by Aliens

Athena wakes up in hell.
Well…it's an alien slave ship, but it might as well be hell because she only has three choices.
Mate. Become a sex slave. Or be killed.
Great options.
Desperate for freedom, a chance for survival is presented in the handsome rogue alien called Xul.
But Xul is caught up in problems of his own and a mission he cannot afford to let fail—one that could be easily compromised if he dared open his heart.
That doesn't leave her with many options and it doesn't help that she finds him utterly frustrating...
...and strong, hot, irresistible…
She shouldn't really be thinking about him like that. Should she?

Other books in the series: Crex, Yce, Kyris, Kyro

Ajos

Series Title: The Restitution [Spinoff from Captured by Aliens]

She didn't move to the big city just to be kidnapped by aliens.
That wasn't even possible...
Right?
WRONG.
When Kerena wakes up, she's not on Earth anymore.

Heck, she's not even in the same galaxy, and the face hovering so close she can make out every detail? That face is definitely...not...human.

But before she can really figure out what's going on, Kerena realizes she's caught in the middle of a war—one she was thrust into as soon as she was ripped from Earth.

She's surrounded by aliens in a rebellion, but there's one—the one with the strange golden eyes, minty-teal skin, and rippling muscles—that holds her attention.

His presence is magnetic and his heated gaze makes something stir deep within her.

He's battling something that has nothing to do with the war and his warning that she should stay away does not go unheeded.

He's a dangerous rebel fighter. She gets that. So...why is he still hovering so close? And why is he growling at everyone that so much as looks in her direction?

Most of all, why does he keep looking at her like she belongs to ... HIM?

Other books in the series: V'Alen

Riv's Sanctuary

Series Title: Riv's Sanctuary

Abducted from Earth over a year ago, Lauren spent most of that time getting accustomed to her new life as one of the "animals" in an alien zoo.

When she's sold by the zookeeper, her life takes a turn she wasn't expecting. She has no idea where she'll end up till she's brought to a sanctuary owned by a tall blue hunk of an alien called Riv.

Riv's life is quiet and peaceful in a place as far away from civilization as he can manage. So when an annoying chatterbox of a human ends up on his doorstep, he's less than pleased. The human disrupts his life and his solitude and he can't wait to get rid of her.

He's not interested in helping her, and he's definitely not interested in love.

Except…she's managed to wheedle her way in and suddenly those barriers around his heart don't seem so strong anymore.

He has two options: Let her go.

Or let her in.

Other books in the series: Sohut's Protection, Ka'Cit's Haven

Arrival

Series Title: Captured Earth

Adira

The machines came, and they trampled us all.

I have nothing left. No family. No friends. No home.

They harvest us. They breed us. They feed from us…

There is no hope…Not until one fateful moment when my eyes open and I see something streaking across the skies.

What appears is like a demon before my eyes…

But can they be worse than the evil already upon us?

I will just have to wait and see.

Fer'ro

Sailing across the stars for what feels like eons…we have followed our enemy to a little blue planet.

We had wanted to arrive before them…now I think we may be too late.

But when we kill the first Scrit and I see the being drowning within its depths, I know I have to save it.

And *it*…turns out to be a *her*. **A female.**

This planet has hope yet. I will save her and her kind.

…Little do I know…she's the one who ends up saving me instead.

Dark. Steamy. Gritty. A thrilling romance intertwined in a plot that will give you chills.

Other books in the series: Base Zero, Cataclysm, War

Claiming His Mate

Series Title: Fated Mates of the Atari

When I get a once-in-a-lifetime chance to go on a luxury space cruise, I jump at it.

This cruise is the beginning of something amazing, and nothing is going to stop me from going.

But when things go wrong shortly after departure, it's clear I have made a mistake.

Suddenly thrown into a world where I have no way of defending myself, the last thing I expect is an Atari warrior coming to my rescue.

This cruise has been full of surprises…but the Atari is the biggest one of all.

He's tall, growly, possessive, and he sends my pulse into over-drive with just the slightest look.

Why the heck is my body reacting this way to this stranger?

And did he just declare that I am his mate?

Other books in the series: Craving His Mate, Fighting for His Mate, Guarding His Mate

Outlaw

Series Title: The Midnight Seven

Our colony is dying.

We're out of time. Out of hope. Out of options—*unless I risk everything on him.*

The outlaw.

One not bound by rules or mercy.

With lives at stake, I offer him a deal he can't refuse. And one I can't go back on.

Bargaining with a demon to save my people, only time will tell if I've sealed their fate, or found their salvation.

And mine.

Find on Amazon

An Alien for the Farm

Series Title: A New Home

Eleanor

I thought starting over on this quiet farm would finally give me a chance to heal. But the moment that towering alien walks through my door, I know real trouble has found me. Zynar is all corded muscle and raw masculinity—nothing like the weak men who've used me. Worse, this alien hunk stirs feelings in me

I swore were long dead. Each time his intense yellow gaze locks onto mine, my resolve weakens. I tell myself to keep my distance, that this attraction can only lead to heartbreak. But as Zynar proves himself gentle yet strong, passionate yet restrained, I start to crave the pleasure his touch promises to unlock in me once more.

Zynar

From the moment I lay eyes on the delicate creature named Eleanor, my core-beat quickens in a way I hadn't thought possible. This fragile flower survived abduction and abuse, yet her spirit remains unbroken. I want nothing more than to make her feel safe and cherished. But this female threatens to expose vulnerabilities I've long tried to bury. As a displaced Kari without a homeworld, getting close means entertaining the thought of something I never thought possible. But keeping my distance is torture. How can I resist a female who awakens feelings I swore were dead?

Other books in the series: An Alien for Her Heart, An Alien for the Future

***

Scan the QR code to view all books

ABOUT THE AUTHOR

A. G. Wilde is an avid reader, a gamer, a lover of all things space, alien, and sci-fi.

She is addicted to intense romance, irresistible heroes, and deliciously naughty things.

facebook.com/agwilde

instagram.com/authoragwilde

tiktok.com/@authoragwilde

x.com/authoragwilde

bookbub.com/profile/a-g-wilde

amazon.com/author/agwilde

www.ingramcontent.com/pod-product-compliance
Lightning Source LLC
Chambersburg PA
CBHW051254210726

48287CB00002B/494